The Stars Have Lost Their Glitter

By Dennis Brown

This is a work of fiction. Names, characters, businesses, places, events and incidents are either the products of the author's imagination or used in a fictitious manner. Any resemblance to actual persons, living or dead, or actual events is purely coincidental.

This effort at a cozy mystery is dedicated to my wife whether she wants it or not.

Chapter One

It had been twenty years since I had been back to Clanton Academy, my alma mater, an all-boys' boarding school in Central Virginia for the affluent, the almost affluent, and the few like me who attended on need-based scholarships, and I wondered how the remaining faculty and staff would remember me. Hopefully not as the class clown given to sarcasm, which I was. That version of me had long since been supplanted by the new me, a sometimes respected private eye glad to take a week off from snooping on philandering husbands and missing persons that invariably were missing by choice.

The secretary of the new president responded to my "ahem" by turning her head toward me, scowling just as she had twenty years before and revealing her glasses through which she could easily see Mars. Students in my day were ever careful never to stand between her and the sun lest her glasses catch the sun's rays and convert them into death beams. Her personality and breath were equally fearsome. "Remember me, Miss Foss?" I asked. "Danny Wright, class of 2001."

"Vaguely. The one the faculty called Danny Never Right? As a general rule I forget students as soon as they leave, sometimes before then. You were particularly obnoxious, if memory serves, leaving an indelible stain on my memory. Is there a reason you're wasting my time?" Her toxic personality had remained intact.

Choosing to ignore the temptation to repay her insult with one of my own, I said, "I'd like to talk with the new president if he's available. Tell him that I am thinking of sending my son here." I have no son.

Death Ray seemed somewhat miffed when the president instructed her to send me in.

The office of the president had changed as little as Death Ray's personality. Same massive cherry desk that had previously been a fixture in the West Wing of the White House, thick crewel drapes a bit faded but still rich looking, and two well-worn leather wing chairs across from the desk meant, I suppose, to create a gap between the president and whoever else was in the room. The new president was a study in contrast between him and his predecessor. Whereas the man he replaced was likable and approachable, especially after he'd downed a few drinks, the new president seemed cold as he greeted me with a smug smile on an otherwise dour countenance.

Without standing or extending a hand to shake, he said, "I'm H. Michael Madison. I understand you're thinking of sending your son to Clanton Academy."

I nodded vaguely.

"I can assure you that Clanton Academy is no longer the morally slack breeding ground of iniquity it was when you graced our halls." He smoothed the gray hair on both sides of his otherwise bald head and adjusted his tie, which needed no adjusting. His suit was well tailored, dark gray and obviously expensive. I felt shabby in my Macy's two-for-one-sale sport coat that didn't drape well on my 6'2" lean frame.

His unsolicited statement was unexpected and a little unnerving. Sanctimony emanated from him with more intensity than his secretary's death rays. As he continued with an unfettered vehemence proclaiming with obvious pride that he was born again, his face assumed a contrived look of beatification.

His smarmy piety triggered an uncomfortable memory. In Literary Criticism when I was a Third Year at The University of Virginia, or UVA, I sat in front of a student who had little use of his withered legs and lurched along on crutches. Though everyone disliked him because he was obnoxious and snide, no one voiced criticism because he was handicapped. One day, in response to the professor's question about the Lost Generation in Paris, he slowly and awkwardly stood up, his crutches precariously supporting him, and sang loudly off key "How you gonna keep them down on the farm once they've seen Paree?" Even the professor cringed, and to a one, the class cast their eyes downward as if that could disguise their discomfort. As I had back in Literary Criticism, I cast my eyes downward momentarily, then managed to produce a half smile at H. Michael that I hoped he would interpret as approval of the newly spawned piety. I hadn't particularly enjoyed my stay there as a student, and an overdose of piety seemed unlikely to improve the place.

I was off to a bad start. Lying was probably going to get me booted out of his office. "Actually, sir, I wanted to speak to you about my nephew who already attends Clanton."

Unlike the son I had invented to gain access, my nephew actually does exist. He had invited me to visit him despite knowing that I held no fond memories of these hallowed grounds. I had no children of my own from my two unsuccessful marriages and was fond of the boy, who seemed to be flourishing here despite his less than pious nature. I had emailed him that I'd arrive today and agreed to meet him at his dorm, then go to the cafeteria for lunch.

"I don't have a son. I wasn't sure if you'd see me if I told you all I wanted was a favor. With your permission, I'd like to eat lunch with him today. Do I need some sort of pass? Because of the rash of shootings at schools, I assume there's some sort protocol that wasn't around back in my day."

Expecting to be consigned to Hell, I was surprised when, without hesitation, he stood up, shook my hand, and said, "Tell the manager of the cafeteria that you're my guest. Good to meet you, Mr. Wright. By the way, what is the name of your nephew? I don't recall that we have a student by the name of Wright."

"That's because he's my sister's son. His name is Rex Hardy."

The smarmy smile disappeared instantly. "Oh, yes, Mr. Wright, I do indeed know your nephew."

Chapter Two

My nephew Rex smiled broadly when he saw me approaching him in the dorm lounge. Standing 6'2" tall like me and weighing a solid 190 pounds, he was probably his full height at age seventeen. He resembled his father more than my sister except for his blue eyes and toothy smile, both salient characteristics of my sister Katherine, who, though ten years older than I, looked five years younger. Clean living, I guess. Never had been guilty of that.

"Uncle Danny, thanks for coming!" I was happy to see that he hadn't succumbed to the prep school uniform of rep tie, white shirt, and baggy khakis. A tee-shirt and jeans suited him well.

"How could I refuse my favorite, albeit only, nephew? How long do you have for lunch, Rex?"

"Forty-five minutes," Rex answered. "I know it's not enough time to go over what I need to talk with you about, but we can meet again here after classes are over in a couple hours, OK?"

Rex seemed fidgety and more serious than usual, and that piqued my curiosity. Like me, he disliked pompousness, humblebraggers, and whiners and threw the occasional barb their way. Always with a smile, though. Perceptiveness didn't justify meanness to Rex, which was one reason I enjoyed seeing him whenever I could. He was good company. He was also good-natured about his unfortunate appellation. Why Katherine thought that Rex was a good choice to inflict upon her only son was a mystery to me. Throughout childhood, he dealt with the usual jibes: Tyrannosaurus Rex lasted though elementary school, Train and Car Rex through middle school, and more recently Et-a-pussy Rex. Greek tragedy was never my favorite, either.

"Has the cafeteria improved its fare since I was a student here, Rex?" I asked as we walked across the quad toward the cafeteria that had served me such dubious delicacies as pineapple stew, planetarium sandwiches (white bread topped with an ice cream scooper blob of mashed potatoes and gray gravy), and meat that shimmered with rainbows. Never a good sign when meat assumes colors.

"You can decide that for yourself," Rex said as we entered the building I swore I would never again set foot in after I had eaten my last meal there twenty years ago.

The first thing I noticed was that the décor had remained as unappealing as it was then: Mustard colored walls and flecked floor tiles that I assumed were intended to disguise the spills of food. Why else would anyone select something so ugly?

Ahead of us in line were three faculty members, two of whom I knew had been there for at least thirty years. I noticed that Mr. Jenkins, an English teacher who had taught me and was now teaching Rex, opted for the swollen knockwurst. Serving the unappetizing choices was the same lady who had served swill to us twenty years ago. We dubbed her Cafeteria Katie.

"Is the library still standing?" she asked who I assumed was the librarian behind Mr. Jenkins. The librarian giggled and asked for whatever wouldn't poison him. Cafeteria Katie plopped a glob of some sort of stew on his tray.

Directly ahead of us was the most bitter, pontificating man I had ever met, Mr. Hal Wood, still weighing in at over 350 pounds and unencumbered by hygiene ritual that might reduce some of the odor of sweat mixed with cloying cologne wafting our way. Apparently they didn't remember me, as neither spoke to me or acknowledged Rex. Or maybe they remembered and chose not to greet me. In either case, I was glad not to have to interact with them, as I was eager to learn the reason my nephew had summoned me, even if it was the *Readers Digest* version.

Mr. Wood sighed theatrically and muttered, "This food is an abomination, but one has to eat something," then instructed Cafeteria Katie to load up his tray with what he called beef spew. His face lit up when he saw the chocolate pie next to the breads. After selecting six rolls and an empty sleeve from a loaf of white bread that he filled with slices of bologna and American cheese presumably for a snack before dinner, he lifted the whole pie with his left hand as he deftly cleared space with his right hand on what I had erroneously thought was his already filled-to-capacity tray, leaving no dessert for Rex or me. Not that I minded. It was no secret that the pies were rejects from a nearby frozen-pie factory.

Scanning the cafeteria for a table with two empty seats, I frowned when I realized that the only available table was next to the three faculty in front of us in line. It was the table for two occupied in my day by the alcoholic director of the cafeteria, who'd sit there surveying the culinary domain he detested working in, his eyes glazed and, after eating corn on the cob, kernels stuck to his chin. We used to wonder how, missing so many teeth, he could eat corn on the cob. Somehow he managed, obviously. Today the table sat empty, our sole option. "Sorry about that," Rex said as we sat, knowing that the duo preceding us in line was not among my favorite memories of Clanton Academy.

"Not a problem," I assured him. And it wasn't. I really couldn't have cared less about ancient faculty and ancient history.

Beside us, the three were gossiping, seemingly unconcerned that they'd be overheard. Actually, it was more of a monologue, with Mr. Wood commenting on teachers and their wives and children, and any student within his range of vision. "Will you look at the derriere on Mr. Walker's wife? They ought to call this school Fat Ass Academy," said Mr. Wood, who seemed not to invite notice of his own prodigious keister. "And look at that pusillanimous ort with his wife who breeds so prolifically that she should be incarcerated for overpopulating the world. She may look sweet and innocent, but she'd cut your balls off in a heartbeat – if she had a heart."

The librarian giggled and cooed, "Ooh, you are terrible."

"You see that new teacher walking across the room? I don't know him, but I don't like him. Oh! There's that scurrilous Bill Weaver who convinced our feckless principal to share my office space. To think that I once spoke to him. I've embraced a viper! Look at those Negro savages," he said loudly enough to be heard by everyone sitting at the tables around him, pointing to six African American upperclassmen. "They should issue them spears, not eating utensils."

The librarian interrupted the monologue. "Ooh, there's Coach Tolliver. Has anyone heard whether his wife had her baby? I heard they had to seduce labor." Mr. Wood ignored both the interruption and the malapropism. In an eating mode, he focused only on defiling character and ingesting whatever filled his tray. Knowing from my previous experiences with him that he required being center stage, I figured he'd likely get around later to cautioning his tablemates not to speak when he was speaking. If "speaking" was the right word for his diatribe. As I listened to him trash everyone in the room, his loud eating sounds serving as a contrapuntal harmony, I flashed back to all those dreary days in his classroom, listening to his intonation of the long list of useless, often archaic words he required us to learn. His extensive vocabulary was sometimes perceived as erudition when in fact it was his ego trying to gain the upper hand on students who were often brighter than he was. Besides, grading vocabulary quizzes required less work than grading essays.

Rex couldn't help laughing at the caustic conversation beside us.

"Listen to that braying jackass beside us," Mr. Wood sniffed, referring to Rex, then returned to the task at hand – eating.

'How can anyone enjoy food *that* much?' I thought.

Beads of sweat broke out on Mr. Wood's brow as he shoveled into his gaping mouth the last bite of the pie he had snatched.

Mr. Jenkins, who had been mostly silent during Mr. Wood's pontifications, looked glumly at the knockwurst that remained intact on his tray and announced, "Would anyone like a big fat dick?"

With surprising dexterity, Mr. Wood instantly stabbed the knockwurst, declaring, "Need you ask?" In three bites he downed the sausage.

"That's gross," said Rex intentionally loud enough to be overheard.

"Almost as gross as this food," I added. "Never mind them. Give me a truncated version of what has been bothering you?" Hearing the barrage of SAT words from the table beside me must have triggered the use of "truncated." With a little guilt, I added, "I mean abbreviated version. God forbid I should become a snollygoster."

Remembering Mr. Wood's class, Rex grinned. Briefly. "Uncle Danny, I really am worried that something bad is going to happen at Clanton."

"Why do you say that, Rex?"

Before he could answer, we were distracted by a loud belch emanating from the table beside us. Turning to see who was guilty of this breach of etiquette, we saw Mr. Wood's eyes suddenly widen and a nanosecond later, his stomach explode. Literally. The contents of his meal and bits of flesh and pulverized bone fragments became projectiles that covered Mr. Jenkins and the librarian, and sprayed the table of students beyond them, covering a ten-foot wide swath of tables, faculty, and students. Mr. Wood's head snapped back from the impact of the explosion that left a hole where his stomach had been seconds ago, then flopped forward onto the empty tray. Screams filled the room, and Mr. Jenkins and the librarian sat as if frozen, seemingly unable to move or speak. The remains of Mr. Wood dripped to the floor that not even speckled tile could disguise.

Spared of the spray of human debris, we sat momentarily stunned during the mayhem. Finally Rex nervously smiled and weakly said, "Mr. Wood is ubiquitous."

Chapter Three

The cafeteria sealed off, everyone sat quietly, most averting looking at the table where what was obviously a murder had occurred. The local sheriff, a Barney Fife clone, had arrived ten minutes after the explosion and declared it a crime scene after talking with me and several other witnesses, the only ones who had actually seen it. Inflated by the power he felt in controlling the scene, he strutted around the room, small notebook in hand, asking every diner for an eye witness account even though he had to know they had nothing to add. Unfortunately, declaring the room a crime scene meant that the ectoplasm that had been Mr. Wood was still covering two tables and a large area of floor till a forensics team could make the hour and a half drive from Richmond. Those who were coated with Mr. Wood were allowed only to wash their faces and hands in the cafeteria sink.

Four of Rex's friends joined us at our table. "Guess Mr. Wood went out with a bang," said one, giggling. "Yeah, remember when he told us not to use dead wood in our writing? Well, look who's dead Wood now," added another, laughing loudly at what he must have considered a witticism. "Taco Tuesdays used to be Belly Bomb Day. Guess that Beef Stew Mondays can be added to the list," said a third. It seemed as if each was competing to be the most callous and sophomorically witty. "Well, at least he went out doing what he liked best – eating," added the fourth, unable to come up with a bon mot exceeding the others.

Clearly there was no need for grief counselors if these students were any indication.

"Guys, this is my Uncle Danny I have told you about," Rex added.

They briefly looked me over, then resumed making light of what I had thought would be a traumatic situation. True, Mr. Wood was a racist, sour, mean-spirited misogynist, but even he deserved a modicum of respect in death.

"Glad to meet you, though I would have preferred to meet under better circumstances." I gave them my sternest look that I usually reserved for clients who balked at my fees. Too many clients had the wrong idea of what a private eye does. They probably saw too many old Bogart movies, which I, by the way, loved. I didn't "pack heat," had never been involved in a fight on the job, and definitely never waived a dame's fee because I fell for her come-hither looks. Most of my work was done on a computer, and that took time, patience, and a lot of coffee. Besides, Bogart was six inches shorter than I and not nearly as good looking.

"Just a heads-up, guys. The police will be asking you for statements. I suggest you can the sarcasm and start trying to recollect exactly what you remember. In case you haven't figured it out yet, this was a murder."

Rex must have detected a note of disapproval in my tone and sidled up to me. "I'm sorry, Uncle Danny. I disliked the man, sure, but I was out of line," he whispered. I would have preferred that he offer an apology his friends could hear, but I settled for what I got. Truth be told, I probably would have reacted just as they had when I was their age.

Noticing that heads were turning to the back entrance of the cafeteria, I turned to see H. Michael stepping gingerly onto a chair flanked by two men. "Who are those two?" I asked Rex quietly.

"The short bald one is his assistant, and the other is the academic dean," he answered.

"Listen up, students and faculty and families," H. Michael announced loudly. "This unfortunate occurrence will be dealt with by the appropriate authorities and of course the school administration. Faculty, we will meet in the auditorium as soon as the police release you. Students, you will return directly to the dorms. Families, you will return to your homes on campus. Any faculty wives who live off campus will report to the police investigator in charge to find out when you may leave campus. No one – I repeat *no one* – will speak to any outside sources or media without first contacting me. I will be the only conduit to the media." His brief comments over, he stepped down and hastily left the cafeteria with his dean and assistant in tow.

'Pretty efficient damage control,' I thought. My opinion of him improved significantly since our first meeting. No hypocritical lamentation for the unpopular Mr. Wood. No waffling. No signs of distress. He was in charge and exuded confidence. Best of all, he hadn't noticed I was there and given any directive to me.

I motioned with a nod for Rex to follow me as I walked to the back of the cafeteria. Looking around to make sure no one would overhear our conversation, I said, "Rex, we still need to talk about what was concerning you when you asked me to come visit. Did it have anything to do with what happened here today?"

"I don't know, Uncle Danny. I mean, I can't understand what happened here. Was he a target, and how did someone get his gut to explode?"

"I don't have any idea of how or why this was done, Rex. I don't even know if Mr. Wood was the intended victim. I suspect that whatever was detonated was in something he ate for lunch, though it could have been something he had eaten earlier."

"But not early enough to be digested," I added after considering the digestive process. "If it was a random act, any one of us could have suffered the same fate. I am as puzzled as you as to how whatever he swallowed was detonated. I hope the forensics team will know that after they examine what's left of Mr. Wood's body and possibly the fragments of himself scattered around the cafeteria. Questions. All I have at this point are questions."

Rex surveyed the room, and his face seemed to harden.

"Uncle Danny, I asked you to visit because I sensed that there is something evil here. And it may involve both students and teachers. I just don't know. It's gotten to the point that whenever certain teachers and students are around me, they stop talking as if they don't want me to hear anything. Maybe I'm just being paranoid, but I swear there's something they don't want me to hear." He looked into my eyes as if to search what I was thinking. If he could, he'd know that I was concerned. Very concerned.

Chapter Four

"Uncle Danny, promise me you'll stick around for a while. Please. If you leave now, so will I."

Now, that was out of character. I wouldn't say that Rex was fearless, but he was more upset than I had ever seen him. I had no cases pending and figured the least I could do was lend moral support. And if I could help Barney in his investigation, I'd do that, too. Not so much for my not-so-dear alma mater as for my nephew.

"Hey, Rex. I'm here for as long as you need me. Or as long as they'll let me stay. Have you ever heard the old saying, 'Fish and guests start smelling bad after three days'? There's some truth to that." I hoped a little humor might reduce his stress.

Rex chuckled weakly and seemed relieved that there would be someone he could rely on. Having met his friends, I knew they would not be much support.

"For starters, Rex, I need to talk with H. Michael. I'd like to stay in the Alumni House if he'll let me. I need to have unfettered mobility if possible."

Barney broke our conversation. "Attention, everyone. As of now, you may leave and report to where the president instructed." He puffed out his concave chest as much as he could muster and almost obscenely felt his pistol holstered on his scrawny hip. This investigation would be the high point of his otherwise dull existence. As distasteful as it would be, I needed to ingratiate myself with him. Appealing to his ego would be a cinch. Not retching while doing so would be considerably more difficult.

I watched Rex and his friends hurriedly leave for their dorm and casually approached Barney. "You did an outstanding job of keeping a bad situation from getting worse, Sheriff. As a detective, I have seen my share of crime scenes, and I know a pro when I see one. You must have a lot of experience dealing with tight situations." God, I was shameless.

Barney hiked up his pants and in his deepest voice said, "I ain't no rookie, that's a fact."

I wondered if the murderer knew Barney. If *he* did – in my experience no woman would commit such a violent murder – he must be brimming with confidence that he would escape detection.

"I hope I'm not being presumptuous, but if the president allows me to hang around for a while, I sure would appreciate shadowing you. You know, learning from the master."

I thought Barney would mull that over for a while. I was wrong. "Son, if you don't mind being up at all hours and dealing with criminal elements, you sure can. I'm without a deputy for the time being, and I could bounce my ideas off you. Kinda like a springboard, ya know?"

That was almost too easy. "I'd like nothing better than being a sounding…er, *spring*board for you. What's your name? Or do you prefer the formal title of Sheriff?"

That weighty question seemed to puzzle him momentarily, but in a moment of magnanimity, he told me his name was Gladstone Dixon, but I could dispense with formality and call him Gladstone. Gladstone it would be. "Great, Gladstone. I'll catch up with you later. Gonna try to catch the president in his office. Where will you be operating your investigation from?"

Judging by the frown on Barney's face, I assumed he hadn't given that much, if any, thought. "I figured you'd use the auditorium, but you may have somewhere else in mind."

"You read my mind, Danno. I bet lots of people tell you to book 'em, Danno." He chortled at his joke. No one had ever told me to book 'em.

"OK, Gladstone. I'll see you there later. Maybe you could fill me in on any reports you get from the forensics experts? That scientific business is Greek to me." I hoped Barney didn't see me roll my eyes.

"Don't you worry none, Danno. I'll explain it in everyday terms you can understand."

Armed with a new ally, I left to find the president.

Chapter Five

Walking across the campus nestled in the foothills of the Blue Ridge Mountains, I noticed how much better the grounds were groomed than when I attended. Flower beds appeared where previously there had been weed-infested, rotting mulch, and much care had obviously been given to the grassed areas. The window trim of red brick buildings no longer had peeling paint, and the pristine sidewalks bespoke of a maintenance plan sadly lacking twenty years ago. Another check in the plus column for H. Michael. Had I misread him this morning?

There was no way to avoid the human gargoyle running interference for H. Michael. "Good afternoon, Miss Foss. It seems I have need of seeing your boss again today. Would you mind checking to see if I can meet with him after he returns from his meeting with his staff?" I reeked of forced pleasantness and smiled as sincerely as I could.

Without answering, she scowled, jerked her cell phone from her purse, and stabbed in a number of what must have been his cell phone. "I am terribly sorry to bother you, sir, but Rex Hardy's uncle is here again wanting to know if he can see you after you're finished with your meeting. I will gladly send him on his way if —"

H. Michael must have cut her off, and unless I misinterpreted her pursed lips and squinted eyes, she wasn't pleased with his reply.

Not looking up from her computer, she said icily, "He said for you to stay here, that he'd be here in ten minutes. You may sit on the sofa in the hallway, not in my office. *Some* of us have work to do."

"Yes, you must have a lot on your plate after the…er, incident in the cafeteria." I was curious to see if she had a shred of remorse.

"Yes, I do, and you're not helping matters. Anything else?"

"No. I can see by your demeanor that you are grieving and having a hard time holding back tears."

If looks could kill, I'd be the second murder victim of the day.

H. Michael was unexpectedly prompt. I had no idea why he seemed eager to meet with me, and I was more curious about his motive than I was about Death Ray's heart of stone.

"Please come into my office, Mr. Wright. I hope I haven't kept you waiting too long." He actually smiled. Did he think I was going to write a large check to Clanton Academy?

"Not at all. Was just having a nice chat with your lovely secretary." At the mention of the adjective "lovely," did I just see him do a very modified version of a double take as he turned to Miss Foss?

"No calls, please, Miss Foss," he instructed as we entered his office.

Taking the same chair I had selected earlier, I sat back and waited a few seconds to see if he would tip his hand before I did. He didn't.

"I have a favor to ask of you, Mr. Madison. If you'll recall, I am Rex Hardy's uncle and was eating lunch with him when the explosion happened. We sat beside the table where it occurred, and I am concerned that witnessing it close at hand may have traumatized him." Remembering Rex's and his friends' reactions to the belly bomb, I had to force myself to keep a serious face at my white lie. OK, maybe more of a beige lie. "I feel the need to stay with him for at least a few days. You know, kind of monitoring his state of mind to report to my sister. I'm wondering if possibly I could bunk at the Alumni House so that I'll have freedom to see him as often as I can. I'll gladly pay any fees you charge, of course."

H. Michael's face showed no sign of what he might have been thinking. Then abruptly he opened the top right drawer of his desk and pulled out a manila file holder. Hesitating for a couple seconds, he finally spoke. "Mr. Wright, you may stay at the Alumni House on one condition."

"What would that be?" I answered warily.

"Do you remember my saying at our first meeting that I am aware of who your nephew is?"

"Yes, I –"

"Don't interrupt me, Mr. Wright. The reason I know of your nephew isn't a good one. Allow me to be blunt, as is my wont."

Did he really say, "…as is my wont"? It was getting harder to keep a poker face.

"You see, the contents of this folder seem to indicate that he is a drug dealer at Clanton Academy."

I was stunned at that pronouncement but was determined not to show that to H. Michael. My nephew a drug dealer? No way. He was as sensible a kid as you'd ever meet.

"May I see what's in that folder, Mr. Madison? I have a hard time – a *very* hard time – believing that Rex would deal drugs."

H. Michael threw me his smug smile and carefully pushed the folder across his desk with two fingertips as if it were contagious. "See for yourself, Mr. Wright."

Inside the folder was only one piece of paper. On it were the printed words "Rex Hardy is selling durgs."

"This is it?" I asked. "It's not even signed, and it seems more than possible that whoever wrote it said 'On to durgs.'"

"How droll, Mr. Wright. There's more to it than that. When my assistant received that, of course he immediately came to me and asked what he should do."

"Nothing like quick thinking from your second in command," I interrupted despite his earlier admonition.

His wrinkled brow revealed he was enjoying my company less and less. "As I was saying, he asked what he should do, and I advised him to send out feelers -- discreetly, of course -- to his sources in the student body. We like to keep a close read on the pulse, as it were."

"And just what did he hear from his suck-ups?" It was becoming increasingly difficult for me not to show my contempt for everything Clanton Academy. I reminded myself of the purpose of my meeting, however, and added, "What is the one condition you referred to, Mr. Madison?"

He paused, and for the first time since I met him, he seemed uncertain of himself. He cleared his throat softly. "I'm not quite sure if you're really of any value to me, Mr.

Wright, but the sheriff told me that you're a private investigator. Is that right?"

"Guilty as charged," I said, resisting the temptation to blow my own horn by touting my credentials and success stories. I needed to find out what he wanted from me. The convenience of campus housing was probably worth dealing with H. Michael.

"Well, then, perhaps we can help each other. I will allow you to stay free of charge in the Alumni House if you'll track down the source of this allegation. Would you be willing to risk finding out more if it meant exposing your nephew to charges?"

There was zero risk of that happening. Rex was guilty only of occasional tasteless humor, not crime. "It's a deal, Mr. Madison. I'll see what I can find out and report directly to you, not anyone else. Especially your assistant. I wouldn't want to tax his already overwrought brain. Where can I pick up a key to a room?"

It was likely both of us wanted the meeting to be done ASAP.

"From my secretary, Mr. Wright."

He didn't extend his hand to shake on the deal.

Chapter Six

With the memory of the exploding Mr. Wood fresh in my mind, there was no way I was going to eat in the cafeteria any time soon, so I headed to Whole Foods in nearby Charlottesville to stock up on essentials – salad in a bag, four kinds of cheeses, crostini and crackers, coffee, and six bottles of sauvignon blanc. My idea of the food pyramid.

Forty-five minutes later I was back on campus. After a quick walk-through of the Alumni House guest quarters, I was pleased. Two small rooms were reasonably clean and furnished with inexpensive but comfortable furniture and a double bed with a firm mattress, which suited well my sometimes bothersome back. The tiny kitchenette was equipped with a few plastic plates and bowls, flatware suspiciously like the cafeteria's, a Mr. Coffee with filters, and, to my delight, a cork screw. My finely honed powers of deduction concluded that the presence of a cork screw made it highly unlikely that H. Michael had ever stayed here. Alumni apparently didn't share the president's opinion that alcohol was Satan's nectar.

When I opened the small refrigerator to store the cheeses, wine, and salad, I noticed that the previous tenant had left behind what I guessed to be a lime in the crisper. Closer scrutiny revealed the lime to be the desiccated remains of what had been a head of lettuce. The irony of calling the drawer a crisper wasn't lost on me. Most ironies weren't, in fact. I generally surveyed life as a series of ironies, often at my expense.

My cell buzzed impatiently. It was Rex, calling from what I assumed was an unauthorized cell phone. "Uncle Danny, I'm free for a couple hours. The police said we are free to go anywhere on campus but not off. Where are you?"

"Staying at the Alumni House. Figured I'd hang around for a while."

"Great! May I come over?"

"You read my mind, Rex. I'm in the first room to the left of the entrance. See you in a few minutes."

A couple hours would give me time to pick Rex's brain. Did he know of anyone who wanted Mr. Wood dead? Had he noticed any political extremists among faculty or students? What was the prevailing mood of students after the murder? Did any students seem especially uneasy? I'd like some idea of the kinds of people who inhabited this place these days. I figured I'd be busy with Barney early next morning and needed Rex's insights before hooking up with Barney and whoever else might be involved in the investigation.

Rex must have sprinted the distance between his dorm and the Alumni House, which was on the perimeter of the campus. "Have a seat, Rex. Cheese and crackers? Don't have any sodas," I offered.

"No thanks, Uncle Danny. Don't have much of an appetite." Understandable. Taking in the guest quarters, he added, "Maybe someday I'll be staying here. Hopefully under different circumstances."

Rex didn't appear to be nervous but was less exuberant than he usually was. Not being around him for months at a time, though, I couldn't tell if maybe he was just maturing, gaining a little more self-confidence. At that age, I would have been a wreck after seeing what he had just hours earlier. Before I called his mother later, I wanted to be assured that he wasn't effecting a stoic front while broiling inside.

"Of course, Rex. You'll come back for Alumni Weekends, I'm sure. Friends you make here are friends for a lifetime." That was another beige lie. I kept up with only a couple guys I had thought were like brothers – my junior and senior year roommates – and even then it was usually an exchange of emails maybe twice a year. I paused long enough to see if he wanted to speak. He didn't. "Rex, it would probably help us both if you told me more about the people you hang out with here. And what you know about those you don't associate with, either by choice or because of lack of anything in common. Let's start with your friends I met in the cafeteria."

"What about them, Uncle Danny? They're all good guys. One is on the basketball team with me, and the others have been on my hall in the dorm for three years. We're tight. Sometimes we visit each other's homes on weekend passes. I trust them as much as I trust anyone. They don't do drugs…well, maybe a little yerba."

"What's yerba?" I interrupted.

"Marijuana."

"Nothing harder? Is there a lot of drug use here?" The note H. Michael showed me seemed to indicate there was.

Hesitating momentarily, Rex said, "Me and my friends do smoke once in a while – please don't tell Mom – but never on campus. I've heard that some others, though, are using drugs. Bad drugs. Coke, heroin, meth. I don't know that for a fact. It's just campus talk, you know?"

That posed more questions than answers. If there was drug distribution on campus, why would anyone want to focus on Rex? Rex would never use hard drugs, but did he know more than what he was saying? I didn't want to interrupt the flow of this conversation by sidetracking the questions, however, and decided to take him at his word. At least for the time being.

"How could anyone get away with using those drugs here, Rex? Surely their behavior would cause the staff, if not students, to become suspicious." I remembered well the code of silence we students followed: No one ratted on another student. Period. But it was one thing to keep quiet about sneaking out of the dorm at night; quite another to overlook dangerous drugs. Could today's students willingly overlook a felony just to follow the Code?

"Like I said, Uncle Danny, I haven't seen anything myself. If I had to guess who it might be, though, I could come up with a few names."

That was good enough for me. I would do some sleuthing on my own while working with Barney.

"Go ahead, Rex, hazard your guesses. And tell me why them in particular."

Without hesitating, Rex blurted three names. Obviously he had given this some thought before today. "Addison Witt, Brandon Van Verdenburg, and Whitey Jensen. They're all from filthy rich families, and they're assholes, brutally hazing freshmen, getting all sorts of special privileges from Hmmm because their parents donate money – lots of it – to Clanton, and talking racist smack. No one I know likes them. I steer clear of them. Besides, they're the guys who hush up whenever I'm around them. There's obviously something they don't want me to know."

"Hmmm? Who's Hmmm?" I asked.

"That's what we call H. Michael Madison." Obviously my generation wasn't the only one to have a nickname for every faculty.

"Do they know you, Rex?" Could one of them be the anonymous writer naming Rex as a drug dealer? And why would any of them, if guilty of using and maybe dealing drugs, want to implicate Rex?

"Yeah, they do. I jacked Witt up against a locker room wall last year when he started picking on one of my friends after gym class. 'You want to mess with Tony, you gotta mess with me first,' I told him. He mumbled some shit under his breath about how sorry I'd be. I told him, 'Whatever' and haven't spoken to him since. He gives me his idea of a threatening look whenever he sees me around campus. I laugh at him and keep walking."

Suspect Number One, at least for drug dealing and trying to get Rex in trouble. But could he be tied to the murder? I made a mental note to myself to check him out tomorrow.

"Thanks, Rex. What you said about them makes sense to me. I have to make a couple calls now. I'll see you tomorrow before classes."

Rex seemed a little less tense as he exited my rooms. Rex was a strong kid, but dealing with bullies and dealing with a murderer were different animals.

Opening a bottle of wine and allowing myself a hefty pour in a plastic glass from the cupboard, I needed to make three calls before calling it a day. My secretary back in Virginia Beach would have no new clients to report, I hoped, and I had to allay any concerns my sister might have about Rex before checking in with Bethany, who so far was happy to be my lover, not my wife. With ex-wife Number 2 rejoining the ranks of the married, I was no longer obligated to pay alimony, and that was one expenditure I didn't plan on resurrecting. Not even the most beautiful supermodel could get me to walk down the aisle again.

Chapter Seven

Barney was pacing the floor, thinking, I assumed, giving him the benefit of the doubt. After insufficient coffee, I decided to sit back and see how he conducted an investigation.

"Now, Danny Boy, I know you're eager to learn, but you gotta keep your mouth shut unless I give you the OK, OK? See, it's all about the rhythm. Once I get my rhythm of interrogating going, it never fails – unless it's interrupted. Now, before I call in the first student to question, I'll give you the condensed version of this report I got from those forensics people. In a nutshell, it says here that his stomach exploded from a tiny unsophisticated bomb he unintentionally ate at lunch. They figure the killer had to be within twenty-five feet to detonate it with some sort of radio signal. It also gives a catalog of the contents of his stomach. The guy put on the feedbag, yes sir, he sure did." Sheriff Gladstone Dixon – always to be Barney to me – had probably never seen a forensic report before. In a small village in a rural county, the nearest thing to criminal activity was teenagers drinking beer in the Meatland parking lot.

When Barney said "REport," my confidence in his abilities waned somewhat further. I didn't change my expression, though, and asked what the contents of Wood's stomach were to confirm what I had observed him eat at the ill-fated lunch.

"Lemme see…beef stew, potatoes, lots of bread, knockwurst, and a ton of chocolate pie."

"That was it? Nothing else?"

"Nope. But ain't that enough?" He chuckled.

I smiled at Barney and pretended to be writing down notes. I had wanted to confirm that Mr. Wood hadn't ingested the bomb prior to eating in the cafeteria but didn't feel a compelling urge to share that information with Barney.

"OK, now, Danny Boy —"

"Please, Gladstone, Danny is sufficient. I haven't been a boy since…well, since attending this school myself."

"Didn't know you was a student here." He looked at me through squinted eyes, and I tried to decipher that look. Did he disapprove of this school? If so, his interrogation could be biased *and* incompetent.

"Yes, a long time ago, Gladstone. Never was too fond of the place but got a good education here that has allowed me to make my massive salary as a private detective."

"So private dicks get a lot of money? Who knew?" He shrugged his narrow shoulders and stroked his holstered pistol.

I made another mental note to myself not to use sarcasm around Barney.

"Well, maybe not massive, Gladstone, just enough to pay alimony." I laughed to let him know that I had been kidding. I was getting antsy to start the questioning.

The first student entered when Barney called his name. "Amos Feinstein? You're lucky number one. Come inside and take a seat."

Amos was short and slim with curly dark hair and brown darting eyes that were taking in everything around him. My money was on Amos to win if it should become a battle of wits.

"So, Amos Feinstein, tell me what you know about what happened in the cafeteria yesterday." Barney apparently was not one to waste time with preliminary chatting.

"Well, I had lunch. And, yeah, the teacher exploded." Amos didn't crack a smile and looked directly at Barney. Was he covering up something or testing Barney?

"Listen here, punk, don't be a smartass, or you'll get on the wrong side of the law, and you don't wanna be there, hear?"

Amos paused, then began to laugh. I didn't like where this was heading. It seemed clear already that Amos was rebellious with incompetent authority and would not reveal anything if he knew it.

"Something funny about this, boy?" Barney said, his teeth clenched. He stood up from his chair and, arms akimbo, glared at Amos.

"Nope. Pitiful, maybe. But funny? Not so much."

Before Barney could respond, I interrupted. "Sheriff, I wonder if you'd allow me to question this student. I know that breaks your protocol, but I..." Seeing Amos smirk, I directed my next words to him. "Amos, if you know what's good for you, you'll wipe that smirk off your face and get serious." I didn't want to intimidate him and get nothing from him, but I had to let Barney think I was supporting him. Turning back to Barney, who was giving Amos what he probably thought was his most menacing look, I said, "How about it, Sheriff? Let me ask him a couple questions before you wrap it up."

Barney looked at Amos, then at me, then at Amos. "If you wanna ruin your day with this punk, go ahead. I'm getting some coffee at the cafeteria. Want some?"

"Yes, that would be great, Sheriff. Black. But only if it isn't the usual sludge."

After Barney left us, I turned to Amos. "I'm Mr. Wright, Rex Hardy's uncle. Know him?"

"Yeah. What business is any of this to you?"

"I am visiting my nephew. I went to Clanton myself and thought I'd lend a hand here. I'm a private detective." I looked for any signs that Amos was relaxing. Not a single change of posture or facial expressions. "Feinstein's a Jewish name, right? Are you Jewish, Amos?"

"Yeah. You got a problem with that?" He glared at me.

Pay dirt! Amos was defensive because he had to be at this place. His sarcasm set off my irony meter like a Geiger counter at Hiroshima.

"Not in the slightest. My roommate when I was here was Jewish, and we got along great. The kid took a lot of insults from a certain element here as the token Jew." My roommate was actually Presbyterian. Was I starting to get a little too comfortable with my beige lies?

"Some jerks call me Jewboy. As if that's supposed to hurt my feelings." He snorted and said in a softer voice. "So, how did your roommate deal with those losers?"

"He didn't. He just ignored them. Eventually they accepted him as some sort of inevitability and reserved most of their puerile remarks for the new Hispanic kid. They called him 'Spic' even though he was from Mexico, not Puerto Rico. That should give you some idea of their mental acumen."

Amos chuckled, perhaps reluctantly. I knew then that he was ready to cooperate.

"So, Amos, will you give me serious answers to a couple questions?"

"Sure, fire away."

"What do you know about the event in the cafeteria?"

"Only what I heard from other guys. Mr. Wood exploded."

"You mean you weren't in the cafeteria when it happened?"

"Not only was I not in the cafeteria but also I wasn't even on campus. I was on a field trip to UVA. I'd like to go there if I can get in."

Barney's ineptitude exceeded my previous estimation. I was never one to enjoy or even understand poetry, but one resonated with me, Dryden's skewering of Shadwell in "Mac Flecknoe," in which Shadwell, mature in dullness from his tender years, waged immortal war with wit. Barney lost that war long ago. I assumed Amos's alibi would be easily verified.

"Amos, I'll make a quick inquiry to check on that, but my feeling is that we have wasted your time. Wait in the hall for a minute while I call the dean's office. I'll excuse you as soon as I hear something."

Amos started to say something, then must have reconsidered and left the room. A quick call to the academic dean's secretary confirmed that Amos's class was indeed away on a field trip at the time of the murder. I poked my head out the door and told Amos he could leave just as Barney approached with our coffees.

"Hey, Danny, what are you doing letting him go? He's a suspect!" His tense body and stony face indicated he was not pleased with me or Amos.

"Not to worry, Sheriff. I just confirmed his alibi – he wasn't even on campus. Who's next to be interviewed?" I needed to see just how inept this process was going to be.

"Andy Swanson, then Archie Patterson."

Fearing the worst, I asked, "I've never done one of these extensive investigations, Gladstone. How do you line up the potential witnesses or suspects?"

"Why, alphabetically of course."

"You alphabetize by first name, Gladstone?"

"Yep. Hey, we need to get cracking. Time's flying."

"How many are you going to question?"

"All 350 students and fifty-some teachers and staff. Can't leave no stone unturned."

For one of the few times in my life I was speechless.

Chapter Eight

"These many, then, shall die. Their names are pricked. Look, with a spot I damn him."

Wielding his pen like an ice pick, he forcefully stabbed a name on a list of faculty names. All but three names were highlighted in yellow. The remaining three were chosen to die.

Peering over his shoulder, the second of three men talking in hushed tones in the small faculty apartment said, "This one we won't explode, right?"

"This one will die less spectacularly. Poison. Wood was a blight on the face of the earth and deserved to die violently. Because he was universally despised, they will think he was the victim of a hate crime until number two. We know better, of course. He had to be sacrificed to disguise our motive. Victim number two will be another necessary sacrifice. We need the police to think there's a serial killer at work before we get to the vermin that ruined our lives. If we wait till the news of the Ponzi scheme that screwed us and five others, the police will immediately zero in on us as prime suspects. This way, he'll just be another victim of a serial killer. Once he's disposed of, let them try to discover a link among the three. They'll be spinning their wheels."

"What do you have in mind?" asked the third man hesitantly.

"Since he teaches chemistry, I think it suitable for him to die in his lab. Preferably while teaching those worthless pricks. Leave the details to me. I'll figure out a way for him to poison himself in the next couple days. The news of the Ponzi scheme will break soon, and our work has to be finished before then." He burst into mirthless laughter. "When shall we three meet again? In thunder, lightning, or in rain?"

"Oh, for crissakes, talk plain English. This isn't a scene from a play. We're killing two innocent people. We're murderers!"

"You're being weak! Revenge is the only satisfaction left to us. They are innocent only of not duping investors. We'll meet here tomorrow at 7:00."

Alone after the chastised two left the apartment, he turned on his computer and Googled "poisons commonly used in chemistry experiments."

Chapter Nine

Barney is such a fool! If I wait for that idiot to muddle up this investigation, the Feds or Richmond police will get involved, and I will not have any leeway to investigate. No other choice but to see H. Michael again.

Before I went to see the president, I needed to clear my head, and walking the perimeter of the verdant campus on a brisk October day did just that and probably lowered my blood pressure from stroke level. By the time I reached the administration building, I was sure of only two facts: One, there were drug deals going on here, and whoever was behind them wanted to place suspicion on my nephew. Two, there was a murderer most likely living in faculty housing or a dorm, and I had no idea what his motive to kill Mr. Wood was, if there even was one. Maybe he got unlucky and swallowed that belly bomb that could just as easily been ingested by Rex or me or the librarian or Mr. Jenkins. The method of murder, however, nagged at me and seemed to indicate a deep hatred. Murdering someone that violently had to mean the victim was intended; it was personal. Who would derive pleasure from blowing up an innocent victim?

Having mentally prepared myself for dealing with the always unpleasant Miss Foss, I was happily surprised not to find her guarding the president's office. I took full advantage of her absence to knock on the president's door and announce, "It's me, Mr. Madison, Danny Wright. Got a minute?"

"Come on in and close the door behind you," H. Michael answered immediately.

He rose from his seat behind his huge desk and sat in the chair next to mine. I guess this time he didn't want the separation and feeling of authority the desk afforded him. "Mr. Wright, I was just about to call you. I'm eager to know what you've found out so far about drugs on this campus."

"Nothing concrete yet, but I have some leads. There's another issue we need to discuss first. Sheriff Dixon is beyond inept. He could mess up a wet dream…oops, excuse my crude comparison. Anyway, his strategy is to interview every student, then the entire faculty and staff. No checking to see who was even around that day or in another building or teaching. Do you have any idea how long that will take?"

"Umm, actually, no." H. Michael didn't seem overly concerned about a prolonged investigation.

"The longer it takes for the media to get hold of this, the better, it seems to me," he added. His voice and demeanor exuded misplaced confidence. Maybe he'd had a lot of previous experience in damage control, but this time he was wrong.

"Not in this case, Mr. Madison. Sheriff Dixon is so incompetent that whoever killed Mr. Wood will never be found out, and an unsolved mystery is honey to flies in the media. And who's to say the killer won't kill again soon?" I paused for a few seconds to give him time to process.

"I have an idea, but I need your support. Give me carte blanche to see what I can dig up without having that foolish albatross hanging around my neck. If I can't find something within a few days, then we need to call in the FBI. When that happens, expect a shitstorm – er, media frenzy. And that can't be good for Clanton Academy. And I need insider eyes and ears – my nephew and a student named Amos Feinstein. Can you make that happen?"

He seemed to bristle at my question. "I can make that and anything else at this school happen, Mr. Wright. The question I ask myself is, *Will* I make that happen? I don't see the need to involve students in this, especially if they could be put in harm's way."

"They won't be in harm's way, Mr. Madison. I simply need them to be able to report to me at my convenience and keep their eyes and ears open. Other than the two of us and those two, no one else will know of their participation. No disrespect intended to your assistant, but kids, even his narcs, won't tell him much."

He stared into the window behind his desk for almost a minute before responding. "All right, Mr. Wright, I will agree to your request. But I still don't like it. Anything not directly under my control bothers me. And if other authorities get involved in this, the deal is off. I have to think of Clanton Academy first and foremost."

'Not to mention his own ass,' I thought.

"I'll order their dorm proctor to allow them freedom of movement with no explanation. Tell them to be discreet and, for God's sake, not to let any other students know they have this privilege."

The die was cast. I left his office feeling only marginally more confident that I could remove suspicion from Rex or find out anything involving the murder. First item on my agenda was to start questioning faculty while Rex and Amos snooped around students' activities.

I headed over to the library to see the librarian.

Chapter Ten

The library had been completely remodeled since I had attended Clanton and now resembled a computer lab more than the comfortable retreat to read and study as it was in my day. I enjoyed the former often and the latter only sporadically. I had fonder memories of the library than any other part of this school.

The librarian was chatting with a couple students at his checkout desk. With a full head of gray hair, stylish glasses, and only slightly overweight compact body in a tweed sport coat, he seemed the model of academe, almost professorial.

Until he opened his mouth.

"Hello, I am the libarian, Hank Mann. Can I help you?" he asked me in a slightly effeminate voice.

Did I hear him correctly? *Libarian*?

"Actually, yes, you can. I am Rex Hardy's uncle, and I was sitting at the table beside you when the unfortunate explosion occurred in the cafeteria. I am a private investigator, though not officially working on the case. I would like to ask some questions to, if nothing else, satisfy my curiosity and make sure my nephew is safe at this school."

He winced at the mention of the explosion. "Ooh, that was so horrible. Mr. Wood was a friend of mine. To everyone, really. Who would want to do such a terrible thing?"

'Who wouldn't?' I thought. I hadn't ever heard a kind word about the man before now.

"I have no idea. I was hoping you could help me out in that regard. Do you know anyone who works here, for instance, who might harbor a grudge against him? Or even a student."

"Not a soul. What is really sad is that he was almost set to retire. He had just bought a condom in his hometown and planned to move into it next year."

Now, that would be an impressive feat.

"He was counting the days and had already begun to pack. He talked of nothing else."

Not according to the conversation I had overheard. I let it slide. I didn't think this interview was headed anywhere but asked a few more questions that had equally unfruitful results. Suddenly he became agitated and pranced over to the window, which he opened, and fussed at students congregated outside.

Still upset when he returned to his desk, he explained himself. "I swan, those awful boys. They block the view of the fire hydrogen there and then people don't see it and park their cars there. Five times a day or more I have to deal with that. I planted irishes around it hoping the boys would hang out somewhere else, but instead they trampled them all. I report them every week to the president, but he doesn't do anything. It's too annoying for words. As if I don't have too much work to do anyway. I am chained to my desk." He sighed, then added, "Is there anything else I can help you with?"

"Well, yes, you can. I need some reading material. Do you have a copy of Sheridan's *The Rivals*?"

"Never heard of it," he said and turned his attention to some students taking liberties with their computers.

Chapter Eleven

Hard to believe that the frustrated librarian could be a murderer.

Or a librarian.

He had yielded no information of value, and I hoped that the next interview would be more productive.

I headed to the academic dean's office to get a list of faculty and their classroom numbers. The current secretary – or administrative assistant, according to the sign on her desk – greeted me with a smile and was the most pleasant and attractive person I had met at Clanton. Probably in her early forties, she wore a discreet amount of makeup and a tight sweater with a name tag that said Mrs. Clarkson. It was strategically placed to direct attention to her pert breasts. 'Intentionally?' I wondered. Either she had contact lenses that bothered her, or she was flirting with me because her upturned blue eyes batted often and seductively. I hoped she wore no contact lenses.

"What can I do for you?" she asked sweetly.

If only she knew. Focus, Danny, focus. I tried to visualize Bethany to get my mind where it needed to be. "Um, I would appreciate your giving me a list of faculty classrooms and their locations, Mrs. Clarkson. I am working on the murder investigation. You can check with Mr. Madison. Wright. Danny Wright is my name." I expected her to call the president, but instead she rose from her chair and walked around her desk to my side. Her curvaceous figure was as alluring as her face.

She placed her hand gently on my shoulder and guided me out of her office to the hallway, where Mr. Madison was talking with his assistant. "No need to call the president, Mr. Wright. We can check with him in person." She smiled at me, then at Mr. Madison, and said softly, "Mr. Madison, I hate to disturb you, but this gentleman said he's working on the investigation. Could you please corroborate that?"

Mr. Madison's demeanor changed the instant he heard her voice. He turned from his assistant. "Why, yes he is, Mrs. Clarkson." His face was frozen in a broad smile that some less kindly persons might consider lecherous. I immediately dropped my own smile. "Please give him the same level of cooperation as you give to me." Both the president and I watched intently as Mrs. Clarkson walked back into her office to photocopy the list I had requested.

"She's worth her weight in gold," he said to me.

Undoubtedly, I thought.

List in hand, I headed to see if Mr. Jenkins could spare a few minutes. It took only five minutes to reach his classroom on the third floor of the red brick building that housed the history, English, and foreign language departments' classrooms. Hearing that his class was in session, I knocked softly and waited for maybe ten seconds till he opened the door.

"Good to see you again, Mr. Wright," he said dryly. He remembered me after all. "What can I do for you?" He hadn't changed all that much since he taught me. About six feet tall, no sign of a gut, maybe a few lines around the eyes. He seemed to be in good physical shape for a man in his late fifties.

"I apologize for interrupting your class, Mr. Jenkins. Mr. Madison has authorized me to conduct a preliminary investigation into the murder that you so vividly witnessed, and I hope you will be able to meet briefly with me after your classes are finished."

"I won't be able to provide you with much help, but, yes, of course we can meet here in twenty minutes if that suits you." He turned to what must have been students that were violating classroom rules. "Shut your damn mouths unless you want an even lower grade than the mediocre grades you settle for." He glared at them for fully ten seconds, then turned to me. The classroom was silent.

"Twenty minutes will be fine. I'll be prompt. Don't want to incur your wrath," I said jokingly.

I smiled. He didn't. He closed the door in my face.

His personality hadn't mellowed in the twenty years since he had taught me.

Chapter Twelve

For twenty minutes I relaxed in the empty teachers' lounge, sorting my thoughts and drinking coffee that must have been made sometime in the past millennium. Did the murderer have a vendetta against Mr. Wood? How could a drug operation possibly exist here without students being aware of it? No secret lasted long when I was here, and I doubted one would last today either. If two persons knew something, it didn't take long for hundreds to share the knowledge. Were Clanton employees possibly involved? More questions and still nothing close to an answer. This place wasn't much to my liking when I was a student here, but it was safe, if nothing else, and it offered a good education. A possible drug operation and a definite murder made me consider calling my sister and advising her to withdraw Rex from Clanton. Too many good boarding schools with safe environments in Virginia to risk Rex's well-being.

A strident bell interrupted my thinking. Time to see the surly Mr. Jenkins.

His classroom door was open, and I walked into the room that was now empty save Mr. Jenkins hunched over papers on his desk. His red pen a sword, he attacked the papers in front of him, grunting and muttering as students' efforts appalled him.

"Um, excuse me, Mr. Jenkins. Sorry to interrupt you, but it's —"

He flung the red sword across the desk into a pile of books and turned to me. "You've spared me from a stroke, Mr. Wright. I thought you and your classmates were bad, but this crop of what are euphemistically called students has reached heretofore unplumbed depths of ignorance and stupidity." A grunt served as punctuation.

I could have easily rebutted him about my classmates, if not the current students. Among my posse, several finished med school, two became attorneys, and a handful graduated with honors from schools like UVA, UNC, The University of Richmond, and William and Mary. Hardly dolts. But I didn't want to get on his bad side even more than I already was.

"Sorry to hear that, Mr. Jenkins. I'm sure teaching is a frustrating and sometimes unrewarding profession."

His eyes narrowing, he seemed to be appraising me before deciding if he should bother conversing with yet another inferior idiot. I guess I passed his scrutiny sufficiently for him to continue with less hostility in his tone.

With a sigh of resignation, he said, "Mr. Wright, if you only knew the half of it. I haven't heard an intelligent statement in this room in over a decade. To a one, they are lazy, either uninformed or misinformed, and inarticulate. Most are also immoral and vulgar."

I risked an abrupt end to the conversation by asking why he didn't get a position at another school.

"It's only natural that you should wonder why I bother to stay in this goddamn shit-hole. The answer is as simple as my students' brains are. My retirement fund. If I stick around another seven or eight years, I will be able to retire comfortably. If I leave now, I'll have to roll my fund over and not get the full benefit. I think it's something like an annual four percent return if I opt out. If I stay, I will collect double the pension than if I seek greener pastures. So, there you have it. Money, not pastures, is the only green I am seeking."

He looked at me to see my reaction. My expression remained unchanged. That he sought security was not blameworthy. I should probably be thinking along those lines myself. The only difference in his current attitude and when he taught me was his increased use of profanity.

"Is Clanton's pension fund different from most other schools'? Seems that it's set up to reward loyalty and longevity and to punish teachers leaving before falling in the line of duty." Having never worked for an employer other than myself, I had no idea of how retirement funds worked.

"It didn't used to be set up this way under previous presidents. H. Michael Madison engineered this change 'to ensure stability and continuity,' in his words. Motherfucker fucked any of us over forty-five years old. We're too old to start over elsewhere, and he knows it. Outliving him is the only satisfaction available to me. I'll dance on his grave." He seemed surprised at his open vehemence and chuckled. "I guess you think I am a sour, bitter old man, Mr. Wright. But remember, it's you who started it."

"Touché." I smiled at him, trying to put him at ease. "Let's move on to a different subject. How well did you know Mr. Wood? Was he a good friend that you ate with often?"

That generated another chuckle. "I, a friend of that bloated, toxic misanthrope?"

The only difference I could detect in who was more misanthropic, he or Mr. Wood, was Mr. Wood's superior girth.

"Yes, the three of us – Wood, Mr. Mann, and I – ate lunch and supper together every day, but it was not because I enjoyed the company. I could barely tolerate Wood's non-stop sniping, and Mann is even worse than my students when it comes to thinking or speaking, in case you haven't noticed. The only thing we have – er... had in common was a penis. And I'm not too sure that Mann qualifies on that count. There are times when I consider his name a misnomer."

"I don't quite understand, Mr. Jenkins. Are you saying that you ate with those men simply because they're male?"

"That's not what I was saying. Let me finish my explanation, if you don't mind. We ate together because we're bachelors. Period. My colleagues at Clanton consider bachelors pariahs and have nothing to do with us socially. Which suits me fine. I'd rather spend my time alone than endure a henpecking nag, thank you. The only woman at this shit-hole that is tolerable is the wife of the Latin teacher. Even Wood spared her his venom because she baked him pies from time to time with a gentle caveat that he share a piece with Mann and me." He paused briefly. "Hmmm, I hope she doesn't stop providing me the only palatable food at this culinary wasteland now that he's no longer with us." Apparently Mr. Wood went to the Great Beyond unmourned by anyone except possibly Mr. Mann.

"Aside from discriminating against bachelors in general, are you aware of any faculty who might dislike Mr. Wood for reasons other than his marital status or unpleasant personality?"

Mr. Jenkins must have approved of my choice of adjectives. "Unpleasant? Good use of understatement, Mr. Wright. Did you learn that in my class?"

How could I overlook an opportunity to ingratiate myself in the service of seeking truth? "None other, Mr. Jenkins. Your class was the best I ever had. I may not have been as bright as you'd like, but I learned more than I ever thought possible."

Mr. Jenkins actually smiled briefly. "Thank you. Mr. Wright. It is a rarity that someone like me who sets high standards of learning is appreciated."

"I know it is safe to share that with you now. Had I done so twenty years ago, you'd have probably thought I was brown-nosing." I hoped this descent into sycophancy yielded something of value.

"You're quite right, Mr. Wright, which is probably why no students ever tell me that."

Yeah, that was definitely the reason.

"You mentioned that Mr. Madison caused a lot of dislike among those of you of a certain age. Was Mr. Wood among those? It's my understanding he was about to retire. Was his retirement adversely affected by Madison's changes to the pension fund?"

"Wood had saved a lot of money during his time here. He never went anywhere or did anything. He probably had quite a stash. Those of us who actually have lives don't have that sort of nest egg to fall back on. As for our not-so-esteemed president, I was just telling Mann recently, "I told that cocksucker Madison that —"

As if on cue, H. Michael Madison walked by Jenkins' classroom. Seeing him through the open door, Mr. Jenkins jumped from his seat and rushed out into the hallway. "Mr. Madison, it's so good to see you in our halls of learning. May I be of any assistance?"

Mr. Wood would have had a word for Mr. Jenkins. Unctuous. But did being bitter and fawning qualify him as a potential murderer? Yet another question without an answer.

Chapter Thirteen

After killing half an hour chatting with Barney, I figured I could kill two birds with one stone by stopping by the chemistry class to see Rex and Amos and talk with their teacher. The door was open and class was in session. I decided to observe from the hallway and snag Rex and Amos on their way out to arrange a meeting for lunch.

Mr. Thomason was a burly man, maybe 6'4" tall and weighing around 250 pounds. His sharp Slavic features belied his Tidewater accent and ready smile as he interacted with the class. It was soon apparent why Rex had told me how much he enjoyed Mr. Thomason's class.

"Can any of you worthless creatures tell me anything about Boyle's Law?" No one seemed to object to being called a worthless creature, and several hands immediately shot up, including Amos's but not Rex's.

Surveying the class, Mr. Thomason nodded toward Amos. "Mr. Feinstein, you think you can avoid bringing disgrace to your people and get an answer right for a change?"

"My people?" Amos asked with a smile. Not too long ago he had bristled at being questioned about his being

Jewish, and now he was smiling? Mr. Thomason was already disappearing from my list of potential murderers.

"Yes, soccer players."

"Oh, for a minute I thought you were referring to my being Jewish," Amos joked.

"No, Mr. Feinstein, I'll leave that to your friends…if you have any." Like most high-school students, they enjoyed hearing a friend get burned by a teacher – if in jest – and laughed. "Well, we are waiting to hear what you have to say about Mr. Boyle."

"Sir, Boyle proposed that the pressure of a gas increases as its volume decreases."

"Right you are, Mr. Feinstein. Please try to remember that tomorrow when we conduct an experiment in the lab."

Loudly enough for all to hear, someone in the back of the room murmured, "Is there is a connection between Boyle's Law and flatulence?"

"That experiment you can conduct back in the dorm, Mr. Blake. Unless your roommate objects." Again the class laughed, then started assembling their belongings in anticipation of the bell.

"Any last-minute questions before class lets out?" Mr. Thomason asked.

A small blond boy in the back raised his hand tentatively.

"What's your question, Steven? Quickly now, class is almost over."

Steven's slight speech impediment became apparent as soon as he spoke. "Thish morning I huwd a wumow. It's about Mr. Woowd."

"Are you asking about Mr. Wood or Mr. Word?" Mr. Thomason replied.

Frustrated, Steven said, "*Woowd*. I said *Woowd*."

"So, you're asking about Mr. Word?"

"Yes, I alweady told you. Mr. Woowd. Is it twue he exploded?"

"You mean Mr. Wood?"

"No. Mr. *Woowd*. Not Mr. *Woowd*. He died in the cafetewia. What about Mr. Woowd?"

I expected the class to laugh at the exchange, but they surprised me by remaining silent. Finally the boy sitting beside Steven spoke up. "Sir, I think Steven is asking if there's anything to the rumor that Mr. Word also died."

"Ah, I hadn't heard that rumor. Steven, in answer to your question, no, Mr. Word, the Spanish teacher, is very much alive. I spoke with him this morning."

That seemed to satisfy Steven, who stuffed his books into his backpack and whispered something I couldn't hear to the boy who had clarified the question.

The bell rang, and the students filed orderly out of the room. Rex started when he saw me.

"What are you doing here, Uncle Danny?"

"I need to talk with you at lunch. Catch up to Amos and ask if he'll sit with us, too, OK? I'll be there in about ten minutes. I need to see Mr. Thomason briefly."

Rex nodded and ran down the hallway toward Amos.

Unaware that I had entered the room, Mr. Thomason was neatening his desk – or, rather, rearranging stacks of papers, books, Styrofoam coffee cups, and whiteboard markers into a different pattern of dishevelment.

"Mr. Thomason," I said, getting his attention. "May I speak with you briefly? I know it's your lunch break, so I won't keep you long."

Mr. Thomason laughed softly. "You won't be keeping me from lunch. I brownbag it in my office. I'm afraid the cuisine at Clanton Academy is not to my liking. You have the advantage on me, however. May I ask who you are?"

"Stupid of me, sorry. I am Rex Hardy's uncle, and I want —"

"To ask me some questions about Mr. Wood? I was forewarned that you'd be around eventually." He smiled when he finished my sentence.

"And who told you that?"

"Rollie Jenkins, an English teacher here, saw me right before class. He was going up and down the hallway asking every teacher in the building if you'd spoken with him. I was the last teacher he spoke with, and when I said I hadn't seen you, he seemed annoyed and said I'd meet you soon enough because you obviously are questioning every teacher who was in the cafeteria. I told him I hadn't eaten in the cafeteria all year, to which he grunted 'Whatever' and went away in a huff. That's the first time I have ever spoken with him."

Mr. Thomason had inadvertently given himself an alibi when he revealed he hadn't been in the cafeteria. I set him at ease by telling him that his absence from the cafeteria precluded his being a person of interest.

"Damn, Mr. Wright, I was looking forward to being grilled." He laughed and added. "Does that mean the interview's over?"

"Fraid so, Mr. Thomason. I would like to add, though, how highly my nephew holds you in regard, and I could tell by my brief eavesdropping that you seem to have a great rapport with your students. I noticed that none of them laughed at the student with the speech impediment. How did you manage to get them to be so accepting of their peers?"

"I have only a few classroom rules, Mr. Wright, and the most important of them is that no student will *ever* demean another student in my class." He paused briefly. "I leave that job to me." He laughed heartily.

"If you had been my chemistry teacher when I was a student here, maybe I wouldn't have been so inept. I almost blew up your lab once. It's been a pleasure meeting you, Mr. Thomason. Keep on doing what you do and enjoy lunch. Regrettably, I am forced to eat at the cafeteria. My last meal there was more than I had bargained for, and I'm not talking about the food. "

"I'd share my lunch with you, Mr. Wright, but I'm afraid I have only enough food to assuage my rather large appetite." We both laughed, and I left his classroom feeling better than I had in two days.

Quite a contrast in pedagogical styles between Mr. Thomason and Mr. Jenkins. And what prompted Mr. Jenkins to become the town crier after our meeting?

Chapter Fourteen

When I entered the cafeteria, I scanned the full room to see where Rex was seated. Waving to me from a table far in the back under one of the windows, Rex sat alone. The cafeteria rarely was noisy when I was a student, with most people softly chatting. Only the occasional squalling baby disrupted the white noise, and today was no exception. Talking in confidence should be relatively easy in the back of the room without my having to raise my voice to be heard.

Apparently I was the last person to go through the line during this lunch shift. Cafeteria Katie was the server today, and I took advantage of my being the sole person in line to ask her a few questions.

"Good morning, Katie. Remember me? Danny Wright."

"I'm sorry. Mr. Wright. I don't remember names too good, but I do remember your face. You was here when the man who eats five hamburgers exploded, right? That was a terrible day for me," she said. A couple seconds later, she added, "For him, too, I reckon."

"You called Mr. Wood 'the man who eats five hamburgers'? I think I can figure out how you came up with that name."

"Yes, sir, that man could sure put it away. Who'd want to do such a thing as explode the poor guy?"

"That's a good question, Katie. I don't have an answer to that, but I do have a couple questions that maybe you could answer."

Wiping food spills off the area between serving trays, she nodded and said, "Go ahead, Mr. -- um, what was the name again?"

"Wright. Danny Wright. Katie, on that day, who brought in the trays of food you served?"

"I did. I always carry the trays in from the kitchen. Those kitchen folks are trifling. Don't want no one interfering with my system."

Her answer provided one of the first solid facts to surface. It was highly doubtful that Katie had sabotaged the food, and if no one else besides her handled the food in the cafeteria, then someone back in the kitchen could have inserted the bomb into a knockwurst. Opportunity, yes, but what motive to kill a random victim would a cafeteria worker have? Or – and this seemed a stretch – Mr. Jenkins also had opportunity to slip in the miniature bomb but didn't seem to have a motive. What was now clear was that only cafeteria employees and Mr. Jenkins had opportunity, but any motive remained unknown. After eating, I needed to get a list of kitchen workers who were working that morning.

"Thanks, Katie. You're a great help." I scanned the trays of food in front of me. "Any suggestions as to what food I should choose today?"

"Sure enough, Mr. Wright." Looking around to make sure no one overheard her, she added, "Ain't nothing here worth eating in my opinion, but if you're starving, then I expect the mac and cheese won't kill you."

"After the last time I ate lunch here, I am not too sure about that."

Cafeteria Katie let loose a loud cackle. "You are too funny, Mr. Wright!"

I wasn't so sure I was kidding.

Katie loaded my tray with her recommended swill du jour, and I headed to the table Rex had secured for us.

Chapter Fifteen

I wended my way through the crowded room, holding my tray in front of me like a shield until I reached Rex's table.

"I reserved this by squatter's right," Rex proudly announced. "Amos is running late."

"That's OK. I am, too. I enjoyed meeting your teacher, Rex. You're lucky to have him. I wasn't as fortunate. My chemistry teacher had the personality of a copperhead, and I hated every minute in that class. Thomason's only the second adult I've come across here so far that has been friendly to me."

"There are a few others, Uncle Danny. On the whole, though, most of the teachers and staff hired by Hmmm are too damn sour, and the ones that stuck around like Wood and Jenkins are even worse. Er, *were* worse. I keep forgetting, or maybe trying to forget, that Wood was murdered right next to me." He seemed preoccupied for a few seconds. "Hey, Uncle Danny, do you have a Facebook account?"

"Hell no! I don't even have time to read a newspaper most days, and when I have time to spare, the last thing I want is to see rampant narcissism. Why do you ask?"

"Because I thought you might have seen the pictures going viral of post-explosion Mr. Wood."

Oh, oh. This was bad. Really bad. I had hoped for at least another day to dig around while Barney was making his way through the alphabet, but now that the murder was public, it wouldn't be long before real investigators arrived and relieved Barney of his responsibility.

"Damn, Rex! How long have those pictures been on Facebook?"

"Since this morning, maybe late last night."

I should have foreseen that kids would be using their unauthorized cell phones for more than idle chatter. "Are you Facebook friends with any adults here, Rex?" I needed to know if H. Michael had been informed.

"Just one. Mrs. Clarkson."

Red flags were popping up all over the place.

"Rex, I won't embarrass you and stick my nose where it doesn't belong, but have you and Mrs. Clarkson been more than Facebook friends?"

Rex turned red and blurted, "How'd you —" His head slumped to his chest.

"Rex, I have met the lady, remember? She's beautiful. And she's trouble. As I said, I won't pry, but here's some avuncular advice. If you and she are friends with benefits rather than just Facebook friends, cut the ties. Now. You have no idea how badly that could end up."

Clearly ashamed, Rex said, avoiding eye contact with me, "It's not just me, Uncle Danny. I know of at least six other seniors who meet with her, usually after clubs she sponsors."

"What those guys are doing is none of my business. You are, however, and let me repeat myself – cut the cord. I wasn't going to tell you until I could clear you, but someone, most likely a student, sent an anonymous letter to Mr. Madison saying you're dealing drugs here. I'll find out sooner or later who actually is dealing drugs, but what do you think this would look like if it came out before then? And you know that eventually this will surface. I feel confident that Mr. Madison will not look kindly upon Tea and Sympathy on his watch."

"Huh? Tea and Sympathy?"

"An old movie about – never mind."

"Someone said I deal drugs? Uncle Danny, that is crazy. I would never do that. Never!" He looked crestfallen. I had tried to avoid adding more emotional baggage. He was already dealing with more than any kid his age should have to. I was left with no choice, though, after learning about the amorous Mrs. Clarkson.

"I believe you, Rex. Just do as I say, OK?"

"Do what?" asked Amos who, unnoticed, had approached us. I hoped he hadn't overheard more of this conversation. The old axiom that there is no such thing as a secret once two students knew something had been proven time and again within these old brick walls.

"Nothing, Amos," replied Rex. He probably had learned that same axiom by mid-semester his first year at Clanton. "Uncle Danny was just reminding me that I need to call my mom tonight."

When Amos didn't pursue it, I felt certain he hadn't heard any more of the conversation. Amos put down his tray containing only two rolls, a small plastic packet of peanut butter and another of margarine, and a glass of a purple liquid that didn't look promising. We had a Pepsi machine when I was a student here, and some days that was the only edible food to be had in the cafeteria.

"Fellas, any suspicious activity among students that you observed? Now that Facebook has become involved, this place will be crawling with Feds and police soon, and my freedom of movement will be severely curtailed. I figure I have till tomorrow morning."

Amos and Rex looked at each other and shrugged. Almost in sync, they replied, "Nah, nothing to report."

Another disappointment. I had hoped for something concrete to remove suspicion from Rex.

"Well, keep your eyes and ears open and report to me as soon as you have something. Even the slightest change of someone's behavior may be important. For instance, if you see someone nodding off mid-morning, he may be on drugs."

"Or he may be in Davidson's class," Rex said, laughing.

I ignored the levity. They simply didn't understand the gravity of the situation, and I didn't really want to make it known to them.

"In the meantime, look around the cafeteria and tell me if these people are always here during this lunch shift."

Both boys did a quick scan of every table. "All these students and teachers eat here first lunch. Sometimes not their families, though."

"So, no other people eat here during this lunch period?" I asked. It would be more than a little helpful if I knew that only someone in this room could have detonated the belly bomb.

"Well, once in a while the president comes in, but other than him, nope, these are all the regulars," Rex said looking at Amos. Amos nodded in agreement.

"Good to know," I said. "Since you are both observant guys, how'd you like to give me a quick character analysis of every adult here?"

Judging by their immediate affirmative response, I got the impression they seemed eager to dish the goods on adults ordinarily off-limits to their criticism.

I was counting on it.

Chapter Sixteen

I surveyed the room and mentally scratched teachers who had taught me, and Mr. Jenkins and Mr. Mann, whom I had already interviewed, leaving a dozen persons who had been hired since my departure. Eliminating the four women among them because the nature of the murder seemed too violent and messy for a woman, I was left with eight men for Amos and Rex to profile.

At the table farthest away from us near the front of the cafeteria were seated three women and a middle-aged, thin man who was given to sweeping use of his arms and hands while conversing animatedly with the three ladies. "Let's start with the guy in the brown suit sitting with three ladies up front, guys," I said, pointing to the table I had referenced. "What's his position at Clanton and what's your opinion of him?"

Rex answered immediately. "Oh, that's Mr. Harland…teaches US Government. He's a good guy who likes to argue politics at the drop of a hat. Extremely conservative, of course. There are maybe only three liberals on the staff."

That was a significant change since I had attended Clanton. Back then the mixture of liberals and conservatives was probably fifty-fifty, and students enjoyed listening to entertaining, impromptu debates by faculty in the hallways, the cafeteria, and even bleachers during basketball games.

"Yeah, I have Harland next semester, and other students have told me I'll enjoy the class – as long as I don't let on I am a liberal. Fat chance of *that* happening," Amos said, laughing.

"OK, next is the table to our left with four young men, maybe in their twenties. Obviously they can't have been here very long."

Rex stared at them intensely for a few seconds. It was unlikely he had ever been asked to provide character analyses before, and I assumed he was sorting through previous interactions, if he had any, to come up with opinions.

Finally he spoke. "The tall, skinny guy in the navy blue sport coat and rumpled khakis, he's in the math department. Actually they all are. I had him for Trig last year. He worked us hard, but he cares about his students. My SAT math score went up over 100 points after taking that class."

"Mine, too," said Amos. "Say, Mr. Wright, you went to UVA, right?" I nodded a yes. "Do you think I'll get in with 2150 on my SAT and a 4.4 GPA with plenty of advanced placement classes?"

"You're in-state, aren't you?" I asked

"Yes, Virginia Beach. Does that matter?"

"It matters a lot, Amos, or at least it did when I went there. If you are from a rural county, I'd say your chances are better than excellent. From Northern Virginia or Virginia Beach/ Norfolk areas that have probably thousands of kids applying, you're probably a good but not a safe bet. Being a state school, UVA makes sure it has all areas and counties in Virginia represented in its student body. It became apparent to me within a week of talking with everyone in my dorm that the only reason I was even there was because I grew up in rural Cumberland County, where not many high-school graduates continued their education. It wasn't as if we all had sloping foreheads and extra fingers, Amos. It's just that most of us stuck around and got jobs. My mother wanted us to explore the world, and Rex's mother and I took advantage of being in a rural county and applied to and were accepted by UVA and William and Mary even though we had lesser credentials and a whole lot less money than most of our peers. Unless admissions policies have changed, you'd be smart to also apply to a couple good back-up schools that are very likely to accept you."

Amos frowned. "That's pretty much what my guidance counselor told me. I want to go to UVA so badly it hurts."

We would have to discuss colleges some other time. I needed to redirect the discussion to the remaining six men.

"How about the other three math teachers?" I asked.

"They're all low-key bachelors…no temper flare-ups, no noticeable idiosyncrasies. They hang out together and I've seen them sniffing around the secretaries a lot. Doesn't seem to be much social life around here for them. I doubt there's a violent bone in their bodies. I took Algebra from the African-American guy – Mr. Stewart – and Geometry from the redheaded guy with the receding hairline – Mr. Reynolds. I don't think they party much because I see them almost every night in the dorm helping guys who are having trouble keeping up in their classes," Amos said.

Not one of the teachers seemed a person of interest so far.

"One table left, fellas," I said, pointing to a table with four large men, one an African-American about mid-thirties wearing an expensive pin-striped black suit; another huge African-American, who, even seated, looked to be well over 6'8" tall with broad shoulders; and two white guys wearing warm-up suits and running shoes.

"The really tall guy is the Varsity basketball coach and athletic director, Uncle Danny. He's respected by everyone here. The two guys in athletic clothes are football coaches who don't work here – they come in from town to coach and then go home."

That was another change since I was here as a student. Non-teaching coaches? Not sure that was a good idea for many reasons.

"What do you know about those two?" I asked.

"Not much, Uncle Danny. Neither Amos nor I play football. From my limited dealings and what my friends on the football team have said, I guess they're OK. They stick to themselves and don't hang out with Clanton employees as far as I can tell."

Down to the last unknown, the well-dressed large man wearing a suit that cost more money than I made last month.

Chapter Seventeen

Both Amos and Rex seemed stumped.

"Uncle Danny, I really can't help you with that one. He's new this year and works in administration. Don't know what he does, but I heard he played college football."

'He must be doing something right to afford that suit. Probably an Armani?' I thought. Who was I kidding? I couldn't tell one expensive suit from another. Armani was the *only* expensive brand I had heard of.

"How about you, Amos? Know anything about him, even if it's just student gossip?"

Amos scratched his head vigorously, and his brow wrinkled. "Sir, I haven't heard word one about him. The only time I have ever seen him is in the cafeteria. Oops, no, make that at football games, too. But he always stands by himself on the sidewalk above the bleachers."

Engrossed in this disappointing exchange, we didn't notice H. Michael standing above us holding a tray with only a dab of cottage cheese in it. Seems that he wasn't too fond of the cafeteria cuisine, either.

"Well, well, gentlemen, how are three of Clanton's finest doing today?" It was more a question to find out why we were eating together than an inquiry about our well-being.

Rather than let the boys fumble my opportunity to see what H. Michael thought of Mr. Armani, I spoke up. "They're here by my invitation, Mr. Madison. I was hoping they could provide me with students' perspective on the staff that eat lunch this period. You'll be happy to know that they gave their stamp of approval to all but one. They haven't had any contact with that large African-American gentleman sitting with three coaches over there."

H. Michael turned to see which table I was pointing to. "Ah, you must mean Mr. Merrick Bobson. He's the new CFO I hired last summer. As you may well realize, Mr. Wright, a man in my position, responsible for the well-being of this academy, must be an expert in personnel. And I pride myself in judging the character of applicants for any position from maintenance staff to faculty and administration. Only the highest moral character belongs here, and I make sure that all hires are exceptional in that regard."

"That's a pretty tall order, Mr. Madison," I said. "How can you be sure of that no matter how thoroughly you vet someone?"

That damn smug smile reappeared on his face. "Nothing else is important, Mr. Wright, except a man's belief in the Lord. If an applicant knows and abides by Romans, I don't care if he doesn't know pedagogical principles or lacks experience. Those things can be learned under my watch and tutelage."

I glanced at Amos. He clearly was not happy with the message that H. Madison conveyed, nor was I, but I couldn't allow myself the luxury of debate at this time.

"How perceptive of you, Mr. Madison," I said, trying to hold down the little bit of vomit that rose to my throat.

"Certainly, though, you'd want your CFO to be certified and savvy with budgets and investments and bottom lines."

"Of course, Mr. Wright. That goes without saying. I checked Mr. Bobson's credentials thoroughly as soon as he left the interview. I knew in my heart after hearing his impassioned pronouncement of his Christian beliefs that he is incapable of wrongdoing. The man is a paragon of virtue, maybe my best hire."

"High praise, Mr. Madison," I said. "I hope for Clanton's sake that you're as perceptive in hiring as you claim. I know you don't have the highest of opinions about most of the staff that worked here when I was a student, but from my experience, they were dedicated teachers and coaches who prepared us well for both college and life. My biggest complaint about them was that they were too strict. Maybe, in retrospect, their strictness wasn't all that bad."

Not wanting H. Michael to think I was criticizing him, even though I subtly was doing just that, I added, "But I suppose all alumni think the good ole days were better. You probably think that yourself."

"Not so, Mr. Wright. The public school I attended was rife with depravity, and as for my college...well, let's just say that not all Catholic institutions live up to the Church's claims."

I couldn't imagine any college that could meet his expectations of morality. "Which college did you attend, Mr. Madison? Georgetown?"

"No, but I wish I had. No, I attended that Sodom otherwise known as Notre Dame. Can you imagine that the Church actually condones having a graven idol on campus? Worse, they mock the Lord by calling it Touchdown Jesus! I vowed there would be none of that heresy when I took the reins here." He was getting red in the face – and not from embarrassment. I feared a sermon was imminent.

To change the direction of this dialog, I asked him where Mr. Merrick Bobson played football.

Visibly calming himself down, H. Michael paused, then said, "Not that it's relevant, but he played at Mr. Jefferson's university."

Another UVA man. Mr. Bobson had at least one check mark in the plus column. Maybe it was time to meet the man myself.

"Thank you so much for your insights, Mr. Madison. It's reassuring that Clanton has a man of perception and integrity at the helm."

I could tell by his smile that H. Michael was not immune to flattery. As he continued to the table where other staff members sat, Rex and Amos rolled their eyes. Though they knew little of Mr. Merrick Bobson, they knew more than they wanted about H. Michael Madison.

Chapter Eighteen

I drank another cup of coffee after the cafeteria cleared out
to give the kitchen workers time to finish their lunch duties.
How I could intrude on their activities to ask questions still
had me at sea, but I needed to speak with them now, so I
figured I'd introduce myself and dive right in. A page out
of Barney's book, yes, but necessary under the
circumstances. The Feds and Richmond law enforcement
team had probably already called ahead to H. Michael, and
I wanted to get as much snooping done as possible before
their arrival.

I didn't think it possible, but the kitchen was more
unappealing than the dining area. Ancient oven doors
blackened with cooked-on grease lined one wall, and four
large refrigerators and freezers with grimy surfaces filled
the wall opposite them. Against the back wall were four
deep stainless steel sinks and a stainless steel counter.
Dinged cooking utensils were hanging above them from
racks. Around a large island in the center of the room were
huddled four kitchen workers, all men who were talking
and laughing loudly, though not loudly enough for me to
distinguish what they were saying from where I stood by
the swinging door I had entered.

'Here goes nothing,' I thought as I strode toward them. The first man to notice me approaching them, a short, rotund man of indeterminate age, had turned toward me and cleared his throat loudly, nodding his head toward me. Immediate silence.

"Good afternoon, gentlemen. I would like to ask you all a few questions about the murder in the cafeteria two days ago. One at a time, if you don't mind. May I have your names first?" If they asked for ID, I'd be at a dead end.

The rotund man who had alerted them of my presence spoke first. "I am Eugene Griffin, to my right is Jake Griffin, to my left is Snake Griffin, and behind me is Eustice Shaflay. We don't mind answering any questions you got long as it don't interfere with our break." Apparently Mr. Griffin Number One was the spokesman.

"Thank you, Mr. – may I call you Gene?"

"Call me anything you want. I ain't got nothing to hide."

Now, why would he think I thought he had something to hide?

"OK, Gene. How about we go to that corner to talk. If you other gentlemen wouldn't mind, please stay where we are right now. This won't take but a few minutes, and I'll ask the cafeteria supervisor to give you an extra fifteen minutes break time." My lies were starting to mount up. I didn't have any idea who their supervisor was or where he or she had an office. They smiled broadly at my deception.

Leaning against the only open wall space in the room, Gene seemed pleased to talk once he thought he'd have an extra break. "So, whadda you wanna know?"

"Well, for starters, are you four always the only employees that work this lunch shift?"

"Yeah, both this one and the one before it. The next shift don't start till two o'clock. Most of them is part-timers who work only five hours. They must not need no benefits."

His missing teeth indicated that perhaps dental benefits weren't available to him either.

"You guys must work as a team, right? Are all of you side by side as you prepare the tubs of food that Katie carries out to serve? In other words, do any of you work alone at any time?"

"That bitch Katie thinks she's the queen of the Nile, thinking we ain't smart enough to carry tubs of food. In case no one told her, that ain't rocket science." Rolling his eyes and sniffing, he must have thought he had provided a deep insight.

I glanced over at the three men waiting. All were intently staring at us, no doubt trying to figure out what we were talking about. They shuffled nervously and avoided talking with one another.

"So, just to be sure, at all times, you four are working together within close proximity?"

"Yep. We been working together so long that we have teamwork. That next shift of part-timers couldn't get done what we does in five hours to our two. The boss knows it, too."

"How do you all feel about the people who eat the foods you prepare? Do you ever interact with them?"

"We don't even know who's out there. As I said, we work like a well-oiled machine in here and don't have no time to socialize like that jabberbox Katie."

I thanked him for his time and asked him to please send over another Griffin.

When the other three workers' accounts matched Gene's, it seemed reasonable to remove them as persons of interest. Still, it wouldn't hurt to talk with the cafeteria supervisor to confirm their accounts.

"Fellas, I sure do appreciate your talking with me." They grinned and seemed more at ease now that we had finished our business. "I'd like to ask your boss right now about that extra break for you. Where can I find him?"

"Out the door and to the left down the hallway," offered the only non-Griffin.

I felt comfortable believing them, and that left me stymied. If they or Katie didn't tamper with the food, and it seemed highly unlikely that Mr. Mann or Mr. Jenkins could have done so, how in hell did that bomb end up in the knockwurst?

Chapter Nineteen

The door to the cafeteria supervisor's office was open, but I knocked anyway to get his attention, as he was on the phone. He motioned with a wagging finger to hold on for a second while he ended the call.

"Damn parents! What do they expect for their lousy tuition money, cordon bleu? I get a hundred of those complaint calls a year."

He sighed and slumped his shoulders. I didn't want to add to his resignation that his world was both disappointing and unsatisfying. If I had his dead-end job, I'd be sighing and slumping, too.

"So, what can I do for you, mister? If it's a complaint that brought you here, I'm not in the mood to talk." He remained seated and looked up at me, his face wearing a slight grimace that may have been permanent.

"Not to worry, Mr. – um, I'm sorry. I forgot your name." I tried to look as contrite as I could. Truth be told, I wasn't all *that* concerned for his minor despair, though even the indigestible excuse for food he served didn't warrant explosions of his patrons. I'd feel bad, too, if my sausages were lethal weapons.

"Mark, just call me Mark."

"OK, Mark, I won't keep you long. I just need to get your confirmation of your staff's work routine. I'm an investigator working on the murder that took place here a couple days ago." I didn't feel a pressing need to add that I was unofficial at best.

He stood up abruptly and extended a hand to shake. "Good to meet you – um, I don't know your name. What's your handle?"

"Wright's the name. Danny Wright."

"Well, Mr. Wright, I'd be glad to answer any questions," he said with a stronger voice than he had a minute ago. "Unless you want to know any of my secret recipes," he added, softly laughing at what he probably thought was a mood lightener.

I repressed the urge to cringe. "Not to worry on that count, Mark. I don't cook. No, what I want to know is how do the four workers operate during the lunch shifts? Do they stay together within eyesight of one another at all times, that sort of thing?"

"For about an hour and a half, yes, they are almost in each other's pockets. Our kitchen is too small to have separate work stations."

"OK, thanks, that's pretty much what they told me. I took the liberty of asking them a few quick questions ten minutes ago." He didn't seem to have any particular interest in my intrusion into their work space and sat back down again. "They seemed to be trustworthy guys, Mark, but I am curious that three quarters of your lunch staff have the same name. Are they related? They do share facial similarities."

That triggered a generous snort and hearty laugh. "Of my fifteen employees, seven are Griffins and five are

Shaflays. I think they're all related to one another. You can't move around the hollows down the road without bumping into a Griffin or a Shaflay. They're smarter than they look and don't mind putting in a hard day's work. I wish a few more of them could read better, but I take what I can get, and they're honest and don't complain like the damn parents do." Apparently the disgruntled parent's call still rankled.

"Yeah, I imagine it's annoying when you don't get the appreciation you deserve." I needed to butter him up a bit. "Ah, one more thing. I told the four workers that I'd ask if you'd give them an extra fifteen minutes of break time since I took up some of theirs."

"Consider it done, Mr. Wright."

Mission accomplished. Sort of. With the kitchen staff off the hook as far as I was concerned, I still was nowhere. It seemed the only explanation was that Mann or Jenkins somehow planted the bomb in the knockwurst, and that seemed highly unlikely. Besides, what possible motive could either of them have to murder Mr. Wood so violently as he sat and ate beside them? It wasn't adding up.

Deep in thought as I walked down the hallway, I almost bumped into Barney walking in my direction.

"Whoa, slow down there, pardner," Barney admonished as he put his arm around my shoulder and led me to the side. "Let's compare notes for a spell."

Not part of my game plan, but what could it hurt?

"Good idea, Gladstone. You go first."

Barney fondled the handle of his gun, hiked up his narrow shoulders, and plowed right into a lengthy account of his detective work. He was especially proud that he had already reached the Rs – Randy Hawthorne was the last student he had interviewed – but disappointed that all the questioning had yielded little, if any, information of value. "I figure I'll be done with all the students by noon tomorrow. Then I'll start in on the teachers and staff. How's your investigating goin'? Proberly not as good as mine but no harm in asking. Might recognize something that seemed unimportant to your untrained eyes but might be a solid clue. My highly honed skills can cull out a clue in a blizzard."

I had no idea what that metaphor was supposed to mean.

"I wish I had something better to share with you, Gladstone, but I work slower than you and have talked with only a couple teachers and cafeteria workers."

Barney patted me on the back to console me. "I coulda told you that you're barking up the wrong tree asking them questions. No doubt in my mind that it was an inside job and the killer is a student. Lot of punks at this hoity toity place."

"You're absolutely right as usual, Gladstone." Why I had hoped that he could provide anything of value indicated to me just how frustrated I was at coming up empty at every turn. "Oh, one more thing. Kids posted pictures of the exploded body all over Facebook and Instagram. I figure the Feds and Richmond special investigators will be here soon. You going to work with them?" It was highly unlikely they'd welcome his input. Or mine.

"Hmmm, hadn't counted on the big boys poking around. I reckon I'll have to allow them leeway, but they'd better report to me if they dig something up. This is my case, and I don't want no outsiders messing things up."

Delusions can be so gratifying.

Chapter Twenty

The transaction went as smoothly as he could have wished for. Paying the unscrupulous jeweler two thousand dollars for 600 mg. of potassium cyanide was money well spent, he reasoned. Wearing a gray wig, padding through his midriff, and dark oversized glasses, and speaking in a flawless German accent should suffice to conceal his identity should the jeweler ever get caught selling on the black market.

'Now all that remains is for me to determine an opportune time to visit Thomason at his classroom and present him with a plastic container of my special gift – extra hot curried chicken laced with my secret ingredient. The best plan is the simplest plan. Fewer moving parts and less chance of error,' he thought. 'My revenge will be complete sooner than I had hoped. Merrick, I hope you take notice of these two deaths. Yours will happen soon enough.'

The closest Indian restaurant was almost twenty miles away, and time was of the essence. Not a time to exceed the speed limit to risk being ticketed, however. Having put in for a half day off, he had plenty of time to make the drive, buy the curried chicken, return to campus and head to the chemistry classroom before lunch break.

Arriving at a small strip mall, he easily found the restaurant he had looked for on a Google search. He was almost overly excited to be progressing so easily and stopped to take a deep breath before entering the source of inviting aroma emanating from within. Native intelligence, not experience, dictated the importance of a calm demeanor that would attract no notice.

"I'd like a carton of your hottest curried chicken. May I sample it first?" he politely asked the Indian server.

"Certainly, sir," he replied and spooned out a generous spoonful of chicken coated with a dark red sauce. Holding a napkin under the dripping spoon, he handed it over with an admonition. "Very hot, sir. Be careful."

Even a small dollop caused immediate burning sensation in his mouth. Perfect. 'I could put Drano in this stuff, and it wouldn't affect the taste,' he thought, satisfied with his choice of weapon. "Ah, as hot as I like it! Yes, this is perfect," he said to the waiting server.

After hastily removing the elements of disguise in the car, he clumsily dressed in his customary attire of beige slacks and a rumpled navy blue sport coat, not the typical garb for a man on a pernicious mission.

He listened to the soothing sounds of Enya on the return trip to campus. With not a single flaw in the execution of his plan to mar his day, he couldn't stop smiling. 'The deal is closed. Thomason, if your soul is going to make it to heaven, tonight's the night.' The Bard seemed especially prophetic today, and that pleased him. Hard as he tried, he couldn't stop smiling.

That is, until he saw the four black SUVs with government tags parked in front of the administration building.

Chapter Twenty-one

The black SUVs in themselves were a sign, and the government tags sealed the deal. I knew it was inevitable, but the one time the federal government was on time for anything had to be today? I felt a headache coming on.

Walking back into the math and science building in hopes of getting in one more interview with a science teacher who had taught me and who had been in the cafeteria when the explosion occurred, I passed Mr. Thomason in the hallway. "Top of the morning, Mr. Wright," he said with a wide smile.

"Technically it's now afternoon, and there's not much to recommend it so far," I replied, frowning.

"I have plenty of lunch you could share with me in my office. Maybe that'll improve your mood," he generously offered despite the cloud hovering over my head.

"Rain check? I need to see Mr. Uterhopf before lunch break is finished," I replied and continued down the hall. When he taught me biology, I had tried to make Mr. Uterhopf seem more interesting by imagining that he was a crazed Nazi scientist. It didn't work. He was as bland as tapioca.

Alternately glancing at the classroom assignment sheet and the names above the doors, I found his classroom at the end of the hallway and knocked on the closed door. Waiting for a response, I took in this new science and math building that was far superior to the one I had vexed teachers in as a student. Its predecessor resembled the set of the original Frankenstein movie. It pleased me that the original lab equipment was used in one of my favorite movies, *Young Frankenstein*. Though films have always been a favorite pastime for me, snobbery never infected my tastes. Mel Brooks's comedies were on my list of favorites that included all Bogart and film noir movies, *All about Eve*, *Citizen Kane*, *The Godfather* movies I and II, *Victor Victoria*, and fifty or more from the 1930s through the 1980s. Eclectic, yes, but fun to watch. 'I need to get Rex interested in film that has more to it than shootings and car chases,' I thought, 'though *Bullitt* is first class.' I knocked on the door again, waited another minute, then started down the hallway, hoping that maybe Mr. Thomason's offer still stood. I was both hungry and disappointed. It was only a matter of time before the Feds would find me.

Not much time, it turned out. Two men in dark suits saw me walking toward them, paused for a second, and double-timed it toward me.

"You are Mr. Wright, correct?" the shorter of the two asked. He was probably five foot nine inches tall and packed 230 pounds of muscle that strained against the sleeves and shoulders of his coat. I instantly decided to be cooperative.

"Yes, sir, that's me. And who might you be?"

"FBI. I'm Sloane and this gentleman is Parker." Both flashed identification badges that I didn't have time to scan.

No matter. They reeked of FBI. "We need to speak with you, Mr. Wright. Follow us."

It was not a request.

They had already established headquarters of sorts in the administration building, usurping the office of one of the many superfluous administrators who had taken up residence in the time since I graduated.

Parker was a good eight inches taller than Sloane but weighed twenty pounds less. His dark suit seemed tailored, draping on his lean frame. I was starting to become more aware of my own sartorial shortcomings by the day.

"Mr. Wright, obviously you know why we're here. Mr. Madison told us that you'd be a good choice to begin our investigation, since you were sitting next to the victim and have been poking your nose into this business," Parker said in a monotone.

Poking my nose? This didn't bode well for me. "Well, yes, I am here visiting my nephew who attends Clanton, and we had the dubious pleasure of a rather spectacular first meal together."

"Tell us what you saw leading up to the explosion. Leave out no detail, no matter how insignificant it may seem," Sloane said.

"I know the drill, men. I am a private detective and —"

"Yes, we know. We'll get to that soon," said Parker with a stern look that I knew didn't indicate a favorable opinion of my profession.

"Well, there's not much to tell, really. I watched Mr. Wood load up his tray with entrees and sides and a whole pie. He sat with Mr. Mann to his right and Mr. Jenkins directly across from him. My nephew and I were maybe four feet to their left as you face their table, close enough to hear their conversation. Actually, most of the speaking was done by Mr. Wood, who was criticizing every person within his range of vision, all the while eating ferociously. As if eating enough for three men wasn't enough, he even ate the knockwurst Mr. Jenkins offered from his tray. In three large bites. Watching him eat was like watching a car wreck. Ugly, yes, but impossible not to watch. After he finished eating, I resumed talking with my nephew for maybe a minute, when a really loud belch from that table got our attention. We turned to see Mr. Wood seem almost startled at his gaseous emanation. His eyes were wide as saucers, and then – kaboom! He exploded from his gut."

"That's it? Nothing else to share?" asked Sloane.

"Nope, that pretty much sums it up. Everyone in the cafeteria, of course, was shocked, but no one left the room. The local sheriff arrived soon thereafter and declared it a crime scene. I think he got the names of everyone in the room at the time of the explosion."

"All right. Thanks for your observation, Mr. Wright. Now, as for your doing your own investigation, that officially stops. Now! To be candid, Mr. Wright, taking pictures of people *in flagrante delicto* is not much above a peeping Tom, in my opinion. Your clients may pay money for you to indulge in your pathetic vicarious sex life, but not us. If we hear of you sticking your nose where it doesn't belong, we'll arrest you, *capische*?" Sloane said.

I had never been insulted in three languages before.

"You made yourself crystal clear." I paused for effect. "*Idiota.*"

Two could play at that game.

His smirk made me wish I had the guts to call him an asshole. Maybe someday. I turned slowly and continued down the hallway, seething. Fat chance I wouldn't keep poking my nose into what they thought was their business. Sloane's arrogance was too contemptible to ignore.

Chapter Twenty-two

My pride wounded and my dander up, I headed up to the second floor of the administration building to check out Mr. Armani Suit. FBI goons couldn't stop me from discussing tuition money with the CFO, now, could they?

The number of administration offices had at least doubled in the past twenty years. It was like a maze, and because there were no names or positions labeling the offices, I wondered how I would locate him without disturbing the others by interrupting whatever they were working on. Peeking into offices with open doors, I didn't see anyone particularly busy, however, and the only voices I heard were from administrators chatting in the hallway. I approached two middle-aged men discussing what I surmised to be a football game judging by the few words I overheard.

"Excuse me," I interrupted. "Would you please direct me to the CFO's office?"

Looking at me for all of two seconds, the one with the bad toupee nodded his head to his right and grunted, "Third door down," then resumed his "work."

"Thanks," I said to their backs. They must have taken charm lessons from the FBI.

Mr. Bobson answered from behind the closed door immediately after I knocked. "Enter."

I was awed by his office, which, compared to H. Michael's, was palatial. A huge oriental carpet in mostly red hues covered the center of the room. Original art work, mostly oils, hung on the walls wallpapered with a warm shade of light grey linen. The focus of the room was a large and uncluttered Chippendale desk behind which, in an oversized red leather wing chair, sat the robust, expensively dressed Mr. Merrick Bobson. The room was as masculine as he was and made a statement of wealth and power.

"Hello, Mr. Bobson. I am Danny Wright, the uncle of a student here," I said, offering my hand to shake.

He stood up and leaned across the desk to take my hand. His powerful hand enveloped mine, and his grip was strong – very strong – but not crushing. "Good to meet you, Mr. Wright. To what do I owe this pleasure?" His smile could light up a room.

"I just wanted to meet you. You see, I was sitting next to Mr. Wood when he exploded, and I noticed you were eating in the cafeteria the same lunch period. Would you mind if I ask you a few questions about that day?"

"Fire away, Mr. Wright. I suppose they're the same ones two FBI agents asked not ten minutes ago."

Damn! The other two agents must have been here while I was being insulted by Sloane and Parker.

"I have no idea what they might be asking, Mr. Bobson. I am only concerned with the well-being of my nephew who was sitting with me at the table beside Mr. Wood."

"Of course, Mr. Wright," he said with seeming sincerity. "What an appalling experience for both of you. And of course to all of us at Clanton. I have been employed here for less than a year, but I already feel accepted as part of a community. Or The Clanton Family, as Mr. Madison calls it. What threatens one of us threatens all of us."

I hadn't noticed an overwhelming sense of familial love among the employees. Then again, I had only seen a small number of employees. Perhaps I missed that in all the ado.

"You're so right, Mr. Bobson. That such a terrible thing happened at my alma mater is distressing."

"Didn't know you are an alumni," Bobson said. I didn't wince at his misuse of the plural *alumni*. He hadn't had the same opportunity I had of studying Latin with Mr. Blair Franklin. Clanton was probably one of only a few schools that still offered Latin when I was here.

"Yes, I am a proud alumnus," I said, accentuating *alumnus*.

"Well, as an *alumni*, you have my full cooperation."

Maybe Latin classes had nothing to do with his ignorance of grammar after all.

"I appreciate that. Now, if I may ask, what was your take on the murder? Can you think of anyone who'd want to murder Mr. Wood?"

He hesitated a few seconds before answering. "To be truthful, I didn't know the man all that well. Some of my colleagues here advised me that maybe he wouldn't welcome me as a friend. They told me he had a thing about Blacks and jocks. I believe he referred to the gym as 'that temple of sweat' and Blacks as Ubangis." He vigorously shook his head as if to clear the man from his memory. "I do know the two men he sat with that day, though. In fact, I knew them before I came to Clanton."

Now, here was something of interest.

"Really? What a small world. If you don't mind my being personal, how did you know them?"

"Before I took this position, I was a financial adviser for Ferncliff and Lynch. I set up retirement funds for them and four other Clanton employees. I reckon they were pleased with the twenty percent return they made on their investments and recommended me for this position when the previous CFO left abruptly last year."

"Ah, I wondered how a Clanton employee could afford the expensive clothes you wear. Is that suit you're wearing an Armani? Mine are always off the rack from Macy's, but I recognize quality when I see it."

"What? This old rag?" he laughed. "Yes, I do like good clothes. And I had this office redone on my dime. 'Spend it if you got it' is my motto. Say, are you interested in having me set you up in a retirement account? I moonlight when I am not working here."

If he knew the state of my finances, he'd laugh, but I beat him to the punch. "Thanks for the offer. Skilled as you might be, however, it's hard to make chicken salad out of chicken shit. I'll keep your offer in mind, though, in case I ever make some decent money."

"You wouldn't regret it, Mr. Wright. I enjoy making others rich. And I don't mind helping myself along the way." He laughed and shook my hand again as a signal that our meeting was over.

Walking me to the door, he added, "Don't be a stranger."

His amiable way obviously went a long way toward his success in business. I couldn't help liking him myself. Maybe someday I would have money for him to invest for me. Right now that time was a long, long way off, and I had more pressing matters at hand. Murder and drugs.

Chapter Twenty-three

Addison Witt threw his grey hoodie on the floor beside his bunk, opened his laptop, and typed furiously while sitting on his bunk.

From: D.WittAddison@Clanton.org

To: TheBoss@gmail.com

Subject: heat

Cc: Verdendude@Clanton.org; JensenW@Clanton.org

WTF, Boss? Did you see the Feds crawling all over the place? Are they on to us? ADW

Addison waited for several minutes, staring at the screen as if that would hasten a reply. One finally came, but not from The Boss.

****
****

From: Verdendude@Clanton.org

To: D.WittAddison@Clanton.org

Subject: re:heat

Dude, this is insane! What did the boss say? BVD

****
****

From: D.WittAddison@Clanton.org

To: Verdendude@Clanton.org

Subject: re:heat

Nada. No reply yet. What do you think?

****
****

From: Verdendude@Clanton.org

To: D.WittAddison@Clanton.org

Subject: re:heat

I think we need to call it quits. At least for a while. I'm not taking any more chances. BVD

****
****

From: TheBoss@gmail.com

To: D.WittAddison@Clanton.org

Subject: re:heat

Of course I saw them, Witt. Everybody knows they're here. It's about the murder, Stupid. How dumb can you be to use school email? Delete it all and come see me on the double. Boss

****
****

From: D.WittAddison@Clanton.org

Dudes, my bad. Those guys are here about the murder. The Boss says to erase all our emails and not to use school email again. Later. Gonna see the Boss as soon as I can. I'll get back to you as soon as I know something. ADW

****

Closing his laptop after deleting his emails, Addison Witt took a deep breath and headed out to see The Boss. Being summoned usually meant he was in trouble.

Five minutes later, he reached the administration building, and, taking two steps at a time, he reached the second floor in a matter of seconds. He paused for a few seconds, caught his breath, stood erect, looked around to see if anyone else was in the hallway, and strode to The Boss's office. Without knocking, he entered and said in what he hoped was a nonchalant tone, "Reporting as ordered, Boss. What do you have in mind?"

"Sit down and shut up, stupid. Here's what I have in mind. Listen carefully, because I am not going to repeat myself. We will stop our shipments for four or five days, maybe longer if the Feds stick around. Don't do anything unless you hear from me, got it? And tell Van Verdenburg and Jensen what I just told you."

Shuffling his feet, Witt mumbled, "But what about that piece of shit, Rex Hardy? You want me to —"

"What I want you to do, Addison, is exactly what I told you. No more, no less, you understand? I'll take care of Hardy. Now get the hell out of here. And don't let anyone see you leave, for chrissakes."

Witt meekly backed out of the office and looked furtively up and down the hallway before bolting for the stairwell.

Walking back to his room, he kept asking himself, "Is the money worth being a lackey?"

By the time he got to his room, he knew the answer. "Yes, fuck, yes."

Chapter Twenty-four

Barney, of all people, knocked on my door at the Alumni House. His scowl told the tale.

"Did you talk to those guys from DC, Danno?"

"Yes, about two hours ago. Two of them, anyway. Total jerks. I take it you have, too. How'd it go with you?" I asked, knowing the answer.

Barney hiked his pants up as if preparing for something. Hard to tell with Barney. Seemed as though whenever I saw him, he was hiking his pants, fondling his gun, or trying to swell his chest.

"Not too good. The four of them told me basically to get lost. As if it's *their* case. Well, I got news for them. This is Dixon Country, and no city boys are gonna tell *me* what to do!" He squinted his eyes and started pacing around the small room, then stopped suddenly and looked around as if he noticed something for the first time. "Your digs here are right good, Danno. Better than where I live. They charge you much to stay here?"

I saw no merit in telling him that my stay here was compliments of H. Michael. "Pretty good deal, I think. Alumni get reasonable rates."

"Yeah, I was real surprised when you told me you was an alumni. You don't seem the type, like you was born with a silver spoon in your mouth."

I wasn't quite sure if that was Barney's version of a compliment. I was even less sure if I should form an alliance of sorts with him now that we were both *persona non grata*. It was doubtful that Barney would bring anything of value to the table. Then again, aside from Amos and Rex, I had no allies, and Barney had more legal right to be here than I did.

"Gladstone, I think both us are *real* folks, not like those arrogant pricks from DC. That's probably why we make a good team." Barney smiled at that, and I knew I could count on him to be loyal. At the moment, that seemed better than any other offers I had gotten since visiting my alma mater. "Say, Gladstone, have you seen any Richmond cops? I figured they'd make it their business, too."

"Yeah, saw two of them in the administration building jawing with the federal boys. Didn't look like a cordial conversation, if you get my drift."

Ah, maybe some dissension in the ranks? One could only hope.

"I wouldn't be surprised if the Feds tried to scare them off, too. How about you hanging around in the admin building and keep your eyes and ears open? They have no authority to make you leave. I need to check with my nephew about a few things not related to this case. Stop by here on your way home, OK?"

"Sure thing, Danno. I might introduce myself to those Richmond fellas and see what I can find out from them while I'm there. I'll see you here about 5:00."

Barney left my guest quarters much calmer than he had entered them. Not the sharpest knife in the drawer, but he had every right to be angry. This was his bailiwick, after all.

I needed to clear my head before finding Amos and Rex and decided to take a stroll around the campus. I figured there'd be another couple weeks before the leaves turned color. I had to admit that the campus in October and November looked spectacular with all the maples, sweet gums, red oaks, and hickory trees ablaze in hues of red and yellow, but it also was beautiful in late September. I daydreamed briefly about sitting in the football stands in past Septembers, watching, not the games in progress, but the mass of hardwoods behind the field that I knew would soon be a brilliant backdrop.

Outside, I looked around trying to make up my mind whether to head toward the front gate or wend my way around campus toward the athletic fields. I opted for the athletic fields.

The lacrosse and soccer fields were filled with players and coaches holding practices. The familiarity of the practice uniforms and drills the boys were going through belied that the place was a crime scene. It was as if nothing out of the ordinary had happened. The only disruption from the norm was the presence of the Feds and apparently a couple Richmond cops. Surrounding the manicured football field, which at the moment was devoid of players, was the cinder track, on which maybe forty or fifty boys were doing stretching exercises before negotiating the cross-country course. I strolled toward the far end of the track and felt relaxed for the first time since I arrived here. The sheer beauty of the emerald expanse filled with chattering and grunting and coaches' barked commands was a tonic. In this setting, I felt reconnected to Clanton.

Idly watching the harriers doing their stretching while chatting with one another, I ran through what I already knew. One, a horrific murder had occurred, but because the victim was universally despised, life at Clanton went on much as it had before the murder. Two, no doubt about it – drugs were being dealt here, and it seemed likely that students were involved, possibly, if Rex's instincts could be trusted, three in particular. But could they be acting alone? Didn't seem likely. Too many moving parts for students alone to deal with. Three, the choice of murder weapon, a belly bomb inserted into knockwurst, seemed to indicate both a rudimentary knowledge of science and a deep hatred of the victim. It was a reasonable assumption to rule out Cafeteria Katie and kitchen workers, leaving only Mann and Jenkins as potential killers. But what possible motive could either or both of them have? Did I miss something, maybe another way to load the knockwurst? Four, as much as their arrogance galled me, the Feds would have to be allowed to conduct their investigation. My role here limited for the time being, I might as well go back to Virginia Beach for a while and keep in touch with Rex and Amos by email and Barney by phone. There was nothing more I could do here until the Feds wrapped up their investigation.

Chapter Twenty-five

When the cross-country and track coach's whistle blew to end practice, I realized I'd better head back to the dorm to find Rex before he left for dinner. Scurrying back parallel to the track, I ran into the long-time track coach, an icon at Clanton who had won something like twenty-two consecutive league championships and fifteen state titles, and trained six Olympians that I knew of. Only a few pounds heavier than he was twenty years ago, he had the lanky look of a former runner.

"Good afternoon, Coach Rotherwood. I extended my hand to shake his and was about to identify myself when he said, "Well, I'll be, if it isn't Danny Wright. Haven't seen you in…what, twenty-five years?"

"Just twenty, sir. I finally remembered how to get here." In my freshman year I had run cross-country and actually got lost during an away meet. I wondered if he'd forgotten that embarrassing moment from my modest athletic career at Clanton.

Coach Rotherwood laughed heartily. "Danny, I'm not surprised it took this long to find your way back. You're the only runner I ever coached who got lost during a meet."

It figured that he'd have a memory like an elephant. I hoped he also remembered that by my junior year I was consistently placing in the top five at every cross-country meet. Never made top three – those guys were actually runners; I was just a plodder who worked hard. There were lots of us like that on the team. We got better by training with the all-star guys who pushed us beyond what we thought were our limits. Our depth was the secret to Clanton's cross-country and track teams' success, not simply talent. For every Olympian, there were ten plodders like me. That was Coach's genius – corralling guys in the eighth and ninth grade and training the fool out of them till they could actually contribute something.

"Coach, I'd really like to sit down and reminisce, but right now I am in a hurry to meet someone. Next time I'm back here, I'll make it a point to look you up, OK?" I really would like to hear his thoughts on the changes at Clanton. "One quick question before I dash. What relationship did you have with the unfortunate Mr. Wood?"

"Oh, Mr. Wood held me in the highest esteem, I'm sure." He winked. "I never had the opportunity to break bread or socialize with the gentleman, however. Look me up when you return. You know where to find me."

I shook hands with the legend and jogged to the dorm. If Coach was watching me, I hoped he saw I still had good knees if not lung power. I was wheezing after twenty steps, but I knew he couldn't hear me.

The dorm was astir with hundreds of Clanton men dropping off their books, grabbing quick showers, and making quick unauthorized calls to girlfriends before heading to the cafeteria. Rex almost ran me down as he rushed out of his room without looking to see if anyone was in his path.

"Whoa, Rex, slow down," I said, holding him back from knocking me over.

He flushed. "I am so sorry, Uncle Danny. I was in a big rush to meet my SAT tutor at the cafeteria."

"I won't keep you but a sec, Rex. Just wanted to let you know that I am going back to Virginia Beach till the Feds finish their business here. I feel confident that they'll find out whoever killed Mr. Wood, and they clearly don't want my help. Besides, I need to touch base with my secretary. And I need to remind Bethany I'm still alive."

"Bethany? Who's Bethany?"

"Bethany's my latest Significant Other, Rex."

"Wasn't your second wife's name Bethany, Uncle Danny?"

"No, her name was Beth."

Rex was trying hard to suppress a grin.

"Don't go there, Rex. Life's complicated," I added.

He stood silently, his head lowered enough to avoid making eye contact. Probably didn't know if I was angry. I wasn't and assured him so.

"We need to keep in touch about that other matter you and Amos are helping me with. Let's stay in touch daily with email, but use your Gmail address, not Clanton's. If you hear anything about the murder investigation, let me know that, too. As soon as I can, I'll be back to visit. I'm going to stop by your mom's on the way back. Anything you want me to tell her?"

"Just that I'm fine and I love her. And I need money."

'Don't we all,' I thought, and headed to my quarters to meet Barney before leaving for home.

Chapter Twenty-six

Barney was waiting for me at the entrance of the Alumni Building.

"C'mon in with me, Gladstone. I don't have long. Gotta get back home and tend to some business." Hurriedly packing the few clothes I had, I added, "Find out anything from the Richmond cops?"

Barney's bravado seemed to have wilted. "Not much. Except I don't think that either the Feds or those guys from Richmond want our help, and the Richmond guys have no love lost for the Feds. Not a whole lot of cooperation around here, that's for sure. And as far as I'm concerned they're all disrespecting us. One of those Richmond guys asked me if you was still hanging around, and when I told him you was, he said you wasn't nothing more than a glorified voyager. Don't have no idea what that even means."

I did. Insulted yet again, I thought, 'So, both the Feds and the Richmond cops think I am a professional voyeur. Well, fuck them. My profession may not be the most glorified, but my clients think I am the best thing out there when I present them pictures of philandering spouses.' My so-called voyeurism had resulted in many a divorce settlement, which was more than could be said for those pricks.

"Forget about them, Gladstone. When they run into a brick wall here, they'll take any help they can, trust me. That is, if we decide to give them any."

"Yeah, you got that right, Danno. I may be a small-town sheriff, but I'll match my record of successful arrests to theirs any day." He seemed mollified somewhat. "When you coming back here, Danno? We're keeping in touch, right?"

"Of course we are, Gladstone. Here's my cell phone number. Give me a call when or if you hear anything. I'm staying in Virginia Beach till the Feds and Richmond cops are gone. Or I may come back to visit my nephew, just to annoy them."

Gladstone let loose a belly laugh as if I had said a joke worthy of Jimmy Fallon.

"I plan on hanging around here myself. Let 'em try to get rid of me," Barney added.

After hustling Barney out the door, I checked the fridge to make sure there were no remains of food to rot, and hoofed it to the admin building to let H. Michael know that I was leaving for a while.

H. Michael greeted that news with a shrug that said "whatever" to me. "I assume you haven't gathered any information about drugs on campus, Mr. Wright. Maybe it's time to let these investigators in on the note I received."

"Please hold off on that for a while, Mr. Madison. There won't be any drug deals going down with all the Feds and cops around. My nephew and Feinstein are going to keep alert for any possible usage or dealing and will be in daily contact with me. If I hear anything, you'll be the first person to know."

My hope was that the Feds would catch whoever did in Mr. Wood, after which I would return and resume the drug investigation, and I needed H. Michael's cooperation for that.

"And I hope your generous offer to stay in the Alumni House will continue."

"The offer stands, Mr. Wright – unless, of course, a paying guest wants it. I am charged with the stewardship of the Lord's bounty. Clanton Academy is His school, and whatever I need to do to help it thrive, I will do."

I nodded in agreement as he pointed to the door to indicate our meeting was finished.

What exactly was H. Michael capable of doing in his zeal to protect Clanton Academy? I wondered.

Chapter Twenty-seven

The drive through Central Virginia was scenic but did little to settle my nagging doubt that the Feds' investigation would move quickly. With unlimited resources at their disposal, they had accomplished less than I had, and that wasn't much.

On a whim, I decided to stop by my sister's house before heading to my office. She must surely be more than a little worried about Rex, and if I could assuage her fears, I would. The reality was that I had no news that would accomplish that, however.

Parking on the tree-lined street in front of her spacious brick colonial house in a posh neighborhood, I was happy for the prosperity she had gained through marriage to an ambitious, loving guy. I seemed to be the Wright destined to carry the mantle of lower middle-class living. Majoring in psychology with a sociology minor hadn't propelled me into the world of high finance, but for the time being, I didn't mind that. I was content. For the most part, anyway.

Katherine greeted me with a quick hug and asked if I wanted something to drink. Too early for alcohol, I decided, and I had to get to my office before my secretary was done leafing through catalogues. No work for me translated to no work for her.

"Thanks, but no thanks. Don't have much time, Katherine. Just wanted to report in and assure you that Rex is doing fine and is not in harm's way."

Her furrowed brow indicated that she was less sure of that than I was. "Danny, I sent him to Clanton based on your recommendation that Rex would get a great education in a safe environment. Then a teacher explodes next to him. How is that not in harm's way?"

She had a point, of course. But if she withdrew Rex from Clanton now, he'd exit with suspicion that he was a drug dealer, not to mention that he'd be behind in any new curriculum he found himself in.

"You'll have to trust me on this one, Katherine. He'll be fine where he is."

Typical of a mom whose only child was in danger, she didn't seem convinced of my assessment based solely on what she probably thought was my gut feeling. In truth, it was. But I wouldn't want Rex to be there if I had even the slightest concern for his safety – from a murderer, at any rate. The drug issue was a whole other matter, and I knew better than to bring it up.

"If you're a hundred percent sure, Danny, I'll let him stay there. But if anything should happen to him – well, I would be devastated. And I would never forgive you."

Great. Now I had guilt to deal with.

"Some vote of confidence, Katherine. Look, if you're really uncomfortable with Rex's staying there, pull him out. I doubt he'll want to leave, though. And to my knowledge, only one or two students have been withdrawn by concerned parents, probably temporarily. I came by just to let you know that he's doing fine. No emotional scarring.

No nightmares. No sleeping with one eye open. He witnessed a grisly death, yes, but he's dealing with it. Everybody there is. Truth be told, nobody cared for Mr. Wood, and there's not even a hint of mourning that I observed. I heard that no one from Clanton even attended his funeral. He was a despicable human being, Katherine, and though he certainly didn't deserve to be murdered, his death had little impact on anyone there."

She kept pulling on her ear as she always did when nervous. After an awkward silence of more than thirty seconds, she said, "OK, Danny, I'll heed your advice on this. Reluctantly. Promise me that if there's any change, you'll tell me first thing."

I assured her that I would, and I meant that. Rex's safety was my number one concern.

Number two was getting to my office.

Chapter Twenty-eight

I entered the unassuming office I shared with my secretary, Julia Hawthorne, just as she was stuffing her pile of catalogs into the top drawer of her desk. I doubted that she had had any reason even to turn on her computer. My desk, an old metal schoolroom special I had picked up at a yard sale, was covered with papers as usual, none of which had anything to do with a case.

"Afternoon, Julia. Any calls I need to know about?"

A busty bottle blonde, Julia rolled her eyes, and said, "You were expecting what? Something like a client?"

I ignored her sarcasm out of habit. Having no case to work on was a concern, though it didn't seem overwhelming.

"What is the state of our finances, Julia?" I used the plural "we" to make her feel as if she was invested in the business. "Are we flush enough to pay the bills this month?"

"Yeah, and maybe enough left over to get a coffee maker that works. But, Danny, you have got to stick around and get some work. I'm not going to work like a field hand for free, you know."

I laughed even though I knew I shouldn't have. "You work like a field hand, Julia? Let's not get overly hyperbolic."

"I don't know what that word means, but I do know this: You don't bring in enough money to pay me, and I'm out of here." She seemed serious, and I didn't want to have to interview other catalog readers.

"You're right, Julia. What potential cases do I have?"

"There's a couple angry wives wanting to hire you to spy on their exes. Something about not getting enough alimony. And Grist Insurance Company wants you to look into a guy who claims he's disabled and they don't believe him. Want me to give them a call?"

Grist Insurance was one of my most reliable clients. It didn't seem to me that they wanted to pay any claims, and to me that was money in the bank. Usually I didn't find out any false claims. The few I did, however, were worth their money to continue hiring me.

The thought of eating more cold Burger King Whoppers while sitting in a car for eight hours hoping to catch a guy dodging alimony while living high enough on the hog to afford expensive restaurants held less appeal to me than usual. "Call Grist, Julia. Tell them that I'll start tomorrow morning."

"OK, Danny. Smart move." She called Grist, then stowed her phone in her purse and got up to leave. "Mind if I speak my mind before closing shop?"

Oh, oh. Whenever anyone prefaced a comment with that question, I knew I didn't want to hear whatever followed. In this instance I didn't have much choice in the matter; I knew she would continue no matter what I answered. "Not at all, Julia," I answered. "You know you can speak your mind here."

"Well, excuse me for saying, but what the hell makes you think you have any skills to track down a murderer? You have no training, no resources, no contacts with the police, no experience. You're wasting your time at that school. Let the real law enforcers do their job, and you stick to taking pictures. You got no business wasting time when you got bills piling up here."

Wow, talk about being blindsided. That hurt. Badly. I didn't want Julia to see that her words had wounded me. "Glad you think so highly of my expertise, Julia," I deadpanned.

"Well, somebody had to say it, Danny. You're above your pay grade when trying to hunt down a murderer. Best to stick to what you know."

I needed to let this sink in. Was she right? Was I making a fool of myself? Was I just a college-educated Barney?

"I'll do the Grist job, Julia. Happy? Now run along. I need to see Bethany."

"Oops, I forgot to tell you. She called this morning to ask when you were coming back. Said you hadn't bothered to let her know. You got a real way with the ladies, Danny."

"If you're done dissing me, Julia, I'll take care of *my* business. See you tomorrow morning."

I sighed, fully aware that Bogie would have handled this better. He kept dames in their place.

She was no Ingrid Bergman, but Bethany was good looking by anyone's standards, and I was itching to see her.

Chapter Twenty-nine

Bethany looked hot but projected cold to me. Obviously displeased with me, she stood in the doorway, her arms crossed, and glared at me without speaking. Maybe I shouldn't have called her first. Forewarned was forearmed.

"Don't even think about coming in," she said between clenched teeth. Wearing an emerald green tight tee shirt that accentuated her curves, she had the air of a siren, and I was all too ready to move closer despite her warning.

"Lighten up, sweetie. I can explain why you haven't heard from me." I put up my arms as if to surrender and gave her my winningest smile. That worked about as well as my grandmother's Yugo.

She turned abruptly and went inside her house, slamming the door behind her.

If Bogie was watching from above, he was shaking his head in disappointment of me.

I rang the bell repeatedly, and when that didn't work, I started knocking on the door as hard as my knuckles would bear. Finally she opened the door slightly and said coldly, "Look, Danny, you can't just waltz in here and pretend that everything's cool just because you said it is. I don't want to see you. Now get the hell outta here." She slammed the door again.

Undeterred, I called her from my cell phone. I could hear her phone ringing inside the house. When she finally answered, I said as contritely as I could muster, "Bethany, don't hang up. Let me explain. Please." I was beginning to wonder if she was worth groveling.

Click.

Bethany had just joined the ranks of Danny Wright's exes.

I drove to my apartment and checked out the fridge to see if there was any beer or wine. Or food, though I knew better. Half a bottle of Three-buck Chuck red wine that I had opened two weeks ago stared back at me as if to dare me to drink it. I took a sip and spit it out into the sink. I needed something better than oxidized swill to console me and drove to the Food Lion half a mile away to buy a six pack of Stella Artois and a bottle of sauvignon blanc that actually had a cork. On the way back home, I stopped at a Wendy's, much as it reminded me of stakeout food, and ordered a couple burgers and a large fries to go. I wanted to eat alone and was definitely not in the mood to cook.

Nor was I in the mood to go out or call any friends. I turned on the television and opened the first Stella, settling in for what I hoped would be an uneventful evening of mindless sitcoms and enough alcohol to drown the memory of annoying women and exploding guts.

Three beers in, a weather alert interrupted the stale sitcom. "Record flooding expected in the wake of Hurricane Loretta. Do not drive through flooded areas."

What was next? Biting insects and wild animals? Fiery hail? Locusts?

That cinched it. I called Julia's cell phone and left a message that I was leaving town for a few days till flood waters receded. If she needed me, she could reach me at a Motel 6 or whatever cheap place I could find near Charlottesville. I'd check in later tonight as soon as I found a place.

Loretta was Miss Foss's name, if memory served. Damn dames.

Rummaging through my dresser and a basket of laundry I had washed over a week ago, I found a few clean shirts, two pairs of faded black pants, four pairs of mismatched white socks, and three changes of underwear, threw them into the suitcase I had emptied only a few hours ago, and headed west on I-64 to Charlottesville. I needed a break from estrogen.

Chapter Thirty

Wearing rubber gloves "just in case," he carefully stirred about 300 mgs of potassium cyanide into the carton of curried chicken. Satisfied that the poison was diffused throughout the special meal made for Mr. Thomason, he sang BADA$$'s "Curry Chicken" in his best Julia Child voice. The presence of federal agents and Richmond police served not to dissuade him from his mission but to energize him.

"He will die right under their noses," he said aloud, pleased with his newfound sense of purpose and bravura. 'Bobson may have robbed me of a retirement, but he has also made me more alive than I have ever been. Come the time, I will express my gratitude by killing him more artfully than with poison. Nothing but the best for you, Bobson,' he thought.

'But first things first. Thomason is not a bad sort, really. I almost like the man now that I have met him. He just had the bad luck to be randomly selected to help the cause. We all have to make sacrifices to get satisfaction, right? I wish he'd know how useful he'll be in death. Revenge. Revenge. Revenge. That word has such a sweet ring to it.'

Checking the cuckoo clock in his den, he saw that he had more than forty-five minutes to wait before delivery of his lethal cuisine. The timing had to be perfect – five minutes into lunch period when the hall was empty. No one must see him entering or leaving the chemistry room. The devil was always in the details. He didn't mind waiting patiently. The room was comfortably appointed with an antique writing desk, large leather chair and ottoman, and pen-and-ink drawings he had found on a summer trip to London. Homage to The Bard justified the expense. A pleasing thought occurred to him: Only Shakespeare could adequately capture in words the mission he was on. The kinship he felt with Shakespeare was almost mystical. Of course this would be no tragedy. Oh, no, he had no intention of being caught. The only catharsis his ascent into greatness would generate would be his own.

Who knew killing could seem so natural, so pleasurable? He felt a stirring in his groin as he visualized Thomason in the throes of a painful though quick death. Could it be that he had remained a celibate bachelor because he had not previously discovered what pleasured him?

Lost in his reverie, he didn't realize how quickly the minutes had passed. Jarred to awareness by the bird's raucous announcement of noon, he hastily grabbed his gift and hustled to the classroom that would soon be a tomb. Moving quickly down the hall to Thomason's room, he knocked softly on the door, looking furtively in both directions. Not a stirring of life.

"Come in!" boomed Mr. Thomason, whose voice was as robust as his physique.

He entered the room immediately, trying unsuccessfully to control his racing heartbeat. 'Stay calm. He mustn't detect any nervousness. I am simply a man with a gift. A generous colleague.' Breathing deeply, he said, "Excuse my breathlessness, Mr. Thomason. I ran here because I have only a few minutes before meeting a student for tutoring."

He held out the carton of curried chicken. "A grateful parent gave me this. Regrettably, it's too hot for my palate, and I just can't eat it. I was going to toss it in the garbage when a colleague of ours said that I should give it to you, that you like highly seasoned food. I hope you haven't eaten lunch yet."

"No, I haven't, and, yes, I love me some food with a kick!" Mr. Thomason grabbed the carton and started to open it.

Oh, it has kick. Lots of kick. "Oh, no, Mr. Thomason. You need to nuke it first…only about two minutes. You don't want the chicken to be so hot you can't eat it fast. This is fire alarm level stuff. Eat it as fast as you can because your lips and mouth will be numb within seconds."

"Mmmm. Sounds delicious to me. Thanks so much for sharing."

"Excuse me for dropping this off and running. I apologize for the brevity of this visit. Maybe I could stop by later to see if you liked it?"

"I'd like that. I'll see you later." Mr. Thomason headed to his office to microwave the unexpected gift.

'Doubtful, Mr. Thomason, doubtful. Damn, I wish I could watch him die.'

Chapter Thirty-one

Mr. Bob Thomason was so hungry that he felt foolish exhorting the microwave to hurry up. The odor of curry had him salivating, and as soon as he pulled the carton from the microwave, he gave the curried chicken a quick stir and gulped down the extra-hot concoction so fast that the burn was only an afterthought.

Before he even had time to get a glass of water to rinse his mouth, he collapsed to the floor of his office, and in less than a minute, he was writhing with seizures. The coma came almost immediately thereafter.

Death came fast to Mr. Thomason, who probably had no time even to wonder what was happening to him.

Ten minutes later, sixth period chemistry class started filing in, looking around the room for the absent teacher. Always respectful of the popular Mr. Thomason, everyone took his seat and sat quietly for several minutes until Tommy Finch, a lanky boy in the front row beside Rex, spoke. "It isn't like Mr. Thomason to be late. Maybe I should use the phone in his office to call the dean?"

Mumbling ensued, showing the uncertainty and reluctance to make a decision. Any departure from the norm had the tendency to make Clanton students uneasy ever since the cafeteria explosion. Finally Rex said, "Go ahead, Tommy. We can't just sit here all day."

Tommy slowly extricated himself from his seat, his long legs released from their cramped quarters, and walked slowly to Mr. Thomason's office, looking back at his classmates every couple steps as if to ask if he should really follow through on his suggestion. If Mr. Thomason came into the classroom and found him in his office, there'd be hell to pay.

"Don't be such a wuss, Tommy," said a football player from the rear of the class. Everyone laughed nervously.

Tommy reluctantly knocked on the office door, waited a few seconds, and when he got no response, he opened it.

Unlike as happens in so many mystery movies and television shows, when Tommy saw the prostrate Mr. Thomason curled up on the floor, he didn't shriek or scream. His mouth agape, he stared at the corpse for fully thirty seconds, then shook his head as if he could shake off the sight, and backed out of the office.

Teetering back into the classroom, he stared at his classmates without speaking, shivering violently.

"What's wrong, dude?" asked several of the boys who realized that something in that office had reduced Tommy to this state.

Finally Tommy managed to command himself to speak. "It's Mr. Thomason…he's dead on the floor."

Tommy's statement met with silence. The stillness didn't last long, however, and every student in the class started firing questions at him.

"Are you sure he's dead, man?"

"How could you tell he's dead? Maybe he's just sleeping."

"Sleeping on the floor? Don't be an idiot, Malcolm."

"What should we do, call 911?"

Tommy didn't respond to those or a dozen other questions. Feeling faint, he leaned against the lab table Mr. Thomason had always sat behind.

"Someone needs to run to the dean's office," Amos said after surveying the paralysis of the class. "I'm going to Reasoner's room next door and tell him to come here, that Thomason may be dead in his office."

Rex volunteered to go to inform the dean, and Amos half-ran out the door to Mr. Reasoner's classroom fifty feet down the hall. Mr. Reasoner and Amos returned in less than a minute.

"Everybody stay put. I'm sure the dean will be here ASAP. Anyone in here know CPR?" asked Mr. Reasoner, even though he knew that CPR was of no avail. Poison, not a heart attack, was responsible for what awaited him in Thomason's office.

When no one answered him, Mr. Reasoner made his way to the office, where he knew his friend and colleague would be dead. 'Why did I get myself involved with that fiend?' he thought as he looked down at the sacrifice that he had been told had to be made.

Chapter Thirty-two

I always made it a point whenever I stayed in Charlottesville to eat at least one breakfast at the Tip Top Restaurant on Pantops, and having dined on junk food and wine and beer for over a week, I looked forward to my favorite breakfast, the pancake special: Three buttermilk pancakes, two fried eggs, bacon, and plenty of piping hot coffee. Traffic seemed heavier than the last time I was out this far on RT 250, but noticing new businesses that had sprouted up in my absence plus a new hospital, I wasn't surprised. A little gridlock simply whetted my appetite.

The Tip Top Restaurant, or Double T as we called it when I was attending UVA, hadn't updated its retro décor, and that was one of its charms. I claimed a red vinyl stool at the bar and ordered coffee and the pancake special. It took less than five minutes for me to devour the food, and I was on my second cup of coffee when I decided to buy a copy of *The Daily Progress*, the Charlottesville newspaper I usually read when in town, to check the news, as my cell phone was recharging in my motel room. Its size, like all newspapers, had reduced considerably since I last read one, I noticed.

The headline on page one made me almost spit coffee: "Second Grisly Murder at Clanton Academy in a Week." Skimming the report as fast as I could, I felt weak in the knees and was glad I was seated. "Popular chemistry instructor Bob Thomason was found dead in his office by one of his students. Cause of death, according to FBI investigator James Sloane, who was on site investigating the previous murder, was likely potassium cyanide poisoning. 'Victims of potassium cyanide usually have a pink to red coloration, and Mr. Thomason's skin was quite red. Only a toxicology report can definitively identify the presence of a toxin, but because of the previous murder on campus, we are proceeding with the assumption that Mr. Thomason was poisoned, not succumbed to natural causes.'"

Victim found by a student? Could it have been Rex? Even if he hadn't discovered the body, he'd be unnerved. How could a seventeen year old boy process that two of his teachers had been murdered? Clanton Academy had never experienced even a whiff of scandal or violence in its long history, and murders simply didn't occur at prep schools in bucolic settings. One salient reason I recommended to my sister that Rex attend Clanton was that it had always been a safe environment, and safe educational havens were fast becoming rare commodities in America.

I paid the bill and drove as fast as congested traffic would allow to my motel room. My phone was fully charged, and I made the first of several calls.

That H. Michael picked up on the third ring surprised me. I had assumed he'd be so deluged with calls that I'd have to leave a message in his voice mail. I was going to drive to Clanton regardless of whether or not he answered, but talking to him now would eliminate one hassle.

"Hello, Mr. Madison. This is Danny Wright. I'll keep this short because after reading this morning's paper, I feel certain you're swamped."

"Indeed I am. Actually, Mr. Wright, I answered your call because I had just been informed that the school's lawyer was going to call me immediately, and I thought the call was from him. I can talk for only a few seconds." His voice was strong and measured. More expert damage control in the works, I assumed.

"OK, I'll get right to the point. I want to stay at the Alumni House to be available to see my nephew. It's highly unlikely that drug dealing students had anything to do with murders; this would be purely a favor on your part – I won't be investigating any drug activity."

"Not a problem, Mr. Wright. See Miss Foss to get a key when you arrive on campus. I will be secluded in meetings but will want to talk with you when time permits. I am not pleased with the way the investigation into Mr. Wood's murder has been going, and I assume it'll be even less satisfactory now. I'd like you to get involved and report any findings to me."

After he hung up without a goodbye, I assembled my limited wardrobe, checked out of the motel, and headed to Clanton Academy.

I expected the mood on campus to be much different than it was when Mr. Wood had been murdered. As much as Mr. Wood had been despised, Mr. Thomason had been revered. It seemed highly improbable to me for there to be a link between the two deaths. And the thought of a serial killer being a resident of Clanton exceeded the wildest imagination. No, this was not the work of a crazed serial killer. In a small school where everybody knew everyone else's business and idiosyncrasies, a deranged serial killer would be too conspicuous, especially in the current climate of heightened morality. There had to be a motive for both of these murders, and I had to find it. Soon. The safety of my nephew could depend on it.

Chapter Thirty-three

Recent events had done nothing to improve Miss Foss's disposition. Either she was impervious to stress, or she had a heart of stone. I couldn't care less which applied. All I wanted was to get the key to my quarters in the Alumni House and find Rex ASAP.

After rummaging through her desk drawer, she handed me the key without making eye contact.

Trying to be agreeable, my own level of stress notwithstanding, I said, "Thanks. This latest unfortunate event must have everyone on edge."

She continued to hammer at her keyboard without looking up. How many keyboards have met their demise serving Miss Foss, I wondered. Maybe her method of dealing with a world she found little comfort in?

"Just doing my job, Mr. Wright. I suggest you try doing that yourself, whatever it is you do."

"Always a pleasure seeing you, Miss Foss," I said cheerfully, ignoring her latest dig and headed to the Alumni House to leave my bag.

Rex was lying in his bunk, staring at the ceiling, when I entered his room after a perfunctory knock on the half open door. He leapt out of the bunk as soon as he saw me and ran to me. Squeezing me in a fierce hug that suggested desperate relief more than a glad-to-see-me greeting, he said in a shaky voice, "Uncle Danny, I have never been so happy to see someone in my whole life."

I let him hug me for a good ten seconds before responding and tried to lighten the tension responsible for his anxiety. Smiling, I said, "Got here as soon as I read the news, Rex. You had to know I wouldn't be too far behind."

"Why didn't you reply to my email, Uncle Danny?" He wasn't being accusatory, I thought…just wanted to settle any uncertainty he might have been feeling. Given the circumstances, that was understandable.

After I explained that my cell phone hadn't been charged, he added, "I wondered if you had given up on me. I wasn't thinking straight after Mr. Thomason was —" He couldn't say the word.

"Don't be foolish, Rex. You know I'll always have your back." I didn't know if a tritely expressed reassurance would help, but regardless of my lack of verbal skills, it was how I felt, and I meant it.

Rex sighed deeply and sat on his rumpled bunk. "Thanks, Uncle Danny. I just can't figure out what's happening around here. I mean, who could possibly want to hurt Mr. Thomason? I have never heard a negative word about him. His family must be sick. I know that all of us students are."

Nothing surprising there. I had met the man only briefly, yet was impressed with both his skills in the classroom and his outgoing, friendly personality. His was a senseless death, and if I could do anything to identify whoever murdered him, I'd gladly do so. Good people like him deserved better. The FBI would do likewise, I hoped, though they had little invested in bringing a murderer to justice other than a professional obligation.

"Can I assume you're doing OK, Rex? Or should I call your mother to have her withdraw you?"

"I'm fine now that you're here, Uncle Danny. Don't suggest that to Mom, please. I heard that maybe twenty guys have left because they are afraid for their safety. I'm not afraid for myself. I just feel awful about Mr. Thomason."

He did seem to be more relaxed, and after a quick assessment, I decided he could remain here without undue emotional stress. "OK, Rex. I'll tell her that you're doing fine, that she shouldn't worry. So, how's Amos handling this latest incident? How about your other friends? They all OK?"

"Amos never lets anything get to him, Uncle Danny. He's a rock. My other buddies are…well, how to put it into words? Spooked, maybe? They hated Wood and didn't feel much of anything when he was murdered except curiosity. Like everyone else, they liked Mr. Thomason, though, and are trying to makes sense of it. And not having any luck doing so."

'Aren't we all?' I thought. "Good to hear that they're all coping reasonably well, Rex." Comfortable with the assumption that Rex was also coping as well as could be expected, I continued. "Have classes been suspended? Have you seen or heard anything about the Feds' work?"

"Classes were shortened yesterday. We had a required meeting in the auditorium. Mr. Madison told us that we are all shocked by the death of Mr. Thomason, but we need to stay calm. The FBI will be conducting an ongoing investigation while we continue with our daily schedules starting today." He suddenly checked his watch. "Speaking of which, my free period is almost over and I have to get to class."

Gathering his books, he continued. "He also said if anyone needed to see the guidance counselor or the school psychologist, he should stay after the meeting. I saw a few guys linger afterward. As for the Feds, I haven't seen them. Course, I haven't been around much. I pretty much stick to my room. Oh, and one more thing. You remember when I told you about those assholes that would glare at me whenever they saw me? All of a sudden, they don't bother even looking at me when we pass in a hallway. Weird, huh?"

Weird, indeed. Maybe they were preoccupied with the double homicide? Or maybe they were changing their tactics? Whatever the reason, I felt confident that if they were dealing drugs, they would suspend their operation while the place was crawling with law enforcement.

"Get back to class, Rex. I'm staying in the same quarters at the Alumni House. Use your unauthorized cell phone to call me anytime."

"How'd you know —"

"Please, Rex, I may be a second-rate detective, but I doubt anything has changed since my days here."

Well, at least regarding cell phones.

Chapter Thirty-four

The only email I bothered to open was from H. Michael asking me to meet with him at 4:00 today. That gave me only fifteen minutes to call Julia to see the status of the Grist job and hoof it to H. Michael's office.

"Danny, here's the long and short of it. Grist says that unless you can get the job done by the end of the week, you can forget about it. And any others, too, he added. Danny, we can't afford to lose that client. When can you get back here?" Julia was right. I did need to take care of business.

"Tell them I'm on it and will have what they need by Friday." I wasn't sure how I could manage that, but with any luck the guy they suspected of trying to bilk them would get careless and mow the lawn or go bowling or try out a trampoline or go sky diving while I watched, camera in hand. With nothing but bad news lately, I could use a break.

"I'll let them know right after I hang up, Danny. Say hi to Rex for me. Guess he's probably shook up with what's been going on at that school."

"Not to worry, Julia. He's doing fine. He has the Wright genes," I assured her.

"Was that W.r.i.g.h.t. genes or r.i.g.h.t. genes? If that was your idea of a good pun, you're wrong, Danny." She giggled, probably pleased with herself that she recognized a pun when I hadn't really intended one. "Anyway, say hi from me. He's a good kid."

Eight minutes to get to H. Michael's office, just enough time with none left over to spar with Death Ray.

I breezed by her desk while saying to her that Mr. Madison was expecting me. Before she could protest, as I knew she would, H. Michael opened his door and invited me in. Though I regretted I didn't have the opportunity to observe Miss Foss seething, I entered his office immediately. Murder took priority over gloating. Just barely when it came to Miss Foss. H. Michael closed the door and with a half-smile gestured to the chair he wanted me to take.

"Mr. Wright, I'll get right to the point. I am juggling more than you imagine at the moment."

He did seem a little gray and had bags under his eyes.

"Not getting much sleep, I take it," I said. I sympathized that he had to scramble to minimize the damage to Clanton. "What can I do for you to help make things better?"

"I'm not sure, Mr. Wright. You were right when you said the media would be all over this. They camp outside the front gate and pester anyone they can flag down. And those FBI investigators…well, unfortunately they're unsympathetic to anyone's feelings or Clanton's well-being. What I need is someone whom I can trust to have Clanton's best interests at heart, and I think you do have that, Mr. Wright. For the time being, drug sales on campus are of minor concern to me. We need to get this campus back to being a safe place for all of us."

Of course I agreed with everything he said. I had little use for the imperious Feds, and I wanted no permanent harm to come to Clanton. And above all else, I wanted Rex to be safe and not exposed to more violence.

"I'm not sure how much latitude the Feds will allow me, Mr. Madison. Probably none. I will do what I can under the radar anyway, and you will be the first person to hear of any discoveries I make."

He breathed deeply, rubbed his eyes with his fists, and said so softly that I could barely make out the words, "Thank you, Mr. Wright." I guessed he hadn't said that phrase too often.

"But I do have to get back to Virginia Beach tonight and will be gone for a while…don't know how long at this time. By the way, when and where is the funeral for Mr. Thomason? I'd like to attend if at all possible."

"That's kind of you, Mr. Wright. I didn't know you knew him."

"I met him only a couple times. He impressed me. And my nephew thought the world of him. His death is a blow to Clanton academically, among other things."

"Indeed it is, Mr. Wright. Though academics are not as important as the spiritual experience at Clanton, we are a school, after all, and Mr. Thomason, according to my academic dean, was a first-rate instructor."

We finally had found mutual agreement on something.

"Mr. Thomason's widow asked if the funeral could be held in our chapel, and of course I agreed. It won't be for another couple days. His children need time to travel here from the West Coast. As it stands now, it'll be held Thursday morning at 10:00."

"I am leaving for the Beach after I stop by the cafeteria to get some coffee, Mr. Madison. I'll keep in touch and hope to be back before then." I shook his hand and almost felt sorry for the burden he was carrying.

I decided to leave the bag with the few changes of clothes in my quarters and walked directly to the cafeteria for a mug of coffee to go.

Cafeteria Katie was sitting at the table Rex and I had sat at when the explosion occurred. When she noticed me approaching her, she hurriedly snuffed out the cigarette she had been smoking on her break. Though Clanton was now a smoke-free campus, I figured that more than a few employees and even more students partook of a cigarette whenever they found the chance to do so. I pretended not to notice despite the cloud of smoke surrounding her.

"Good afternoon, Katie. More excitement here, I heard. Not on your watch, though. I'm sure you're relieved about that much at least. Mind if I steal a mug of coffee? I'll return the mug next time I'm here."

"Suit yourself, Mr. – er, what's your name again? I am the worst at remembering names."

"Danny Wright. I'm bad at names, too."

As I turned to fill up a mug with dark sludge at the coffee machine, I noticed out of the corner of my eye two men huddled in the far corner.

I whispered to Katie," Who are those guys?"

"Oh, they're some fuzz outta Richmond. Worthless waste of tax dollars, if you ask me. They're supposed to be investigating these murders, but every day, all day, they just sit in here at that table and play on those small computers they carry all the time. Earlier today I took them a refill of coffee and looked at what was so important on those little computers. Solitaire. They play Solitaire all day. And I bet they make as much money as I do busting my butt working all day." She grunted to show her disgust.

"There's no justice if they do, Katie. I think I'll check that out myself. I'm going to introduce myself to them. I'll grab some coffee on the way out. Thanks. I'll see you around."

I couldn't care less about how much time and tax payers' dollars they wasted. I did want to find out if they'd share information with me, however.

Chapter Thirty-five

Sure enough, the two Richmond cops were engrossed in the games on their tablets. I didn't know if they didn't hear me approach them or they did hear me and chose to ignore me, but in either case, they didn't greet me with so much as a nod or a "hi there."

Clearing my throat, I said, "Good afternoon, fellas. You probably don't know me. I am Danny Wright, and I —"

"Yeah, we know who you are. The private dick meddling in the murder case," said the one closest to me without looking up from his tablet. Lack of even mild exercise might account for his hefty gut. As for his rude candor, I hadn't a clue why he held such a low opinion of my profession.

"I don't know where you heard that I was meddling, but you were misinformed. I'm here looking after my nephew who is a student at Clanton and who was sitting at the table next to the teacher who exploded. You can imagine the trauma. And now another murder right after that one. The poor kid needs some looking after."

The other cop, a balding man with a bulbous nose, tore himself away from his tablet and looked at me through his slits for eyes as if to focus. "Didn't know you had kin here. Sorry about that. Still don't think much of what you do for a living, though." His face was expressionless and hard to read.

"Gotta keep the wolf away from the door somehow. It pays the bills," I replied, trying hard not to show how irritated I was with their condescending attitude.

Almost simultaneously, they both turned off their tablets and looked up at me without speaking for ten or twelve seconds. Finally, the cop nearest me said, "Yeah, I guess we're all entitled to make a living. Wilson's the name. What's yours?" How gracious of him.

"Wright. Danny Wright." I extended my hand to shake, unsure if my gesture would be ignored.

He shook my hand without hesitation and said, "My partner's name is Willy Johnson. A word of advice – no kidding him about it. That's my job," he said laughing.

The ice broken, I shook Johnson's hand and asked if I could join them briefly. They both nodded, and I pulled up a chair. "How is the investigation going? Any good news for me to pass along to my nephew?"

"Don't have a clue ourselves, Danny. The Feds have not allowed us to do anything. And I mean anything. We've been sitting here on our butts for days, bored silly. Our boss wouldn't let us go back to Richmond. Some territorial BS, I reckon. Finally, I called him this morning and begged him to be relieved of this do-nothing case. I mean, it's not as if there's no crime in Richmond to deal with," said Det. Wilson.

"So you have to keep sitting here wasting time?" I asked.

"Nah," Johnson spit out. "We finally get to leave this dump in less than an hour. Hope I never run into those Feds on our turf, especially that douche named Sloane."

In a way, I was glad that I wasn't the only one to be insulted by the Feds. "Don't mean to make light of it, fellas, but hearing that the Feds dissed you, too, has reassured me that maybe I'm not an asshole after all." I grinned widely.

They both laughed a couple snorts. "Oh, I wouldn't go *that* far, Danny," Wilson said, and they both laughed.

"I have to leave for Virginia Beach now, and I probably won't see you again. The circumstances could have been better, but I am glad to have met you. You guys deserve better treatment than the Feds have given you." As unlikely as it was, if I ever ran into them again, I wanted us to be on good terms.

Johnson shrugged. "I've dealt with Feds before. Their arrogance is an affliction they all seem to share. Safe journey, Danny. Hope your nephew copes OK."

That they wouldn't be here when I returned meant one less obstacle in my path. Time now to tend to business back home. Even though I knew the coffee was as old as dirt and strong as Arnold Schwarzenegger, I filled the mug to the top. I needed a clear head and a caffeine jolt to think during the two-hour trip to the Beach.

Chapter-Thirty-six

Driving through Virginia in October presented so many beautiful bucolic distractions that my mind was purged of anxiety by the time I reached home. Since there was no food in my fridge as usual, I drove to a nearby Chick-fil-A for a sandwich and waffle fries. No such thing as being too tired of fast food when it came to Chick-fil-A. Driving home, I wolfed down both the sandwich and fries in record time, and by the time I pulled up to my driveway, all that remained was a crumb or two in my lap.

Plopped comfortably in my favorite – and only – recliner, I texted Julia to find out necessary details about the Grist job, which I knew I had to start early next morning. When a reply came within a few minutes, I knew she was genuinely worried about our financial situation. Nothing appealed to me on television, so after guzzling a beer, I went to bed early and set the alarm for 4:40 a.m.

I must have dozed off immediately because the annoying alarm jarred me out of a heavy sleep. I considered hitting the snooze alarm, then reconsidered, knowing we desperately needed that money to keep the business afloat. Resigned to a boring day, I shaved and showered, made an almost undrinkable cup of instant coffee, and headed to the street address Julia had provided.

Most of the brick ranch houses on the tree-lined street were modest but well maintained, probably a neighborhood that sprang up in the sixties for working class folks. A rusting, ancient Honda Civic was parked in his driveway; no lights were on in his house. I settled back for what I hoped wouldn't be a torturously long wait.

Sometimes it pays to be lucky, not smart, and today fortune smiled down at lucky me. The would-be insurance scammer limped out of his front door, looked up and down the quiet street, and walked slowly to his garage. He pulled up the door by its handle and disappeared – briefly. In less than a couple minutes, out he came, pushing his hand mower. Again surveying the street for what I assumed were any witnesses, he commenced to mow his lawn with the dexterity of a point guard, turning and veering and bending to remove impediments. My camera recorded every beautiful movement. Possibly the fastest $1,500 I had ever made.

I exceeded the speed limit whenever I could and made it to my office by nine o'clock. Julia was already there at her desk. She looked up at me, startled that I was there and not on the job, I assumed.

"Good news and bad news, Julia," I deadpanned. "The good news is that you need to call Grist ASAP and tell them to expect some very interesting photos as soon as I can message them. The bad news is that now that we're on the verge of financial solvency again, I'm leaving for Clanton."

"I thought you said there was bad news," she said without smiling.

"I don't know what is more endearing about you, Julia, your drollness or your slothful work ethic. Let me know if any other jobs come up."

Having insulted each other sufficiently, we both smiled. As soon as Julia phoned Grist and she nodded to me to indicate they were satisfied, I messaged the incriminating photos, then headed out the door with a wave of my hand behind my head to serve as a goodbye. I figured that with this early start, I would be at Clanton in time for me to insinuate my way into the goings-on without the Feds being any the wiser.

Chapter Thirty-seven

Talking in hushed tones even though no one was around to overhear them in Mr. Reasoner's apartment on the fringe of the campus, they were at a stalemate.

"This has gone far enough. I'm over it. There was no reason to kill Thomason. He was a good man and a good friend. I can't sleep without seeing his dead body on the floor. I no longer want to be a part of this insane revenge plot." Reasoner kept shaking his head NO, NO, NO to punctuate his words.

"There's no getting out – unless you want to end up with a lethal injection. Look, I had nothing against the guy. He just had the misfortune to be where my pin landed on the list of faculty. Someone had to be sacrificed, and I didn't hear you coming up with any alternative when he was selected."

Reasoner wasn't having any of it. "BS! *You* decided to kill Wood, *you* decided to kill Thomason, *you* are going to kill Bobson no matter what we say. I think you're enjoying this. You've become a sick bastard." Despite being smaller than Jenkins, Reasoner felt no fear. He knew he was never going to be able to atone for this mortal sin, and if he could, he'd take down Jenkins with him. Remorse and rage did battle within him.

Jenkins shook his head slowly, then directed his comments to Mann. "Well, then, it seems at least one of us got cold feet. How do you feel about our mission?"

Mann shuffled his feet and averted eye contact with either Reasoner or Jenkins. "Don't put me on the spot. Please. I am having trouble dealing with my conscious. And I despise Bobson for what he did to us. I just don't know what to do or even what to think. I am so confused. You do what you think is best. I won't help kill anyone, but I will keep my mouth shut. If we're going to Hell, Bobson will be there to greet us."

"My God, you two haven't a shred of resolve. Mann, you just go about your business and keep your mouth shut. As for you, Reasoner, can I rely on your silence, too?"

Reasoner glared at Jenkins, hatred emanating from him as if it were palpable, and that wasn't lost on Jenkins.

"Well, Reasoner, what's it going to be? Will you keep your yap shut, or will I have to dispose of you, too?"

Reasoner exploded into laughter. "*You* dispose of me? Ha! Ha! You're pathetic. Do you really think in that twisted mind of yours that I'd ever give you a chance to do me harm?" Reasoner took two steps toward Jenkins and was less than a foot away from him, staring directly into his eyes. "But as for your question, yes, you can count on me to stay silent. Not because of any loyalty or fear. I despise you. No, I will not say anything to anyone only because I would incriminate myself. I will face my Maker eventually, but I am in no hurry to do so." It took every ounce of self-control for him not to spit in Jenkins's face.

"You're really a piece of work," Jenkins said through gritted teeth. "Go ahead, convince yourself that it's all my fault. You have conveniently forgotten that it was *you* who approached me about getting revenge."

"Oh, I have not forgotten that. I sold my soul to the devil that day and will regret it for eternity."

"So, suddenly you're *now* an upright Christian. Where was that Christian zeal when you devised the belly bomb?"

"I let anger screw me up. And you, you vile man, you fueled that anger." Reasoner's shoulders slumped as he shuddered. "I will never be able to forgive you. Or myself. I know what awaits us even if you don't. Just stay out of my way, Jenkins, and I hope never to see you till we meet in Hell."

'You'll find yourself there sooner than you think,' Jenkins thought. "Fine, that's how it's going to play out. You go your way, and I'll go mine."

With that, Jenkins stormed out the door.

"And how about you, Mann? You have done nothing except be with us when we talked. You never actually did anything. You could tell the Feds what happened and send both Jenkins and me to prison," said Reasoner.

"Not me! I am not going to grease my loins and fight my conscious. I will pray for me and you. Plus, I am an accomplish, and that's enough to send me away, too," replied Mann.

"Don't waste your prayers on me, Mann. I am beyond redemption."

"In that case, I'll pray for Bobson."

"Don't get carried away, Mann. I mean, there are limits to our collective guilt," Reasoner said laughing bitterly. "Let's go get a few beers and see if they can help us to forget what we've become."

Chapter Thirty-eight

After stopping by Whole Foods to restock my meager provisions at the Alumni House, I stowed my clothes in the inexpensive but spacious pine dresser and walked toward the track, hoping to see Coach Rotherwood. I know he'd have some insights about the changes at Clanton if not the murders. Seeing a tiny figure a half mile past the track, I headed that way. The long-jump pit was there, and I thought that maybe the tiny figure was Coach raking the pit that faculty children had probably been using as a sandbox.

It was. I stood back for a minute to watch him tend to the pit with meticulous attention even though track season was months away. He expertly caressed the sand into a smooth and level surface, and then stood up to survey his handiwork. It must have met his approval because he turned around and started walking toward me.

As soon as I was within earshot, he said, "Ah, glad you made it back so soon, Danny. How's your nephew doing?"

"He's holding up, Coach. How are *you* doing? These murders seem surreal to me."

"That's for sure, Danny. Who'd ever think that there's a murderer among us? It seems out of the realm of possibility. Hundreds of times since these two murders I have gone through the list of faculty and staff and tried to picture any of them blowing Mr. Wood up or poisoning Mr.

Thomason. For the life of me, I can't imagine a single person here being that sick."

It would have surprised me if he had. Whoever was responsible for the two heinous killings must have undergone a troubling psychological change recently.

"That makes two of us, Coach. Maybe you could help me understand something else, though. I have met a handful of folks that weren't here when I was, including Mr. Madison, and to a one, they seemed...well, beyond devout. They all seem to tie their religion to every action here. Am I imagining things?"

Coach laughed and shook his head vigorously. "No, you're not, Danny. The atmosphere – actually, a lot of things – have changed considerably since you were here. It started with the hiring of Mr. Madison. He is imminently qualified and does a great job at fundraising, but in his opinion this place was rife with sin before he got here. To be truthful, there had been some unsavory affairs and the usual breaches of propriety and moral lapses here. Every school has that sort of thing. In his mind, this place would be The City upon a Hill, though, and he took it upon himself to make it very uncomfortable for the people he didn't like. Most of the younger teachers he targeted found employment elsewhere. But old farts like me have to stick around. Who'd hire us?"

"Stop talking nonsense, Coach. With your successes here, there's not a school or college that wouldn't love to hire you."

"Still full of that Irish blarney, I see, Danny. Oh, I suppose I could have relocated, but I thought I'd stick around, thinking things would return to a comfort zone eventually. That didn't happen. Every hire for the past dozen years has been based not on talent or experience but on religious beliefs. Or at least professed beliefs. I happen to know for a fact that some of the anointed ones are guilty of the very things they preach against. A few have been exposed and immediately fired. But more than a few have found a home here. It doesn't bother me much, really. They do their thing, and I do mine. Live and let live. So far it hasn't hurt enrollment. These murders, on the other hand, have students bailing out. Up to this point I have been impressed with how Mr. Madison is handling things, though the admin he hired have done nothing to help." He stared at nothing in particular for half a minute. "And I'll give him credit for not hassling me. Any program that is visibly successful like track and swimming he has let be even though he thinks we coaches are heathens." He smiled, but his smile quickly faded.

"I appreciate your sharing your insights, Coach. I have always looked up to you and recognized your wisdom. I never knew of any gross misconduct when I was here, and you and handful of other mentors here are responsible for my being who I am today. Not that you may want to claim responsibility for that," I joked to avoid sentimentality that I knew neither of us liked.

"I figure alumni should be given the inside skinny," he said.

Finally someone here used the correct plural!

"I have to get to the locker room now, Danny. Glad you took the time to seek me out. I trust you're savvy enough to keep what we talked about between us, right? I'm not looking to find a new job."

"You mean you'd be fired for sharing your opinion?"

"In a heartbeat, Danny."

That ended our conversation and my optimism for Clanton's future.

Chapter Thirty-nine

I knew my luck would run out sooner or later but hoped for later. With four Feds working overtime here, it was inevitable I'd have a confrontation, and on the way back to the Alumni House after chatting with Coach Rotherwood, I bumped into two of them. Literally.

"Hey, watch where you're going, mister," said the one I almost knocked down as I turned the corner of the dorm without looking. Focusing on me closely, he must have realized we had already met, and I did likewise. It was Parker, paired up with a Fed I hadn't previously seen, not Sloane. "So, you're still crawling around here. I thought you had better sense than that," he snarled.

"Don't get your panties in a wad, Parker. I'm here visiting my nephew, not doing any investigating." I paused briefly while debating whether I should get in a lick or two. Very briefly. "Speaking of which, I guess you're kind of embarrassed about the second murder, this one on your watch. The FBI's credibility must be tarnished big time." I just couldn't resist deflating a federal ego a bit even if it barely made a dent. Bogie would be proud of me.

"Ha! Ha! Ha! You think we give a rat's ass about what a peeping Tom thinks?"

"Probably not," I said, shrugging my shoulders. "I don't think you guys care what *anyone* thinks. Well, I have a news flash for you. If you keep fucking up this investigation, the school's president will have to call in Sheriff Dixon to clean up behind you. Maybe you could learn a thing or two from the local constabulary." Twisting it in felt so gratifying.

"Well, how about that…a comedian on top of being a peeping Tom. You're just full of surprises."

"Better full of surprises than full of shit," I countered.

I was beginning to think that this conversation was resembling two ten-year-olds sparring verbally, and, in truth, I was half responsible. Before I could summon up a witty rejoinder like "Oh, yeah, so's your face" or "I know you are, but what am I?", I said, "Parker, this conversation is beneath both of us. I apologize for being a jerk." Judging by the bulging veins in his neck, I wasn't especially confident that he would cool down. In fact, I was pretty sure that only his questionable professionalism was holding him back from coldcocking me.

Parker stared daggers at me for well over thirty seconds, and I was starting to feel uncomfortable. If he was weighing the pros and cons of beating my face and damaging his career, I hoped he opted for the latter.

"Maybe you're right for once, Wright," he finally said.

"Even a stopped clock is right twice a day," I joked feebly. "I don't mean to make light of this situation. My nephew is probably freaked out despite trying to look cool about it, and I want to give him family support, not stir the pot with you. Truce?"

"Yeah, why not? Couldn't hurt. Say, when you were poking around, you didn't happen to come up with anything you'd like to share, did you?"

This was an unexpected open invitation for me to pry, and I wasn't going to ignore the opportunity.

"You probably already did this yourself, but I did check out the cafeteria staff and server to see who could have handled the food to insert a belly bomb." If they hadn't, they were a waste of taxpayers' money. And if they had, it wouldn't hurt to verify what I had learned. Mainly, I wanted to give them a little proof of my good intent.

"Of course we did that first thing we arrived. Came up dry. Same for you?"

"Not exactly dry. I eliminated as persons of interest the four kitchen workers, who never had opportunity to insert a bomb. And I automatically eliminated Cafeteria Katie, who may be uneducated but who is as honest as the day is long and wouldn't harm a cafeteria cockroach."

"How'd you come up with the idea that the kitchen workers had no opportunity to plant that bomb?"

"I mentally recreated them working at their stations that day. Each of them was in sight of the others at all times, and if one of them broke routine and left to stick that bomb in the knockwurst, the other three would have protested. They work in tandem as a team."

Parker seemed to mull that around for a while. "You may be onto something, Wright. We hadn't gotten that far yet in eliminating anyone." I let him save face hoping that maybe he'd share some information with me.

"The way I figure it, the only people that had opportunity were the two faculty sitting with the victim, Mr. Jenkins and Mr. Mann. Other than opportunity, though, I have nothing – no motive, especially. And it's possible that the knockwurst had been tampered with before being delivered to Clanton. That's about all I was able to determine."

"I appreciate your sharing what you did know, Wright."

"How about the last murder? Do you have anything yet to go on?" I asked. Nothing ventured, nothing gained.

"Nothing much. Even less than the first one. Tox reports confirmed that he was poisoned by eating a curried chicken dish laced with potassium cyanide – a large dose that likely killed him rapidly."

"Curried chicken? That's not a cafeteria offering. Have any idea where it came from?"

"Yes, it was take-out from an Indian restaurant in Charlottesville. We've already checked it out. They sell fifty or more of that dish every day. We showed the two employees who work the cash register a yearbook that has every staff member pictured. They couldn't remember seeing any of them. That's what we expected. Who'd be so stupid to order it without disguising himself?"

"You're absolutely right about that. No fingerprints, I assume?"

"Just the victim's. Unless we can find a motive, we're stuck. Two violent murders of two different types of people that we can't find a connection between. If these are random murders by a psychopath, we will have a hard time solving this. In the meantime, we intend to stay here to make sure there's not another one – if we can. A psychopath can strike without motive any chance he gets."

This was worse than I realized.

"I'm planning on sticking around here myself to be available for my nephew. Having gone to this school, I am deeply distressed by all of this. On the outside chance I find out anything, you'll be the first person I'll notify. "

Well, probably not the first. I owed H. Michael and Barney that honor.

Chapter Forty

Because I hadn't remembered to bring a suit to wear to Mr. Thomason's funeral, I decided to arrive as late as possible and sit in the back of the chapel to avoid drawing attention to myself. It wasn't a matter of vanity or breach of decorum. Rather, I didn't even want to hint at disrespect for the deceased.

Arriving at the entrance to the red-brick chapel, I found myself among a crowd of people milling around outside and made my way through them to the narthex. It became instantly obvious that they were outside for one reason: The chapel was filled to capacity. The entire Clanton community was paying their respects to a man they held in high regard.

I scanned the crowd to see whom I knew. Without my taking roll, it appeared at first glance that every faculty and staff member was in attendance, as well as a good portion of the student body. Conspicuously absent were any Feds. Hardly shocking but disappointing nonetheless. Would it kill them to consider a victim a person, not just a case to work on? A waving hand caught my eye – it was Barney motioning to me that I should join him.

Trying to be as inconspicuous as possible, I sidled down the aisle next to the wall. Naturally, everyone rubbernecked. I hoped they would overlook my wearing a plaid shirt and khaki pants. And if they couldn't do that, I decided not to worry about it. I wasn't there to make a fashion statement. Not that I could have if I wanted to.

Barney patted the empty place beside him and whispered, "I saved this just in case you was able to be here."

Though Barney was a bit shy on intellect, there was no faulting his heart. He had generosity of spirit, which was more than I could say for the Feds.

"Thanks, Gladstone. I appreciate this." And I really did.

The organist, struggling with tempo as she played Bach and Chopin while we waited for the chaplain to begin the service, must have found her comfort zone when she launched into "How Great Thou Art." Ignoring any dynamics that she might have exercised on a piano, she played as loud and fast as she could. Oddly, that seemed to work in her favor, providing an element of emotion lacking in her assault on the classics.

As she drew out the last note, she turned to the chaplain and nodded. He stood and walked solemnly to the pulpit. How many chapel services had I daydreamed or slept through in my years here? The chaplain during my stay here was a good man who was popular with and respected by students. I had never heard him say an unkind word about anyone, and he preached love and understanding. My inattentiveness had nothing to do with the quality of his sermonizing. After we had been sitting in classrooms for hours, it was almost impossible to focus on anything except getting a snack or checking email from our girlfriends or family. I was curious how the newest chaplain would address us in the Era of Piety. For the sake of Mr. Thomason's family, I hoped he would not pontificate or use the funeral service as an opportunity to remind us that we were going to Hell.

My concerns were quickly allayed. The new chaplain spoke with compassion, and expertly put everyone at ease. Surely H. Michael wouldn't hold that against him.

His homily was succinct and most likely comforting to Mr. Thomason's family, focusing on an eternity of peace. I couldn't help wondering if his murderer was in attendance. If he was, what did he think about the massive turn-out of mourners? Did he take pleasure in causing so much discomfort and grief?

The service concluded with an invitation extended by the chaplain. "Please greet Mr. Thomason's family and partake of refreshments at the cafeteria. Extra tables and chairs have also been set up in the area immediately outside the front entrance, as the cafeteria cannot accommodate all of us."

I had mixed feelings about gathering at the site of a recent brutal murder. "Let's hope that whoever murdered Mr. Wood and Mr. Thomason has no plans for an encore today," I said to Barney as we made our way with the other mourners to the cafeteria.

Chapter Forty-one

The amount and variety of finger foods awed me. I just couldn't envision the kitchen staff I had met coming up with such delectables, and my instincts were correct. Cafeteria Katie, who was moonlighting this event, said "Hi there again" without saying my name and informed me that Mr. Thomason's friends and family had contributed all of the food on display, plus a refrigerator full of other delicious offerings in the kitchen. I loaded up a plate, found a coffee urn, and with Barney in tow, found a couple empty seats outside.

"This must be what it's like to live in a small town," I said to Barney as I started to savor actual home-made food for the first time in a long time.

"What do you mean, Danno…er, Danny?"

Pointing to the mounds of food, I said, "This. All this food that was contributed. That doesn't happen in a city."

"Yep. Well, it's right commonplace around here."

Barney didn't seem as excited about this heartwarming small-town custom as I did. Probably was used to seeing it since he was a boy and considered it an expected rite.

It took maybe five minutes for me to eat every morsel and crumb on my plate. Sated, I went in search of the Thomason family to introduce myself and express condolences, leaving Barney to fend for himself. They were easy to spot. All were robust, including his widow, and even in this moment of grief, they were smiling at every person they spoke with.

Mrs. Thomason had apparently decided to forego traditional black widow's weeds and wore a purple dress and bright paisley shawl. I still felt ill at ease being here in my everyday clothes. Wearing colors was less objectionable to a traditionalist than wearing something I would wear to a golf course. I hoped she would be as unassuming as her late husband. "Please accept my sincerest condolences, Mrs. Thomason." Seeing the quizzical look on her face that indicated she had no idea who I was, I quickly added, "I am Danny Wright. My nephew Rex was in Mr. Thomason's class and had high praise for him both as a person and as a teacher. Observing his class the other day, I saw why he was so highly regarded and respected. I spoke with him after class and the following day, and in that short time he also impressed me deeply. In no way do I mean to minimize your personal loss, but his death is a tragedy for both you and Clanton Academy."

She was gracious in accepting my sympathy. Sensing the presence of others standing behind me to talk with her, I excused myself and started to drift through the crowd, saying hello to teachers who had taught me and lingering near those I didn't know in hopes of picking up strands of conversation that might be helpful to me in trying to find some meaning in this senseless murder. If the murderer was here, would he be able to conceal his malice or self-satisfaction? It wouldn't hurt to do some subtle eavesdropping even if it produced nothing of value.

Mr. Mann and Mr. Reasoner were in deep conversation and seemed especially distraught, but I couldn't move in close enough to make out what they were saying. Directly behind them was H. Michael, surrounded by fawning staff whom I didn't recognize and whom I had no desire to get to know. H. Michael nodded politely to me as I passed, and I murmured a soft, hurried hello that wouldn't invite more interaction.

I stopped moving to observe Mr. Jenkins talking with Mr. Bobson and one of the coaches I had seen him eating with him in the cafeteria. Seemed like an unlikely grouping, but funerals and weddings made for incongruous pairings of guests. Mr. Bobson talked animatedly, and his coaching buddy was hanging on every word. Mr. Jenkins looked bored.

Mr. Bobson was dressed to the nines in a navy blue expensive suit and a subdued burgundy silk tie. Mr. Jenkins was only slightly more formally attired than I in a moss green sweater that was beading and baggy brown pants that were shiny from wear. They were opposites in appearance and body language, and, as deduced from my previous interactions with them, personalities as well. Curious to hear how they were getting along, I worked my way through clusters of mourners till I was beside them.

"Good morning, Mr. Jenkins and Mr. Bobson." Looking directly at the unknown coach, I said, "Haven't had the pleasure, Mr. – er? I'm Danny Wright, an alumnus."

"O'Sullivan. George. Nice to meet you. Sorry to be so abrupt, but I have to get to the locker room before the animals start getting too frisky. See ya around, Rollie and

Merrick." He peeled away from the crowd and half jogged, half walked, toward the gym.

"Seems like a nice guy," I said. "He wasn't here in my day. What does he coach?"

"JV football," said Mr. Bobson at the same time Mr. Jenkins was saying, "Don't have the slightest idea."

Mr. Bobson laughed briefly. Mr. Jenkins didn't.

"Excuse my candor, Mr. Wright, but these country funerals are only something to be endured. I suppose Thomason was a good enough person, but I barely knew the man and am here primarily because Mr. Madison made it known that attendance was mandatory."

The affable Mr. Bobson looked as surprised as I was at such a callous remark.

When neither Mr. Bobson nor I replied, Jenkins added, "Forgive me. This is not the time or place for me to speak my mind. Merrick, are we still on for drinks tonight in Charlottesville?"

Whereas his bitterness came as no surprise to me, his question did. I didn't know of any two people who had less in common than these two, and yet they were going out for drinks. Curious, very curious.

"Sure thing, Rollie. Do you remember my address…two blocks down Pine Street past the antique shop?" Mr. Jenkins nodded yes. "Pick me up around seven?"

"Not around seven, Merrick. At exactly seven."

Such a personable man. I wondered if he hated dogs and children, too.

Chapter Forty-two

Looking around the posh living room of Bobson's apartment, Jenkins realized that most of the furnishings had changed since the last time he had seen it.

"Have you remodeled this place recently, Merrick?" Jenkins said loud enough for Bobson, who was finishing dressing in his bedroom, to hear him.

"Yeah. You like?" Bobson yelled back as he was admiring his choice of Tommy Bahama silk shirt and slacks. "The stuff cost me a fortune."

Satisfied that he was looking GQ enough to make an impression in a trendy club in Charlottesville, he entered the living room where Jenkins was sitting down in a retro looking chair.

"That chair you're sitting in is an Eames…cost me five grand. This sofa set me back over twenty-five grand, and that Persian carpet was close to a hundred grand. That desk over —"

"Never mind, Merrick. No need to flaunt your money around me. I get it. You're rolling in money."

Bobson's face registered no emotion. If he was put out by Jenkins' lack of deferential treatment, he wasn't showing it. "Let's head out, Rollie. I am thirsty and in need of some liquid alternative to the gloom of Thomason's funeral."

"Yeah, whatever. You want me to drive?"

"I'll buy if you fly, if you don't mind. I'm in the mood to tie one on."

'Which is exactly what I want you to do,' thought Jenkins.

The short drive to Charlottesville passed quickly with little conversation. Bobson was glued to his smart phone, and Jenkins hummed along to the Mozart CD he selected.

Having struck out at finding a place to park on a side street of the downtown mall, which was not open to traffic, Jenkins reluctantly entered the Water Street parking garage.

"We should go to a place that validates parking, Merrick. I can't afford to pay the hefty parking rate."

"Don't worry about that, Rollie. I'll take care of it," Bobson said as he looked for the exit he preferred. "There's the exit we want. Let's go – party time!"

Bobson opted for the priciest club, of course, and after they found a small table in the far back, Bobson signaled for the waitress.

"What are you having, Rollie?" Bobson asked, and after Jenkins told him that any craft beer on tap would do, he placed the order. "Your most expensive craft beer on tap for my friend, and I'll have an appletini. And have the bartender make it with Stolichnaya Elit vodka."

As soon as the waitress left to get their orders, Jenkins laughed and asked Bobson, "You're drinking appletinis? I figured a jock like you would stick to manly drinks."

Bobson scowled. "Quit stereotyping, Rollie. I'll drink what I like. My tastes in all things have grown more refined since I made my fortune. I remember all too well not having money for anything but rotgut wine when I was in college playing football with all those guys from money. Now I drink whatever I want, and the more expensive it is, the better it tastes."

"Sorry, Merrick. I didn't mean to impugn your virility."

"You are so damn conventional, Rollie. I bet you have never done anything outside the box."

"You're right, Merrick. That's me, ole Victorian school marm Mr. Jenkins." He laughed for Bobson's benefit while thinking, 'If you only knew, Bobson. If you only knew. Soon you *will* know.'

The harried waitress delivered their drinks in under three minutes, surprising both of them.

Bobson raised his glass and said, "Salute!" Instead of sipping his appletini, he downed it in two gulps and again signaled to the waitress.

"That was fast," the waitress said, grinning. "Special celebration?"

"You might say that," Jenkins said, a sly smile briefly crossing his face.

"You bet, Sugar. Bring me another of the same. Come to think of it, bring me a chocolate Cosmo, too."

"Are you sure you shouldn't slow down, Merrick? The night is still young," Jenkins said disingenuously.

"Tend to your knitting, Rollie. I can drink you under the table anytime."

"Such immodest bragging, Merrick. As George said to Martha, 'There isn't an abomination award going that you haven't won.'"

"Huh, what's that supposed to mean? Should I be pissed off at you?"

"Lighten up, Merrick. I was just kidding. Drink up. Here comes our waitress."

"Thanks, Sugar. Keep 'em coming." Directing his attention to Jenkins, he said, "Rollie, you ready for another?"

"No more for me. I'm the designated driver, remember?"

A drunk Bobson would be a perfect ending to an already outstanding day.

Chapter Forty-three

"Damn, he weighs a ton!" Jenkins muttered to himself as he half steered, half supported, the wasted Bobson draped on his shoulder. Surveying the three flights of stairs to the level where his car was parked, he cursed the elevator that was out of operation. Even though it was a chilly evening, beads of sweat popped out on Jenkins's forehead as he maneuvered his cargo toward the car.

Ten laborious minutes later, he reached his car, only to realize that he couldn't simultaneously retrieve his keys in his pocket and support the semiconscious Bobson. Easy decision. Jenkins let Bobson drop to the concrete floor like a 250 pound bag of potatoes and fished out his keys.

"Oops," tittered Jenkins as he looked with distaste at Bobson lying in a heap. "Sorry about that. You OK?"

Only a soft moan was Bobson's answer.

"I'll take that as a yes," Jenkins said, expecting no further conversation as he unlocked the door.

His next task proved to be even more difficult – dragging the dead weight into the back seat of his car. He opened the door over Bobson's body and maneuvered one of his arms onto the back seat, then walked around the back of the car to the opposite door. Crouching in the back seat, he grabbed the arm he had positioned to the seat and tugged as hard as he could. The only result of his efforts was a torn sleeve of Bobson's silk shirt.

"Pity. Such a nice shirt." Jenkins laughed.

'No way I can get him into the car if he's passed out,' he thought.

He suppressed the urge to leave him in the parking garage and leaned over far enough to slap Bobson's face as hard as he could. No response. He slapped him five more times before Bobson groggily slurred, "Hey, what's going on?"

"Wake up, you drunken idiot. Help me get you into the car. I need to drive you home."

A comical looking struggle ensued, Jenkins tugging and yelling at the giggling Bobson, who finally pushed himself far enough into the car that Jenkins could let go of Bobson's arm, and go around to the other side to push the rest of Bobson all the way into the back seat.

Fifteen minutes later, they arrived at Bobson's apartment. Tired from the struggle to get him into the car, Jenkins had no intention of repeating the process to get him out of the car and into his apartment. He turned around to face Bobson. Slapping his face vigorously – maybe a few times more than necessary – Jenkins finally was able to get Bobson to lift his head and open his already bloodshot eyes. At least a dozen drinks, even girly ones, packed a wallop.

"Merrick, we're at your apartment now. You're too heavy. I can't carry you inside. You have to get out of the car."

Bobson nodded heavily, and unsteadily moved his bulk out of the back seat, then leaned against the car and breathed deeply.

"Where is your house key, Merrick?" Jenkins asked.

Holding up both hands, he laughed and said, "I don't know." He must have thought that was hilarious and threw back his head, laughing so hard that he almost lost his balance.

"Great," Jenkins growled. "How in the hell are we supposed to get inside?"

"No problem, Rollie. I never lock the door."

Jenkins smiled broadly and patted Bobson on the back. "Good to know, Merrick, very good to know."

Leading the complacent Bobson like a trained elephant, Jenkins directed him into the apartment. Before Jenkins could decide where to deposit him, Bobson plopped down on the twenty-five thousand dollar sofa and passed out.

"That's good enough, you thieving piece of shit," Jenkins spat. Standing over the snoring body, Jenkins thought, 'I could kill you so easily right here, right now. Have to delay gratification, though. Your time is coming soon enough.'

A more pressing matter was how to dispose of Reasoner first.

Before letting himself out of the apartment, Jenkins urinated on the 100,000 dollar carpet. To make sure that Bobson would assume he himself had done it, he pulled down Bobson's fly.

Yes, indeed, a perfect ending to a perfect day.

Chapter Forty-four

October was slipping by, and I hated to see the end of the beauty of the brilliantly colored leaves. Clanton's abundance of hardwoods – especially maples, sweet gums, red oaks, hickories, and a few elms – made for a scenic campus that temporarily disguised the evil that resided there of late. I decided to absorb the last gasp of autumn's splendor with a leisurely walk around campus prior to meeting with Amos and Rex before their classes began and with H. Michael shortly thereafter.

Lost in my mindless and desultory stroll, I lost track of time. Glancing at my watch, I panicked. With only fifteen minutes till classes would begin, I sprinted to their dorm. This would be a brief meeting.

"Uncle Danny, you're late. We had almost given up on you. We have to leave in five minutes, you know," Rex gently scolded.

"Sorry, fellas. I just lost track of time. I'll get right to the point. I wanted to see you to check on what you've noticed among students. Any behaviors that you've questioned?"

Amos was the first to answer. "Unusual in what way? I mean, there have been two violent murders in a month, and lots of people are freaking out."

"I get that, Amos. I was wondering about signs of drug use. Rex, are any of those students you mentioned before still giving you the fisheye?"

"Nah. As I said last time we talked, they ignore me lately. There's only one thing on people's minds right now – when can they go home for Fall Break? A few days away from this place will lower stress levels a lot. Most of us seniors are also stressing over getting our college admissions process finished. As for me, I need to raise my SATs at least 150 points to have a shot at UVA or William and Mary, and next Saturday is the most important SAT I will ever take. I've been obsessing about it. "

No need for me to add more stress. "OK, fellas, thanks a lot. I'll check with you in a day or two. Rex, relax – worrying about it won't increase your SAT score." His expression didn't seem to indicate he put much stock in my reassurance. "I have another appointment now. I'll see you later."

We left Rex's room together, and as they peeled off to their academic buildings, I headed to the administration offices. It was one thing to be late for a meeting with Rex and Amos, quite another to be late to see H. Michael, who made it clear by being prompt for every meeting with me that he expected the same from me.

Three minutes later the memory of glorious autumn leaves was squelched by the scowling visage of Death Ray.

"You're like a bad penny, Mr. Wright. You keep coming back. What do you want this time?"

"For your information, Miss Foss, your boss asked me to meet with him." I grinned at her, savoring my little triumph.

Like all sycophants, she couldn't bear to incur any disfavor from her superior, and I knew that she had to struggle to keep her contempt of me from showing lest I share her comments with H. Michael.

"I'll buzz him to check if he's free," she replied through pursed lips.

A pinch of salt in the wounds seemed to be in order. "Not necessary, Miss Foss. I'll let myself in."

Before she could react to my brazen effrontery, I breezed by her desk and, after a perfunctory knock on his door, let myself in to H. Michael's office. I hoped she was at least a little worried that her boss would blame her for my intrusion. Before closing the door behind me, I wanted her to see H. Michael stand to greet me with his version of a smile. Then I flashed my biggest grin at her and closed the door.

Yes, I could be petty. And I was unrepentant about it.

Chapter Forty-five

H. Michael's face was more deeply lined than usual, and his complexion looked a bit gray, both signs of worry and sleepless nights.

With a half-smile and pointing to the empty chairs, he indicated for me to take a seat. "Mr. Wright, I'll get right to the point. Clanton is suffering in many ways from the recent ghastly murders, and the worst of the problems is that more than forty students have withdrawn from school, maybe permanently, maybe temporarily. Solving these murders quickly would go a long way toward restoring a sense of calm normalcy that is necessary to stop the bleeding. Many more withdrawals and the school will face financial insolvency. The Board of Directors is meeting with me tomorrow, and I have a suspicion that they won't approve of raiding the endowment fund any time soon."

"And how do I figure in that, Mr. Madison? The Feds are actively investigating the cases."

"Give me some credit, Mr. Wright. Do you not think I realize that? Where you would come in is to investigate under the radar as I told you before. You would have better luck mingling with faculty and students, and if one or more of them is guilty of murder, they would be more likely to let their guard down around you than around the Feds. They've come up with a big fat zero after using all their resources. You couldn't do any worse. I know you agreed to keep your eyes and ears open, but I need more than that now. I need you to work on this full-time."

His shoulders slumped for a moment and he sucked his breath in. He was obviously dealing with more stress than he was accustomed to contending with.

"You may or may not be right in that regard, Mr. Madison. I have had little luck so far in finding much about the drugs on campus, though I think that the murders have driven that deeper underground. My biggest problem with helping you out, however, is the time spent here amounts to time *not* spent at my job. The bills don't stop coming in just because I have more pressing matters than my work. I am going to have to spend more time in Virginia Beach."

H. Michael looked directly at me for what seemed like minutes but was probably only ten seconds. Being stared at always makes me uncomfortable.

His face remaining expressionless, he said, "I fully understand your concern, Mr. Wright. Clanton's bills have the same habit of being relentless. Naturally, the school could not pay you to investigate. The Board would never agree to such an expenditure." He paused to read my reaction, and when he must have assumed none was immediately forthcoming, he continued. "But I have no restrictions on how I spend *my* money. To be blunt, it's not only Clanton's future at stake. Mine is, too. If Clanton doesn't weather this storm, I'll be terminated. And, Mr. Wright, that is not an acceptable option for me. What would you charge for your services?"

His offer blindsided me. I had not even considered being employed here a remote possibility. After doing some quick figuring in my head, I said, "Two thousand a week would cover my expenses." That amount would cover a lot more, but being in the driver's seat, I figured I ought to be compensated for more than the bare minimum.

"Fair enough, Mr. Wright. I will start paying you in cash today, half in advance, half at the end of the week. I do insist that whatever you come up with you run by me first. I will have the final say in how information is shared with the Feds or even Sheriff Dixon. Are we in agreement?"

"Yes, sir," I instantly replied. "I do have an idea for your consideration. Though I don't have access to FBI resources, I do have a friend since our days at UVA who is a highly regarded psychologist. I figure her two PhDs could qualify her as a profiler of sorts. Any objection to my asking her for her opinion of what might drive this person or persons to commit such grisly murders? She is the model of discretion and will not breathe a word of this to anyone if I insist on for-my-eyes-only information."

I figured it couldn't hurt to get an expert opinion gratis, and I owed her a telephone call anyway.

"No objection from me, Mr. Wright. Get started as soon as you can." He rose from his chair and walked to the door. Not the most subtle way to let me know the meeting was over, but I knew that I was only one of many people he had to communicate with today.

I shook his hand on the way out, and, as I had hoped, Miss Foss saw our friendly departure.

"Top of the morning to you, Miss Foss," I said cheerfully. "I'll be seeing much more of you in the near future."

I knew that would make her day.

Chapter Forty-six

Relieved that my finances had picked up, for a while at least, I looked forward to an evening with a glass of wine and a call to my psychologist friend, Dr. Angelina Sharp. The best laid plans, however...

Just as I was about to leave the administration building, I heard a woman's voice calling my name, twice. Turning around to see who was calling me, I saw Mrs. Clarkson scurrying toward me. Wearing a black bra under a sheer white top was probably not going to win her any fashion awards, but I had to admit it accentuated her ample chest.

Huffing a bit from her running down the hall, she said, "Let me catch my breath, Mr. Wright. Or may I call you Danny?" Her smile was radiant.

"Danny's fine with me."

"Danny, I am having a small get-together at my house tonight and would love for you to come join us. Very informal. Interested?"

That I was. It would be refreshing to talk with adults about something other than murder and drugs. Not to mention she was more than a little attractive. And, yes, sexy.

"I'd like that," I said earnestly. "May I call you by your first name?"

"By all means," she purred. "It's Rebecca, but almost everyone calls me Becky or Miss Becky."

It was obvious to me that she was mildly flirting, and I did nothing to discourage her.

"What can I bring, Becky?" I asked, hoping for a negative reply. I doubted that she or any of her other guests would enjoy stale crackers with moldy cheese, and I didn't feel like driving to Charlottesville.

"Just bring yourself, handsome. Seven o'clock, last house on the right across from the Academy pond."

"Looking forward to it," I said and watched her walk all the way down the hall.

As I walked back to the Alumni House, it occurred to me that I didn't even know her marital status. If she wasn't divorced or widowed, her husband would probably be there, and I was fully prepared to dislike him. Well, maybe not dislike…more like envy. But, according to Rex, she was promiscuous, and I doubted she'd be so reckless as to have affairs with students if her husband was around.

I called Julia to relay the good news about our finances, then had a long chat with my sister, assuring her that Rex was doing fine and would probably appreciate a care package to help allay the stress of the SAT that loomed large. I had plenty of time for a long shower, and fifteen minutes later was feeling like a teenager going to a prom. For my introduction into Clanton's social life, I decided on a fairly clean blue dress shirt and black slacks that were relatively free of creases. Though I seldom spent time looking in mirrors, I checked myself out – not bad, I concluded. No Benedict Cumberbatch but not likely to scare little children.

The walk to her house took less than ten minutes, and not wanting to appear overly eager, I walked around the pond a couple times to kill time. At 7:15, I knocked on the door of the attractive brick two-story house. I knew the Academy provided housing for many of the faculty and staff, but I wasn't aware that included all the administrative assistants. I couldn't remember any faculty or staff named Clarkson from my stay at Clanton. If she was married, maybe her husband was a recent hire. It should have bothered me a little that I hoped there was no current Mr. Clarkson. Moral ambiguity was just one more of my character flaws I tried halfheartedly to discourage.

Opening the door, Becky Clarkson flashed that alluring smile and invited me in.

Chapter Forty-seven

Becky Clarkson's house was decorated with an appealing mixture of antiques and comfortable modern furniture complemented by a host of deep red oriental rugs here and there. I took a seat next to Coach Rotherwood on a three cushion leather sofa.

"How are things, Coach?" I asked. It seemed a bit strange to be in a social setting with teachers whom I knew twenty years ago as a student.

Just then Becky came over and asked what I would like to drink.

"Any beer would be good, thanks," I replied. "I'm not particular." Not about beer, at any rate.

After asking Coach Rotherwood if he needed a fresh drink, she left to retrieve my beer and another glass of merlot for Coach. Watching her weave through the assembled teachers and staff, I must have been too obvious in my interest.

"Danny, you know she's married, don't you?" Coach said.

"Sure. No harm looking, though, right?"

"You and half the men here," he said, smiling. "She's separated from her husband. Waiting for a divorce, I heard.

He used to work in administration, then moved on to a sales job in Norfolk. She told him she wasn't moving and somehow wrangled her way into being allowed to stay in this house. No one could figure out how she managed to do that with so many growing families on the faculty."

I thought I could figure out the reason for that, and I knew that Coach did, too. I had seen the way H. Michael eyed her, and I would bet a day's pay that he had, too.

"I'm sure it had a lot to do with her professional abilities as much as anything," I said, knowing that neither of us believed a word of it.

We both smiled as she maneuvered her way through the guests to deliver my beer.

"Here you are," she said as she handed me a Coors Light and Coach a full pour of merlot.

Spotting my World History teacher holding up an empty wine glass, she excused herself and left to continue her hosting duties.

Coach and I had a long chat about sports, politics, and the state of the world. Not mentioning Clanton or murder put me in a better than usual frame of mind recently. Three beers later, the crowd had thinned out, leaving only two married couples and Becky and me.

I got up to say good night and thank her for having me over.

"Please don't leave yet, Danny. Have a nightcap with me after I shoo away the others. I need to put my feet up and relax but don't want to drink alone."

How could I refuse that offer?

The two remaining couples left minutes later, and Becky came over to the sofa with a beer for me and a glass of white wine for her.

"I enjoyed the party, Becky. It sure was a trip being with people who taught me."

"Glad you enjoyed," she said and moved closer to me. "But you look a little tense. Did being with them make you uncomfortable?"

"Not so much that I couldn't handle it. Just a little weird is all." I chugged my beer hard.

She set her wine glass down on the coffee table and said, "Get comfortable. Slip off your shoes, and I'll massage your feet to help you relax."

I had a good idea where this was headed and was trying to decide how I could end it when she slipped off my shoes and started working on my tired feet. It felt too good to protest. Her strong fingers seemed to erase any trace of tension from recent events, and soon they were massaging my ankles, then my calves, and moving steadily north.

"I think we'd be more comfortable if you lay on your back," she said softy and led me to her bedroom.

Her bed was a huge round thing with pink satin sheets, and even though I knew that she had shared it with many others, I didn't seem to mind at the moment.

The day was destined to have a happy ending.

Chapter Forty-eight

After tip-toeing out of Becky's bedroom as soon as she fell asleep, I walked back to the Alumni House with feelings of ambivalence I had a hard time sorting through. On the one hand, I knew full well that tonight was a huge lapse of good sense. But on the other hand, a boost to my battered ego couldn't be all that bad. Nevertheless, I promised myself that last night was a one-night stand in the truest sense of the phrase.

My father was one of the male Wrights whose contribution to my gene pool was probably responsible for my occasional forays into less than wholesome behavior. A hard drinker – no, make that a drunk – Leonard Wright was never considered father-of-the-year material by either my sister or me, and when his liver finally gave out after years of cirrhosis at the age of fifty-two, leaving my mother with nothing but a stack of bills, we didn't observe an extended period of mourning. Not even a day, actually. The only good he ever did was dying so impoverished that I qualified for a scholarship to Clanton.

Battering myself with guilt and bad memories was counterproductive, I knew, and I went to bed resolved not to follow in his footsteps or indulge myself in self-pity. Tomorrow I would call my longtime friend Angelina and see if she could help me profile whoever killed Wood and Thomason. A better boost to my ego would be to help uncover the evil here.

The following morning, three cups of strong coffee and a bagel with cream cheese at the cafeteria recharged my batteries, and after stopping by Rex's room to make sure he was studying for the upcoming SAT, I went back to my quarters and called Angelina.

She answered groggily after four rings.

"Sorry to call so early, Angelina, but I wanted to reach you before you left for work. Got time to talk?"

"Do you know what time it is in California, Danny?" she barked, sounding none too pleased to hear from me. "It's six a.m., and I don't do six a.m.'s."

"I do apologize, Angelina, but I'm in desperate need of picking your brain." She was not the type to be moved by flattery, but I hoped our friendship would allow her to get past her anger.

It did.

"OK, Danny," she sighed. "What's on your mind?"

"Thanks, Angelina, you're a real pal. Long story short is that I am at Clanton Academy, where I went to high school and where my nephew Rex is now attending. My years here probably did more than anything to help me get into UVA and make a life for myself, and I don't want to see the school go down the drain."

"What are you saying, Danny? Is the school in jeopardy of closing? Money problems? You know I don't have any extra money."

"No, nothing like that. Two murders – really bad murders – happened here in one month. Both teachers. One was a despised man who exploded in the cafeteria from ingesting a belly bomb. The other was a well-liked and highly respected teacher who was poisoned with cyanide. One of the impacts of those brutal murders is that lots of students have been withdrawn by their parents who fear for their kids' safety, and if withdrawals continue, Clanton's future is dismal."

"How awful for you and your nephew, Danny. But how do you figure in this? Don't you do missing persons work, that sort of thing? I didn't know you investigated homicides."

"I don't do homicides, Angelina. This is the first and hopefully the last. The FBI is currently here investigating, but they have been as unsuccessful in discovering the culprit as they have been successful in alienating themselves with everyone here. The president of the school, desperate for this to go away as soon as possible, has employed me to do my own investigating without the Feds being any the wiser."

"I see. Well, how can I be of help, Danny?"

"As you can imagine, the FBI has vast resources, and I have none. I was hoping you could become a resource of sorts by profiling what you think the killer might be like. Think you can do that? I know you wouldn't try to do anything that would even hint at lack of professionalism. I am simply asking for a friend's opinion. And my friend just happens to be a highly knowledgeable shrink."

There was a long pause, and I expected a negative reply. I hated putting her on the spot and was ready to apologize when she answered, "Danny, the best I can do is to think out loud if you tell me a little more about the murders."

Whatever thinking out loud she could do was more than I would come up with on my own.

"My best guess, and the FBI's and local law enforcement's, too, is that the murderer is someone on the staff here. Problem is, I don't have any idea why those two were victims. They had nothing in common, and for the life of me, I can't think of a motive."

I provided her with the short list of those who were in the cafeteria at the time of Wood's murder and explained that the cafeteria staff had no opportunity to sabotage the knockwurst. I didn't add that Mr. Jenkins and Mr. Mann had the only apparent opportunity because I didn't want her to be prejudiced by circumstances. I wanted only a psychological assessment of a killer who probably had lived and worked at Clanton for years without ever having murdered anyone. Besides, there was the outside chance that the knockwurst had arrived at the cafeteria already outfitted with the bomb, and the second murder was unrelated to the first.

"Danny, given so few details, I can't provide any accurate assessment of a specific nature, such as age, ethnicity, background, and so forth. However, if both murders were the work of one killer, I can say with confidence that the victims didn't necessarily have to be related in any way. They could have been simply the end product of a mind that has become warped by anger. The nature of the murders suggests two things: One, this killer – and he is almost certainly a man – selected means of murder he knows are spectacular. Not a typical gunshot or stabbing. No, he is finding pleasure in creative means of killing, and since he is probably known by everyone there, he is cunning enough to murder victims that wouldn't be traced back to him. You really do need to find a motive to find this man. And he may kill again. These murders may have whetted his appetite for more, or maybe they were just a prelude for a subsequent murder of a victim who may be linked to him. If that is true, and I have no way of knowing that, he's ruthless, consumed by anger."

"Is there anything in any behaviors that I can look for that may help get this killer to reveal himself, Angelina?"

"Probably not, Danny. If this man has been living in that secluded, small environment where everybody knows one another and their business, as well, I suspect, he must be unassuming and nonviolent on the surface, or else there would have been talk. All I can suggest is that you and everybody else there be super vigilant and spend as little time alone as possible. And that includes you, Danny."

"Me?" I hadn't even considered myself in any degree of danger.

"Yes, you, Danny. If this killer has yet to kill the person who has generated this intense anger, he may kill others before getting to him. Or if this is a man who has simply become unhinged, he may strike at random until he makes a mistake and is apprehended. Be careful, very careful. I'm sorry for being so imprecise. Really, Danny, without knowing more information, this is the best I can do, and it would never pass muster if scrutinized by other professionals. I am just offering an opinion formed on very little information. It's an act of friendship not to be confused with genuine profiling. If you tell anyone that I said this, I'll deny it."

"It's more than I thought of, Angelina. Thank you so much. And not to worry about my telling anyone. This was for-your-ears-only, and I'd appreciate your keeping mum. Anything else you can throw my way would be for my-eyes-only. I owe you one. Big time."

"You can buy me drinks and dinner at our next UVA reunion. My fee is nonnegotiable," she said laughing briefly before adding, "but seriously, Danny, you could be in danger yourself. This man is the hardest kind of killer to find because he has no pattern. He may have seemed normal for a long time, but he is a psychopath. Now, goodbye – I am going back to sleep. Call at a more civilized hour next time, OK? And don't wait till another murder to do that."

Civilized? Such a strange word considering the circumstances at Clanton.

Chapter Forty-nine

Less than two weeks ago, Rollie Jenkins would not have considered killing anyone, let alone a friend, but having tasted the thrill of murder, he looked forward to removing one more impediment – Ted Reasoner. Armed with resolve, a bag of confiscated marijuana, a bottle of wine, and Belgian chocolates laced with potassium cyanide, he waited till nightfall to visit Reasoner at his campus house. Darkness became his ally, affording no one a glimpse of him as he climbed the three steps to the porch, knocked softly on the door, and waited for Reasoner to answer.

"Jenkins, what in the hell are you doing here? I told you before that I want nothing more to do with you," Reasoner growled while shutting the door.

"Hold on, Reasoner. Don't close the door. I am here to apologize. Look," Jenkins said holding out a bottle of wine, "I brought a peace offering. Let's drink a couple glasses and bury the hatchet, OK?"

Jenkins hoped that Reasoner would make it easier on him and let him in, but even if he didn't, he would push his way in and use his superior size to subdue Reasoner.

Nothing and no one would stop him from executing this necessary part of the grand plan.

Reasoner held the door open for a moment, then started to close it, saying, "Thanks, but no thanks."

Wedging his foot between the door and its frame, Jenkins put on the most sincere appearance he was capable of and said, "Please, Reasoner. Give me a chance, for crissakes. What have you got to lose by taking the high road and letting me in?"

If he only knew, Reasoner wouldn't have shrugged his shoulders and reopened the door. "OK, Jenkins, but I don't have a lot of time for this. I have a stack of papers a mile high to grade."

"Oh, this won't take long. Thanks so much." He presented Reasoner the bottle of cabernet sauvignon and waited for Reasoner to lead him to the living room.

As they walked down the hallway, Reasoner said, "Have a seat in the living room, Jenkins. I'll go to the kitchen and look for a cork screw to uncork this and share one glass with you."

"Make mine a short one, Reasoner. I have papers to grade, too."

Surveying the living room quickly, Jenkins spotted what he wanted to find: Reasoner's laptop. So far, so good. He could feel his excitement growing.

Reasoner came with two glasses a quarter filled and handed one to Jenkins. "Here's to letting bygones be bygones, Jenkins. I will never forgive myself – or you – for what we did, but we may as well wallow in our guilt together. Misery loves company." He gently clinked Jenkins's glass and took a sip, nodding his head in approval. "You always did have good taste in wine, Jenkins."

Taking a sip of his wine, Jenkins smiled. "Mmmm, yes, this is a pleasant surprise. I bought this one blind, not knowing if it would be any good. Say, if you have your computer handy, how about doing a Google search for me? I want to see more about this brand…won't take but a sec."

Reasoner cleared a space on the oval coffee table and set his glass down, then walked to the laptop at his desk. Jenkins shadowed him and looked over Reasoner's shoulder as he typed in his password. Once it was booted up, Reasoner started keying in "Google.com" in the URL space and got only as far as "Goo" when Jenkins interrupted him.

"That can wait a while, Reasoner. Let's finish this bottle and say to hell with papers."

After a brief pause, Reasoner said, "That's an offer I can't refuse, Jenkins. I am more than eager to relieve my stress level for a while, and getting a buzz seems much more agreeable than grading papers."

Together they walked back to their seats. Jenkins filled their glasses to the brim and said, "For a few hours at least, let's forget everything, Reasoner. Skoal."

'In a few hours Reasoner will forget everything permanently if things go right,' Jenkins thought, and that provoked a smile that Reasoner interpreted as a sign of camaraderie.

Reasoner's bad decisions were mounting and heading to an outcome he couldn't foresee.

Chapter Fifty

The bottle of excellent cabernet sauvignon went down easily, with Reasoner enjoying two thirds of it. The more they drank, the more easily and freely they conversed about a dozen subjects, avoiding any mention of murder.

"You know, Jenkins, this wine hit the spot. I have a bottle of chilled pinot grigio in the fridge. Should I open it?"

"I have a better idea," Jenkins replied, smiling. He pulled out a bag containing four joints. "I confiscated these from a kid's desk in the dorm, figuring we needed relaxation more than he did. Let's revisit our college days and get ripped."

"Grass? I haven't smoked in probably twenty years. I don't know about this."

"Loosen up, Reasoner. No chance of us getting caught, and we need to unwind. Let's do it!"

In yet another bad decision, Reasoner agreed. "Sure, why not? I have nothing to lose."

Except his life.

Jenkins handed Reasoner the fattest joint. "No need to share that. We can each smoke our own."

Reasoner lit up and inhaled deeply, coughing from lack of practice, then said, "Whoever you stole this from has a good supplier." He inhaled deeply again and this time held the smoke in his lungs much longer without coughing.

"Confiscated, not stole," Jenkins said, laughing. The joint he was smoking was ninety percent tobacco, ten percent marijuana. He wanted to produce the characteristic odor of marijuana but needed to keep a clear head.

Halfway through their second joints, Jenkins said, "Damn, I am so ravenous. I brought along some great Belgian chocolates I was going to leave with you, but I think I deserve to share them. Hungry?"

"Famished," Reasoner said and swallowed the cyanide-laced chocolate without even chewing.

Jenkins savored a chocolate he hadn't doctored. "Mmmm, these do go down easily. Here's another for you," he said, offering Reasoner another dose of death.

This time Reasoner chewed the chocolate. "Kinda bitter," he giggled. "But my taste buds might be a little under the influence." He doubled over in laughter at what, in his stoned condition, he thought was wit.

"I need some wine to wash this down, and I think I have some peanuts we could demolish," Reasoner said as he unsteadily got to his feet. He wobbled ten steps before gasping. A few moments later, he dropped to the floor, dead.

"That's it? That's all there is…a minute of struggle? Not what I hoped for," Jenkins muttered.

'Oh, well, the next one will be much more gratifying. I'll make sure of that,' he thought.

Reasoner's wine glass he placed on the computer desk, and if his staged suicide worked, investigators would assume that Reasoner drank wine to swallow Tylenols he injected with cyanide. Jenkins took his wine glass to the kitchen to wash, dry, and put into a cabinet with other wine glasses. After flushing the remains of the joints down the toilet, he washed and dried the ash tray and opened a couple windows to air out the house.

Though he thought it was probably an unnecessary precaution, he methodically retraced his exact movements from the porch to the living room, wiping off his fingerprints from any object he touched. No sense in not being thorough. There was no hurry.

Reasoner's fingerprints were already on the cork screw, leaving only the wine bottle for Jenkins to deal with. The damp wash rag in the kitchen sink removed all prints from the bottle, which he carried with the rag wrapped around it to the unconscious body. Jenkins slipped on latex gloves and maneuvered Reasoner's left hand around the body of the bottle to leave an impression of his fingerprints, knowing that all right-handed people use the right hand to work the cork screw while holding a bottle with their left hand.

"One more step to go," he said aloud to himself. Watching Reasoner die was his entertainment, the prelude to the completion of a perfect crime; typing the suicide note on Reasoner's computer was all that remained to do.

Leaning over the open laptop, Jenkins started carefully typing, wearing his latex gloves. First he completed the "Goo" that Reasoner had entered to "Google" and keyed in "How to commit suicide with cyanide." When the list of answers popped up, to leave a history of searches, he clicked on the one about the Chicago murders in the early 80s, with the murderer injecting Tylenols with cyanide. After closing it, he opened Word and composed the suicide note that he would leave open for whoever discovered the body.

I simply can't continue living after my monstrous acts. I originally thought my conscience would not bother me. I was wrong. I haven't slept in days, and when I tried, a voice inside me kept calling me a murderer over and over till I gave up trying to sleep. Let me explain my vile acts so that no one else will fall under suspicion, and Clanton Academy can begin the healing process. My descent began with my hatred of Mr. Wood. He was a toxic man, a bloated misanthrope, who was smearing my professional reputation by telling anyone who would listen that I wasn't worth my salary, that my students were being cheated by my ineptitude. That couldn't be further from the truth. I gave my all to this job. It was my life. I confronted him, and he laughed at me. That sealed his fate. Knowing that fat bastard loved sausage, I easily inserted a tiny radio-activated bomb into a sausage that I removed from the serving tray and slipped it back to the top of the serving tub when the cafeteria lady was talking with Mr. Mann. I momentarily panicked when I saw Mr. Jenkins take the sausage. To get an unobstructed view of the table where he and Mr. Jenkins and Mr. Mann sat, I took a seat at a table behind the one where a student and a stranger sat. If Mr. Jenkins had started to cut the sausage, I was going to rush there and bump into him and knock the tray to the floor. Much to my relief, Mr. Wood ate the sausage. Waiting enough time for it to reach his stomach, I then detonated it with a radio transmitter in my pocket and watched him explode. I felt no remorse. But two days later Mr. Thomason was visiting me in my office and saw the radio transmitter on my desk. He asked me what I had that for, and I improvised a lie, but I knew that as smart as he was, when it came out that the bomb was detonated by radio signal, he'd figure it out, and I couldn't have that. I bought some cyanide online and doctored some food I knew he liked. It was after that that I couldn't sleep. Mr. Thomason was a good man who had done me no harm, and I can't live with what I did. I had poison left over from killing him and injected it into Tylenol capsules. I know this is a long, detailed description of my fall from grace, but there is no such thing as TMI for me to clear my conscience and try to make things right. I am going to take the capsules now and hope that my soul finds peace even though it doesn't deserve it. With remorse, Ted Reasoner

'I think I got the level of literacy right. Not overly fluent but essentially correct, something a science major would write. Jenkins, you're getting very good at this.'

He wiped a syringe clean of his own fingerprints and again maneuvered Reasoner's right hand to make impressions with the inside of his middle and index fingers on either side of the barrel and his thumb on the top of the plunger. He carefully placed it on the floor beside the chair with Reasoner's body and an opened bottle of Tylenol.

After taking a final look at the corpse to congratulate himself on a job well done and then carefully scanning the room one last time, Jenkins exited the house.

'Nothing now but to wait on what the FBI concludes,' he thought. 'Even if they don't reach the conclusion I want, they will have no reason to suspect me. Another perfect crime.'

He hummed softly the whole walk home.

Chapter Fifty-one

After picking up cash from H. Michael and happily annoying Miss Foss at 9:00 this morning, I had to admit I liked having a little discretionary income for a change. Surveying my empty refrigerator, I decided to head to Whole Foods to stock up on foods and wines pricier than my usual fare. Armed with Stilton and manchego cheeses, crostini, and three expensive – by my standards – bottles of pinot grigio and three of sauvignon blanc, I headed back to the Alumni House. A quick hot shower later, I headed over to the dorm to see Rex. It was my intention not to mention drugs or murders. Today his focus needed to be on tomorrow's SAT.

"Come on in," Rex yelled from his room, not knowing who was knocking on his door.

Entering his disheveled room, I was pleased to see him at his desk memorizing abstruse vocabulary words.

"I won't bother you long, Rex," I said. "Just wanted to see if you're on task. And that seems pretty obvious. Feeling good about tomorrow's SAT?"

"I guess so. Not super confident, but if I can't make 2200, it won't be from lack of trying."

"You'll be fine regardless of whether you make your goal, Rex. UVA isn't the only excellent option in Virginia, you know."

"Yeah, I know you're right, Uncle Danny. It's just that it's been my dream school since I was a kid."

"Now is not the time to stress about which college you'll end up at, Rex. That'll be settled in the next couple months. Just give the exam tomorrow your best shot and keep those "As" coming. I'll check in with you after the exam tomorrow. Good luck."

"Thanks for caring, Uncle Danny. I really appreciate it."

I excused myself and headed back to the administration building to see if I could locate Agent Parker – if he wasn't with Sloane. While Angelina's input confirmed what I already thought about the killer's mental condition, it did little to get me closer to identifying him. If Parker would share what they'd come up with, I could share that in turn with H. Michael to let him know I was working hard for his cash.

Walking down the hallway, I found, not Parker, but Becky. Before I could register my discomfort at this chance meeting, she breezed by me with not so much as a nod toward H. Michael's office. I hesitantly followed a few steps behind her. What could possibly be so important that she'd not bat her eyes at me?

H. Michael was talking with Miss Foss but abruptly ended that conversation and turned to the approaching Becky. "Any word yet on why Reasoner didn't show up for class this morning, Mrs. Clarkson?"

"Nothing yet, Mr. Madison. I arranged for Jeff Anderson in Marketing to cover his class in the meantime. He didn't seem to be working on anything pressing. After I get the grades entered in Powerschool this morning, I'll get someone to check at his house. It's not like him to not call in when he's sick."

"Good work as always, Mrs. Clarkson," H. Michael said. "Keep me in the loop." He beamed, she smiled, and I scurried back down the hallway. I did not want to engage with her at the moment.

No luck with that, however.

"Mr. Wright, don't rush off so fast. Not even a hello from you this morning?" She flashed her toothy smile at me.

"Um, I was just in a big hurry, sorry," I stammered.

"You sure weren't the other night, Danny," she said and winked at me.

I hoped I wasn't blushing. "Well, er, I…I have to go. Very important matter came up."

Becky laughed softly. "I'd like *you* to come up sometime again."

Unable to make a graceful exit, I turned and walked away, so mortified that I temporarily forgot why I was even there.

Chapter Fifty-two

Frowning, I thought, 'I sure didn't handle that chance meeting well. Bogie would not be impressed.'

Ahead of me in the lobby I spotted Parker, and he was alone. Perfect. I hustled to him and said, "No company today? Is that good news or bad?"

"Neither, Danny. Sloane has scheduled a meeting with our boss to determine if all of us need to stay here. We seem to be at a dead end, and having four of us drinking coffee all day because there are no new leads isn't the best use of manpower."

Unaccustomed to such candor from a Fed, I didn't quite know how to react. In the back of my mind, I still thought that Jenkins, despite having nothing to go on other than his having opportunity, somehow had something to do with Wood's murder, but a hunch and five dollars would get you a jolt of caffeine at Starbucks.

"Have you finished interviewing all persons of interest?" I asked.

"Every damn one of them. Zilch. Ordinarily we have a case pretty much solved within a few days. Either this guy is very skilled or very lucky."

"Sorry to hear that," I replied. And I was. "Let me know if something comes up, and I'll do the same for you. See you later."

"Sure thing, Danny, but I am not too confident that anything new will turn up any time soon."

Mildly disappointed but not surprised, I left Agent Parker and headed to the library to see if Mr. Mann had anything to add to the mixture. If my hunch had any substance, Mann would offer the best chance of verifying it, since apparently he spent more time with Jenkins than anyone else here.

Entering the pleasant library, well-lit with overhead skylights, I wandered over to a reading area and picked up the latest Charlottesville *Daily Progress* to see if the Clanton murders had fallen off the front page yet. They had, the beneficiary of a local political scandal that reflected the goings-on in DC. Even corruption had a silver lining, it seemed.

Eavesdropping unintentionally, I knew that Mr. Mann was preoccupied with gossiping with students, and I hoped he'd have a few minutes to gossip with me as well. As soon as I saw him direct a look at me, I gave him a half wave to acknowledge that I was open to conversation. A couple minutes later, he walked with his tiny steps that reminded me of the David Suchet version of Poirot to greet me. In hushed tones, of course.

"Good afternoon, Mr. Wright. What brings you to my little libary?'

"Just killing time till Happy Hour," I lied.

He tittered. "Oooh, Mr. Wright, don't say that too loud. You know, I'm sure, that Mr. Madison hates drinking. And probably those who do it."

"You don't say," I said with calculated disingenuousness. "I was hoping you'd join me for a glass of wine and an appetizer before dinner. I am staying at the Alumni House and have a cozy little place to bunk. Guess that's out of the question."

He looked around us several times, then whispered conspiratorially, "I'd love to join you for a glass, Mr. Wright. You wouldn't happen to have any pinot gigolo, would you? If not, I can bring my own stash."

"You're in luck, Mr. Mann, I just happened to lay in a couple bottles of pinot gigolo myself. Seems we have taste in wines in common. I'm in the first apartment to the left after you enter. Five o'clock OK for you?"

"Five is perfect. Can I bring something?"

"Not a thing except maybe the latest gossip," I said, winking at him.

"Ooh, wine *and* gossip. You are a wicked influence, Mr. Wright." He chortled and directed his gaze toward several students who were intensely focused on a laptop. "Dollars to donuts they're watching porn, Mr. Wright. I will not allow Satan in my libary!" He bee-lined toward them like a medieval crusader, albeit one with mincing steps.

I left him to complete his mission to eradicate evil and headed to my quarters to prepare cheap cheddar and crostini and uncork the last of the inexpensive bottles of pinot grigio. No Stilton for Mr. Mann, and if he couldn't pronounce it correctly, he certainly would not partake of the twenty-dollar bottles of pinot grigio.

Although I might reconsider if he supplied anything of value that related to my unofficial investigation.

Chapter Fifty-three

Mr. Mann had abandoned his customary tweeds and wore a faded black sweatshirt with "Clanton Academy" in letters that were probably red some years ago but were now closer to a shade of dirty pink. Regrettably, he had chosen to tuck the sweatshirt into his baggy khaki pants a couple inches too large around the waist. A pencil thin red belt held up the pants while offending any normal sense of style. Having exchanged his professorial attire for Good Will chic for this *tete a tete*, he entered as soon as I had yelled, "Come in!"

"I hope I am not too early, Mr. Wright. My social skills are a little rusty."

"Nope, you're right on time. And please call me Danny." He was actually ten minutes early, but that was of little consequence. Stale cheese and cheap wine allowed for social faux pas.

I set a tray loaded with the cheese and crackers on a coffee table and said, "Take either of the two seats in the room. I'll be right back…am getting your wine. Hope you don't mind drinking out of a water glass; it's all that's here."

"As long as my gigolo is cold, I'm fine. 'No fuss' is my motto."

I handed him a generous pour and sat in the remaining chair, watching him take a sip. If he recoiled because of the quality of the wine, I would reluctantly resort to uncorking a better bottle and blaming the store for selling me a wine past its shelf life. He took another bigger sip and smiled. My good wine was safe.

"This is delicious wine, Danny. Thanks for thinking of me."

"Glad you like it, Mr. Mann. Let me know when you need a refill, and please help yourself to cheese and crackers."

"Call me Hank. Thanks." He snatched several pieces of cheese and crackers from the tray.

"My nephew has spoken highly of you," I said, pretending to enjoy a stale cheese and cracker. Another little justified lie to loosen lips. "You've been here quite some time. You must like Clanton."

"Oh, yes. Irregardless of what some others might say, I am devoted to the school."

Interesting opening statement. I had to see where that would lead. "Who would think otherwise, Hank? Here, let me top that glass for you." I took his glass and gave him sufficient time to measure his words if he so chose to do so.

Returning to give him an almost full glass, I waited for an answer. After a long gulp, he said, "Well, there are some Philistines here who look down upon us bachelors like Mr. Wood and Mr. Jenkins as if we are leopards or something."

I shook my head in mock dismay. "Surely not, Hank. Both you and Mr. Jenkins are invaluable assets to my alma mater."

"I know. Shocking, right? Well, it's true. We are *persona non gratis*."

"I am appalled. Have more cheese and crackers, Hank. I hate to throw away expensive food."

He snatched a few more and ate them as if they were cordon bleu cuisine.

"How long have you and Mr. Jenkins been friends here, Hank? I imagine you seek each other's company since others here are so imperceptive of your virtues."

"More than ten years. Though to be truthful, we don't hang out together all that much. He prefers his own company – he's a little bit of a loner. Mostly we just eat together in the cafeteria. I do drop in to see him occasionally at his apartment when we have business to discuss."

"Business?"

"Yes, you know, stuff like pension plans, committee work, watering plants for each other when one of us is away…that sort of thing." He swallowed the last of the full glass and held it up. "Would you mind if I had one more, sort of to put a stopper on it?"

I didn't even know what he meant by that, but there was enough of the bottle for another generous pour.

"But of course, Hank. I may have another bottle somewhere in case that's not enough."

"Oh, no, Danny. One glass is usually my limit."

Who was he kidding? I knew a souse when I saw one.

"Here you go, Hank. Drink up." I smiled and took only my third sip. "So, as a third of the triumvirate of bachelors, Mr. Jenkins was very upset when Mr. Wood was murdered, I guess?"

He must have considered his answer weighty enough to justify his long pause. "Funny you should ask that, Danny. Just between you and me, I think he couldn't have cared less."

"What makes you say that, Hank?"

He flashed a Cheshire cat grin and said, "Because I know things, Danny. I know things." He slammed down the rest of his wine. "This has been lovely, Danny, but I must be on my way. The cafeteria closes in half an hour, and I think they're serving my favorite tonight, fried catfish. Let's do this again sometime, Danny. Soon."

I smiled graciously and said, "Soon, Hank, soon. You bet."

I needed to calculate just how much wine I needed to get him to guzzle before he would share what he knew. At the rate he just downed his pinot gigolo, my estimate was climbing. Mr. Madison would have to include several cheap bottles of wine in his budget. I could, if I were feeling particularly sensitive to his need for pious decorum, list them as incidental expenses to preclude his conscience from flaring up. Or not.

Chapter Fifty-four

Damn, I sure didn't see this one coming! Mr. Reasoner committed suicide out of remorse from killing two fellow teachers? Could the news spreading through the cafeteria this morning possibly be true?

I gulped down the last of my coffee and headed to the administration building to get verification from anyone in the know in admin but preferably from the Feds. The first person I encountered was the last I wanted to see, however – Becky Clarkson. Her somber clothing and demeanor were telling.

"You don't need to ask, Danny. Yes, it's true. When he didn't show up for classes yesterday, I sent someone over to his apartment. What he found was horrible. He had killed himself with the same poison he had used on Mr. Thomason." For once she was not flirting.

"How do you know that? Suicide note?"

"Yes, apparently it was a lengthy explanation of how and why he did it. He was so consumed with guilt, as well he should have been, that he couldn't go on any longer. If nothing else, I hope this ends this ugly chapter in Clanton's history."

"I hope so, too, Becky, but I am not sure how this will play out in the media and with concerned parents." Not to mention my nagging doubt. This seemed too pat. "Have you seen the Feds this morning?"

"Yes, they're down in the boss's office. I have a lot on my plate at the moment, Danny, and have to get back to my office. See you later?"

"Sure thing, Becky." But not if I could help it.

The hall was strangely devoid of voices despite phones ringing everywhere. Given the way H. Michael ran this place, I thought his administrative staff was paralyzed by reluctance to do or say anything that might not meet with the boss's approval. Surrounding himself with yes men might be good for his ego but bad for problem solving.

Even Miss Foss seemed numb. This latest bombshell stunted my desire to rattle her cage, and I simply greeted her with an innocuous "good morning."

Without looking at me, she said softly, "What's good about it? Should I be honing my resume to find employment at a place that isn't going under? I have put my faith in Mr. Madison and hope that he can reverse the damage, but I fear the worst."

For the only time since I returned here, I agreed with her. If H. Michael couldn't manipulate the media and parents enough to stop the bleeding, Clanton's future was in jeopardy.

"Let's hope so, Miss Foss. Any idea how long the Feds will be in there?"

"Probably not much longer. They went in over an hour ago, and I know that Mr. Madison needs to take care of a lot of business today."

The words were not long out of her mouth when the door to H. Michael's office opened and out filed four Feds.

Sloane, of course, ignored me, but Parker walked up to me and shook hands. "You won't be seeing much of us anymore, Danny. Now that we know who murdered the two victims, there's no need for us to stay here any longer. We're headed back to DC, and only if the toxicology report contradicts Reasoner's suicide note will we return. Frankly, we don't foresee that happening."

"Is there any way I could see what was on the suicide note just to satisfy my curiosity?" I wasn't about to mention that I had nagging doubts.

"I don't see why not. It'll be in the media soon anyway. Follow me to where I can open my laptop without Sloane looking over my shoulder. He's not one of your biggest fans."

"Oh, he made that clear enough," I said and turned to Miss Foss. "Please tell Mr. Madison that I will stop by today or tomorrow to touch base with him, Miss Foss."

"I will, Mr. Wright, but understand that he will be busy. Very busy," she said emphatically.

Parker and I peeled off from the group and headed to the visitors' lounge for my private viewing of Reasoner's last words.

Chapter Fifty-five

Parker's files on the two murders were more extensive than I thought they'd be, given his expressed frustration at having learned little of value in the investigation. I wasn't invited to skim those files, however, even after hinting that I would like to take a closer look.

"You know I can't do that, Danny. Only something that will be accessible to the public is fair game."

He scrolled through what seemed to be hundreds of files before finding the suicide letter. Clearly, it was too lengthy to be termed a note. A thorough reading did nothing to confirm my gut feeling that Reasoner wasn't the only person involved. Yet there was still that something nagging at the back of mind.

Parker must have seen my doubt in my expression.

"Something about this bothering you, Danny?" he asked.

"Nothing I can put my finger on. There's something about it that's just not right, though. I just can't shake the feeling that there's more to the story." Seeing that my groundless doubt wasn't registering much enthusiasm from Parker, I quickly added, "Hell, it could just be my mind swirling. I've never worked a murder case before."

Parker laughed softly. "It happens to all of us when we first enter the darkness of a murder investigation, Danny. Murder is essentially illogical. It runs against every instinct we have, and when we run across an aberration, we have a hard time processing it. I hope you never have to investigate another murder, Danny, but if you do, be aware of your own mode of thinking. It can skew your perceptions that need to be totally free of emotion or bias. Objectivity is essential." He paused to read my expression, I guess, and finding little in it to indicate that I objected, he said, smiling, "And that concludes my unsolicited lesson for the day, Danny."

"I appreciate your sharing that with me. I know I have been out of my league. I need to stick to tracking down unfaithful husbands and scam artists. Navigating a computer and patiently sitting in my car waiting for them to make a mistake seem to be my best skill set."

"Hey, now, for a rookie, you've done just fine. I wouldn't have bothered talking with you if I didn't think that."

"Thanks." And I meant that sincerely. "I hope we meet again sometime. Without Sloane, if possible."

We both laughed. Parker closed his files and his laptop and headed down the hall to find his colleagues.

'He's probably right about my instincts being influenced by inexperience,' I thought. Still, that little nagging voice in the back of my mind didn't go away.

With the Feds and all their experience, skills, and resources willing to declare the cases closed, I knew I couldn't justify remaining on H. Michael's payroll.

I walked slowly towards H. Michael's office. If he was able to see me, my source of income was about to stop immediately. Assuming that H. Michael would soon end my brief career as a homicide detective, I planned to stay at Clanton, H. Michael willing, till after Rex was finished with the SAT and maybe see Amos to say good-bye. The drug situation seemed a distant memory, but I owed the unofficial sleuths I had recruited a word or two of thanks. Virginia Beach was beckoning. Yet, though I was relieved that the murders had ceased, I was less than enthusiastic about resuming my boring job.

Chapter Fifty-six

When H. Michael curtly instructed Miss Foss not to interrupt our meeting with any phone calls, her scowl directed at me indicated that it was business-as-usual between us. I added a drop of fuel to the fire by winking at her as I followed H. Michael into his office.

H. Michael's desk was in uncharacteristic disarray with stacks of scraps of paper, post-its, and empty coffee cups covering its surface. He had obviously been busy putting out brush fires. Even his slicked back hair was ruffled and bags under his eyes had persisted. Nevertheless, he seemed visibly recharged and actually patted me on the back as I sat in what was becoming my favorite chair.

"This reversal of fortunes has me greatly relieved, Mr. Wright. Tired as I am, I am looking forward to getting in touch with every parent of the students who withdrew recently to assure them that we are once again a safe haven for their sons and blasting an email to all parents to inform them that all is again well at Clanton. If only half of the withdrawn students return, we will make budget."

Though my priority would probably be the security of Clanton if I were in his shoes, I did find it somewhat off-putting that he'd not once, in my presence at least, uttered a word to indicate that the deaths of three of his faculty had affected him in any way other than as a threat to his job. Predictably, he had stopped mouthing his usual God's-will-is-present-at-Clanton mantra. Three deaths didn't figure into H. Madison's vision of Clanton Academy's being God's City upon a Hill.

"I feel certain half or more will return, Mr. Madison. For one thing, withdrawing from school a couple months into the year is fraught with problems, especially for seniors. And for another, other than the supposed work of an unhinged employee, Clanton always has been and will likely always be a safer place than most." Truthfully, my own words seemed hollow. Angelina's profiling of the murderer and the unclear doubts I had seemed to indicate that Clanton was not yet out of the woods.

"Supposed? Why do you say 'supposed,' Mr. Wright? The FBI is firmly convinced that Mr. Reasoner was guilty." The tone of his voice expressed agitation, and I instantly regretted my choice of word. I wanted to remain in his good graces for a while.

"Bad wording, Mr. Madison. I should have said 'supposedly unhinged employee.' What I meant to convey is that we will never know what his state of mind was."

"Ah, that makes better sense, Mr. Wright. I learned long ago to choose my words carefully. I hope you do likewise."

The damn man couldn't even accept an apology without asserting his smug arrogance. Resisting the urge to say something I'd later regret, I said, "You're right, of course. My lame excuse is that I am not responsible for an entire institution as you are. Your deftness with words and gravitas befit your position. I'm just a small-time private dick who can barely take care of himself, let alone hundreds of others."

My hope was that ass kissing would lead to his generously overlooking my inferiority of language and leadership skills. I knew Bogie would never stoop so low, but in my world, occasional kowtowing was necessary.

H. Michael seemed pleased with both of us. "Oh, don't be so hard on yourself, Mr. Wright. One day you may hoist yourself up a wrung or two on the ladder of success, and then you'll have a better appreciation for the burden of responsibility."

I managed – with great effort – to smile. "You're too kind, Mr. Madison."

"So, Mr. Wright, now that the murderer is no longer a threat to Clanton, may I assume that you're here to call an end to our financial agreement?"

The words I had dreaded hearing finally materialized.

I nodded my head in agreement. "Yes, I assume you no longer have need of my services and ask only that you allow me to extend my stay in the Alumni House for another day or two to provide me an opportunity to clear up matters with my nephew and his friend."

"You assumed wrong, Mr. Wright. I still have need of your services. Like you, I am quite confident that the drug dealing on campus was halted simply because of the presence of the FBI. I would appreciate your continuing our arrangement, the only difference being that you now work full time to uproot the drug trafficking that I suspect will resume shortly. Same terms for us, same money. Does that work for you, Mr. Wright?"

I hesitated, pretending not to be pleased with this unexpected offer. After perhaps ten seconds of supposed weighing of my options – and this time the word *supposed* was accurate – I said, "I think I can rearrange my schedule of assignments back in Virginia Beach. Let's kick drug dealing in the ass!"

H. Michael pursed his lips in disapproval at my mildly profane enthusiasm. "As you surely understand, we cannot have even a whiff of further scandal on this campus. Whatever you find out, report it directly to me, and I'll take care of the situation without further damage to Clanton's reputation. Is that clear, Mr. Wright?"

"Clear as a bell, Mr. Madison."

Gently leading me out of his office toward Miss Foss, he said, "I'm glad we have an understanding." As a footnote to my good fortune, he said to Miss Foss, "I have many matters to attend to, Miss Foss. Mr. Wright has agreed to supply his services to the Academy." Extracting his checkbook from his suit pocket, he wrote a check in my name for five hundred dollars. "This is an advance, Mr. Wright. See me next Friday for the remainder." He tore out the check and presented it to Miss Foss. "Take this to Mr. Bobson to cash it. Mr. Wright will accompany you and instruct Mr. Bobson as to what denominations he prefers."

I could swear I heard her teeth gnashing.

"Of course, Mr. Madison. Please follow me, Mr. Wright," she managed to say with as little unpleasantness as she was capable of.

With Mr. Madison back in his office, Miss Foss's venom resurfaced as we walked briskly toward Mr. Bobson's office. "You are a despicable parasite, Mr. Wright. I don't know what scheme you cooked up to convince Mr. Madison that you could offer anything of any value, but I'll be watching you. Most alumni your age donate money to Clanton, not sponge from it. You should be ashamed of yourself."

Hurtful words if said by anyone other than Death Ray. Happy that I could extend my stay at Clanton and be paid for it as well, I refused to take offense.

"I can always depend on you, Miss Foss, to cheer me up," I said as I passed her in the hallway to find Mr. Bobson myself before she could preface the request to cash my check with her verbal cyanide.

Chapter Fifty-seven

I was impressed as ever with Mr. Bobson's opulent office, maybe because mine was shabby and undecorated or maybe because it was genuinely impressive. I noticed he was decked out in yet another Armani suit when he stood up from his chair behind the massive desk. His arms were so long that they stretched across the expanse of desk to shake my hand.

"I never forget a face, but I'm terrible at names," he said with a smile and a firm grip.

"Wright, Danny Wright," I said to refresh his memory.

"Ah, yes, now I remember. You have a nephew here, right? I need to come up with some mnemonic devices. So, how can I be of help today?" His eyes suddenly directed their attention behind me to the open door of his office. "Good morning, Miss Foss. I'm busy at the moment. Can you wait a minute or two outside my office?"

How insulting. He remembered that witch's name and not mine.

"I'm with Mr. Wright, Mr. Bobson. Mr. Madison sent us here with a personal check made out to him that he'd like you to cash." I had to give her an iota of credit: She could keep the malice out of her voice in the blink of an eye, reserving her charm-free tone solely for me.

"Well, then, come in, Miss Foss. May I have the check, please?" He examined it briefly, then escorted us to the safe in the main office. Pulling out a metal petty cash box, he asked, "What denominations would you prefer, Mr. Wright?"

"Four hundred-dollar bills and five twenties, if that's not a problem."

"Not in the least. If we can't trust Mr. Madison's checks not to bounce, whose can we?"

I assumed he meant that as mild humor; Miss Foss interpreted it otherwise.

"Mr. Madison's credit record is impeccable, Mr. Bobson. Please try to remember that!" she hissed and then scurried back to her office, surely satisfied with herself that she had squelched Mr. Bobson's impudence.

Mr. Bobson rolled his eyes and let out a soft, "Geez."

I laughed. "I'm sure you know her well enough to pay her no mind. She can't help herself. She was born that way."

With an odd look on his face that I found impossible to interpret, he said, "We're all born a certain way, aren't we?" He quickly closed the safe and resumed his affable disposition. "Anything else I can do for you today, Mr. Wright?"

"Not a thing, Mr. Bobson. Thanks, and have a great day."

Flush with extra cash, I left the business office to find Rex, hoping that the current string of good news would continue with a positive assessment of his performance on the SAT.

The door to his dorm room that made my disheveled office look like a Martha Stewart project was ajar. I knocked gently and let myself in. Empty. Where would he be on his free period? I wondered.

Too many possibilities. Rather than waste time wandering around the campus like a nomad, I wrote a note asking him to give me call on his unauthorized cell phone. As I placed it on top of textbook I knew he'd need, I couldn't help noticing a note beside it from Becky Clarkson asking him if he'd like to join her and a few other students on a Saturday trip to Charlottesville.

Now I had two things to ask him.

Chapter Fifty-eight

Witt, Van Verdenburg, and Jensen, fidgeting and clearly nervous, sat across from the uncluttered desk of their stone faced boss.

"Why have you called this meeting, Boss? I thought we were suspending operations," Witt asked.

The Boss stared at Witt long enough to make all three of them shift in their chairs and avoid eye contact.

"God, Witt, I can see why your peers say that your middle initial stands for 'Dim.' Now that the Feds are gone, why wouldn't we resume our business?"

"Yeah, Witt," Jensen added in an obvious attempt to ingratiate himself with the boss. If he expected some sort of approval from the boss, he was disappointed.

"Shut your pie hole, Whitey. Like you knew anything," Witt spit out in frustration.

"All of you just shut up and try to act like you graduated from middle school. Here's what you need to do. Tonight I am going to pick up a large shipment of coke from my supplier. Tomorrow morning, report to me how much your buyers here at Clanton will want. As always, cash only. The rest I will send to my contact in Richmond. Whitey, I need you to check with your usual clients to see what other candy we need to get. Brandon, your room will be the buy site because after so many students left, your room is almost the only one on your hall that is occupied. Any questions?"

"Yeah, what about me? What am I supposed to do?" asked Witt, anxious that he had lost favor with The Boss. He needed – or at least wanted – the easy money.

"For the time being, nothing. I'll have need of your services tomorrow evening."

Witt seemed as relieved as the others seemed annoyed.

"How come he don't have to do any work for the money?" Brandon asked The Boss.

"You don't like the way I run things, Brandon? Fine. I'll replace your sorry ass in ten minutes."

Brandon immediately said, "No, Boss. That was me just being stupid. I know you got a good reason for everything."

"You bet your ass The Boss does," said Witt. "Let's get outta here and start doing what we're getting paid for."

As they were filing out the door, the boss said, "Not you, Witt. Stay here for a sec."

Witt remained standing in front of The Boss's desk.

"Witt, make sure you keep those morons on task without any fuck-ups. And as for you, be prepared when you see me tomorrow night. You won't have any trouble sneaking out of the dorm, I trust."

"No trouble at all. Looking forward to our meeting. I aim to please." He smiled.

"Wipe that smile off your face, you fool. The day you stop pleasing me is the day you'll find yourself in more trouble that you ever dreamed of. Now get out of here and look after those idiots."

Witt paused.

"Did you forget something, Witt?"

"Do I need to know a special knock to use at your house door?"

The Boss groaned.

"Did your mother have any children that lived, Witt? Just knock on the door. This isn't a James Bond movie. Be sure to wait till dark and be careful that no one sees you."

It seemed doubtful to The Boss that Witt had enough sense to feel embarrassed. "Anything else, Witt?"

"Nope, I'll be there rarin' to go."

'Good God almighty, is making money worth dealing with these tools?' "Be prompt, Witt. You know I don't like to wait."

Witt executed an unsuccessful version of an about face he had seen in a war movie and exited, unable to see The Boss's look of disgust.

Chapter Fifty-nine

The library was my last stop in my quest to track down Rex, and I was a little surprised to find him secluded in a study carrel poring over his lessons.

"Rex, I've been all over the campus trying to track you down," I said, maybe a little too peevishly. Inconveniencing me was not his intention. "Let's find a quiet place somewhere else to talk," I added, smiling.

Startled, Rex broke his concentration and took a couple seconds to regain his focus.

"Oh, hi, Uncle Danny. You startled me. Didn't hear you approaching."

"Sorry about that, Rex. I should have coughed or something to alert you. What's so interesting that you're studying in your free period?" That was something I never did during my stay at Clanton.

"It's a chapter in my Psychology 1 book. Fascinating explanation of some abnormal behaviors."

"A word of advice, Rex. Two college majors that will get you nowhere fast are psychology and sociology. I speak from experience." I knew that my majors had nothing to do with my failure to climb the ladder of success, but he was like me in so many ways, I didn't want him even to think about following in my footsteps.

Rex laughed softly. "Uncle Danny, just because I enjoy my psychology class doesn't mean I will major in it. And, besides, what's wrong with what you're doing for a living? I think your job is exciting."

"Trust me, Rex, it's anything but. And I'm sure your mom would prefer you pursue a career that's more lucrative. But enough on that. Can you spare a few minutes to talk?"

"Sure thing, Uncle Danny. Let's go to the dorm lounge. I have a good twenty minutes before next class."

They hustled across campus, and I headed to the dorm lounge while Rex dropped off his books and picked up what he needed for his next class.

The lounge was spartan, with a couple worn sofas and six uncomfortable chairs extending their shelf life with ill-fitting slip covers. Considering the tasteful and well-maintained offices in his building, I surmised that H. Michael didn't seem to be bothered by students' lack of amenities. My guess was that he justified the somewhat seedy décor as character building. Not surprised that I was the only person in there, I took a seat on one of the sofas and waited for Rex.

When he entered the lounge, Rex glanced around to see where I was. Not too difficult since I was the sole occupant.

"Nice digs, huh?" Rex said, laughing. "I figured this would be a good place for privacy. No one comes in here if they can avoid it."

Scanning the room, I said, "I have to admit that it isn't too inviting. I think the same furniture was already starting to wear out when I was here. Pull up a chair or sit at the other end of the sofa to make sure uneven weight won't crumble it."

Rex opted to pull up the ugliest chair in the room, a rickety thing covered with a faded mauve cover. At least I thought it was mauve. It could have been red at one time for all I knew.

"So, Uncle Danny, what's on your mind?"

It was like Rex to get right to the point.

"Two things, actually, Rex. The first is that I want to hear how you did on the SAT Saturday."

I could tell by the big grin that he thought he had done well.

"Honestly, I think I got all the questions on the verbal section right and was unsure about only one question on the math. The writing section was a breeze. Of course I won't know for sure for a few weeks, but if my prediction is right, I am applying for early action to UVA. Amos told me he was going to do that, too."

"Great, Rex! You realize that the SAT is only one part of the equation, I'm sure, but at least that would be one hurdle you won't have to worry about."

"What was the second thing you wanted to talk about?" Relaxed and smiling, he looked at me without a glimmer of a thought that it might be something he didn't want to talk about.

Not sure about how to proceed without seeming like a snoop who read someone else's private diary, I stumbled for words momentarily before finally deciding to blurt it out.

"Rex, please don't think that your uncle was deliberately reading through your papers, but when I left a note for you on your desk, I couldn't help seeing that Mrs. Clarkson had invited you to go with her this weekend."

"Stop worrying, Uncle Danny. I know you wouldn't approve, and I already told you I wouldn't see her again."

I was relieved, not only because I didn't want him to get messed up with that cougar but also because I didn't want him ever to find out that he wasn't the only family member to be beguiled by her.

"Good decision, Rex. Tell you what, why don't you and I spend this Saturday in Charlottesville? We can tour the UVA campus and get some decent food. You can ask Amos to join us if you want."

"Wow, that would be terrific! I'll ask Amos at lunch break and let you know." He glanced at his watch. "I have to get to class now. Thanks for everything, Uncle Danny."

As he quickly exited the lounge, I yelled after him, "I'll sign you out in the office. If Amos comes with us, he'll need to have permission to leave campus with an adult other than his parents on file."

Rex waved over his shoulder. "I'll pass that along. Later."

It felt good to return to normalcy on campus. But how long would that last? That damn nagging voice in the back of my mind wouldn't stop.

Chapter Sixty

I finally figured out what that nagging voice was trying to say: Someone within the past couple weeks had characterized Mr. Wood as a "bloated misanthrope," the same phrase that Reasoner used when referring to Mr. Wood in the suicide note. What would be the odds of two different people using that same phrase to describe Mr. Wood? Astronomical.

I closed my eyes, trying to clear my head to induce memories of conversations I'd had the past two weeks. 'Who in the hell said that? Think, Danny, think.' Nothing. Too many conversations with too many people, and most of them had no kind word to say about the departed Mr. Wood. It could have been any of dozens of people. Nevertheless the repetition of those words was significant and made me doubt that Reasoner had committed suicide. If he didn't, that meant that a killer of, not two, but three teachers was still at Clanton Academy. And that was unsettling.

Unable to come up with the name of whoever it was that had said Mr. Wood was a bloated misanthrope, I knew I probably should not share that coincidental information with anyone just yet. Or maybe Barney, who had been with me during a number of conversations. I could rely on him to keep it to himself. It was a long shot at best, in any event.

Besides, I had better things to do tomorrow – enjoy a day in Charlottesville away from Clanton Academy with my nephew and Amos, who had readily agreed to join us and who had checked in the administration office to make sure he had permission from his parents to leave campus with an adult. Presumably I qualified. Because I hadn't been back to UVA in some time, I was looking forward to a leisurely stroll around the beautiful grounds. Bogie and Thomas Jefferson, the founder of The University as we called it, were my mentors in absentia. Not having a father was no reason for me not to find guidance from other men of accomplishment and style.

Weary from an overload of rapid changes, I ate a light dinner at the cafeteria, walked back to my guest quarters, and watched the local news on my tablet. Not a single word about Clanton Academy for a change and a forecast for a dry, sunny day in the low sixties predicted for tomorrow. A daily double of good news.

I had one more item of business to take care of. Two, actually – call Katherine to tell her I was taking Rex out for the day and email Julia to let her know I was staying here for at least another week.

Katherine was pleased that Rex felt confident about his performance on the SAT and that I was willing to spend the day with him.

"I'll reimburse you for any money you have to put out," she said as the conversation was about to end.

I shouldn't have let that bother me, but it did. "Not to worry, Katherine. It's my treat. I'm flush with money these days." I was starting to hate being on the edge of financial insolvency.

I hung up before she could protest and wrote a quick email to Julia. Before I could hit "send," however, my cell phone vibrated. It was Julia texting me.

R u coming back this week? If not, I would like a week off to go see my sister in Philly.

Perfect timing. *Go ahead, Julia. I deposited more money in the account. Pay any bills coming due before you leave. And if you wouldn't mind, would you check my apartment to make sure everything's OK?*

You're aces, Danny. I'll stop by your place tomorrow before leaving town. Is ur key still under the welcome mat?

Yes. Thanks. Throw away any food turning fuzzy blue in the fridge. Enjoy Philly.

Conventional wisdom considered hiding my spare key under the welcome mat a very bad idea. That didn't bother me in the least, however, because conventional wisdom was not aware that there was not a single item of value worth stealing in my apartment. Maybe someday I should get some decent furnishings, I kept telling myself, but unless a career change lay in my future, the chances of that happening were fat and slim.

My duties done, I nursed a small glass of wine and watched two episodes of *Person of Interest* just to confirm that the difference between real-life detectives like me and fictitious ones in *POI* like ex-CIA agent John Reese and reclusive billionaire genius Harold Finch was not simply a matter of my inferiority. Lacking mad fighting skills and an omniscient machine, I had to do the best I could with Old School leg work and outside-the-box thinking.

'Too bad life isn't scripted,' I consoled myself.

Chapter Sixty-one

I woke up later than usual and headed to the library to skim headlines in a couple newspapers before eating at the cafeteria. The place was empty except for Mr. Mann and me, possibly because the place was an inferno.

"Good grief, Hank, why is it so damn hot in here? It's only sixty degrees outside," I asked Mr. Mann, who was fanning his face vigorously if inefficiently with his hands.

"It's awful, isn't it? It's like a Sonia bath in here."

Soni…took me a while to understand his latest malapropism. But he was right: It did feel like a sauna.

"Where's your thermostat, Hank? Let me check it. I have trouble sometimes with my Wi-Fi thermostat. Maybe I can get yours working right if it's like mine."

He directed me to the far end of the first stacks, and I plodded over to it. Sure enough, the thermostat was a Wi-Fi variety, and it was inaccurately reading the inside temperature as fifty-five degrees and thus calling for heat. I simply turned it off and back on, and the problem was instantly solved. Such a tech maestro.

When I relayed the good news, Mr. Mann was as happy as he probably felt when finding wine on sale.

"Ooh, thank you so much, Danny. You are indeed a man of many talons."

I took that as a compliment.

"My technology skills usually are minimal, but every dog has its day. Glad to be of help. Have you put out the Charlottesville and Richmond papers yet? I'd like to skim headlines before going to the cafeteria."

He rustled around behind his counter and pulled out two newspapers.

"Dull news day, Danny. The headlions are boring, but here you go," he said, handing me the newspapers.

He was right about there being no major local news stories – or dangerous felines – and for that I was happy. I wanted this day to be devoid of problems.

I handed the newspapers back to Mr. Mann. "Thanks, Hank. I think if you open a couple windows and the front doors, the place will cool down soon enough. If you've got nothing scheduled for tomorrow evening, you're welcome to come to my place for Happy Hour."

"How kind of you to ask, Danny. Since you hosted last time, though, why don't you come by my place? Last apartment on Faculty Row. Fivish?"

"That would be great, Hank. See you at five."

A fresh opportunity to see what I could wring out of him after he guzzled a few glasses of wine. I wanted to find out the things he mysteriously claimed to know. A gossip like Mr. Mann might actually have heard something that the rest of us hadn't. If not, all I had to endure was a couple glasses of his favorite swill.

Heading to the cafeteria, I sensed a return to normalcy on campus. Students I passed on the sidewalk were laughing and acting foolish, and I hoped that Rex and

Amos were equally free of stress. I never underestimated the resilience of kids and the fragility of adults.

Inside the cafeteria, I was greeted by the smiling faces of Rex and Amos. The ominous SAT and three deaths behind them, neither seemed in the least stressed. Both wore khakis and button-down blue shirts with red and blue striped ties. The murder rate had changed since my time at Clanton but not the travel garb for students. Seeing them dressed so similarly to how I had been required to dress twenty years ago triggered memories of a few memorable teenage weekends. They probably assumed my broad smile was a reaction to seeing them, and I would say nothing to alter that misperception. Those memories would remain unshared with the current company.

It promised to be a good day.

Chapter Sixty-two

On the way to Charlottesville, Rex and Amos argued good-naturedly about who would end up with the higher GPAs and SAT scores and who had the better chance of being accepted by UVA. It was good to hear banter again, even if it wasn't the most mature conversation.

"How's this for a plan?" I interrupted. "Lunch at The Corner, then a tour of the grounds."

They both agreed to let me make all the decisions. That in itself was a welcome change of fortune.

The Corner boasted almost thirty restaurants in its seven blocks when I was attending UVA, but because of their convenient location, lunch at any of those restaurants usually entailed a long wait. Because of The Corner's location across from the Rotunda, however, which I wanted to be the first stop on a walk around the grounds, I drove around for fifteen minutes till I finally found a parking space near one of the many small restaurants.

"Can we walk around first to see what's here, Uncle Danny?" Rex asked.

"Good idea. That will give you a feel for the place. I spent more time here at restaurants and clubs than I did in classrooms, I think," I said, laughing, though there probably was some truth to it. With no home football game today, I assumed there wouldn't be too much congestion, and I was right.

After forty-five minutes of checking out and approving of this adjunct to UVA, they decided on a pizza place for lunch. Its outstanding pizzas notwithstanding, I didn't eat at this restaurant for the last three years of my stay at UVA because when I was a First Year, one of its employees had stolen my only decent sunglasses, which were a luxury, given my meager financial status. I had forgotten them at my table, and when I realized that back at my dorm, I called the manager, who said they'd be waiting for me when I could pick them up. A day later the manager told me the glasses had mysteriously disappeared from his desk.

I relayed this story to Rex and Amos primarily to let them know about UVA's rigid honor code. The deduction that it was an employee who had stolen my glasses was easy. No UVA student would risk expulsion, the only sentence meted out to a student found guilty of a violation of the honor code, for a pair of sunglasses. There were detractors of the single-punishment component of the Honor Court, but I was not among them. The idea of mandated and enforced honorable behavior resonated with me and was a factor in my decision to become a detective.

As a tiny act of protest, I didn't order food for myself. I had vowed never to eat there again after my unfortunate experience, and I intended to be true to my word. The boys inhaled their pizzas, though, and I didn't begrudge them that.

Their stomachs full and eager to see the grounds, they rushed outside and started sprinting toward the Rotunda.

"Slow down, fellas. We have all day, and I don't feel like reliving my track days with Coach Rotherwood. Let's take our time and give Jefferson's academical village the unhasty attention it deserves."

The Rotunda had been completely restored, and it filled me with a kind of reverence. That Thomas Jefferson himself had designed it and the rest of the Lawn, including the Pavilions and fifty-four Lawn rooms that house select professors and students, deepened my appreciation of my four years there. The education was first-rate, the history even more impressive. The neoclassical center of the grounds never failed to impress.

"Did you know that Edgar Alan Poe lived in Room 13 of the West Range?" I said to Rex and Amos.

"With all the grisly deaths at nearby Clanton, he'd probably make a visit to our campus if he were alive. I read that he wandered around Central Virginia during his stay here," Amos said. Taking in the view of the Lawn, he added, "Damn, I want to go here. This place is crawling with history, and I want to major in history, minor in English."

The place was crawling with more than history. Fifty yards ahead of us and walking toward us were three Clanton Academy students and Becky Clarkson.

How could such a perfect day turn sour so fast?

Chapter Sixty-three

I thought I was happily indifferent to Becky's ample allure, but I was wrong. Wearing skin tight black leggings, a very low-cut gold bustier, and Jimmy Choo black stiletto heels, she could easily compete with Mariah Carey or Nicki Minaj for sexiness, though I doubted Becky's audience of five ogling teenagers cared if she could kill a high C.

Ignoring them like bothersome gnats, she sidled up to me and said, her hand on my forearm, "Why, what a pleasant surprise to run into you in Mr. Jefferson's stomping grounds, Mr. Wright. Taking your nephew and his friend on a tour?"

"Something like that, yes." I slowly eyed her from head to toe and added, "Mrs. Clarkson, I see you're wearing your Sunday-go-to-meeting clothes for your little field trip. Our third president would be honored. Or blushing."

She threw back her head and released a hearty laugh. "Do you disapprove, Mr. Wright?" she asked coyly. "Judging by where your nephew's gaze is directed, I don't think he does."

I quickly scanned all five boys, and all of them seemed unaware of anything but Becky's cleavage. Neither our third president's academical village nor I could compete with that, and I was quite certain the boys hadn't heard a word we were saying.

"As you well know, Mrs. Clarkson, you always look good. Sometimes too good, if you get my drift."

If that registered as a criticism, it didn't show in her demeanor. Still smiling, she released my arm and said, "Always a pleasure seeing you, Mr. Wright. We must be on our way now. I hope to see you back at campus." Turning her attention to Rex, she added, "Don't be a stranger, Rex." Just as I had done to her minutes ago, she slowly eyed him from head to toe. "You and your uncle are certainly cut from the same cloth. Drop by my office any time." She winked at him and signaled to her three acolytes to follow her. I noticed that they chose to follow from behind.

Rex was still blushing by the time I turned to him after watching her head toward the Rotunda. "Uncle Danny, what did she mean by 'we're cut from the same cloth'?"

Eager to avoid where that was headed, I said, "Who knows? She probably just meant we look alike."

That seemed to satisfy his curiosity. "Yeah, you're right. I guess we do kinda look alike even though you're really old. No offense." He patted my back as if to console me.

"None taken," I said, happy that the subject was closed.

Amos and Rex looked at each other for all of three seconds with serious expressions, then burst out laughing.

"No secret why she selected those guys for the college visit," Amos said, still laughing.

"Is that a fact, Amos?" I said. "Just who are those guys?"

"The tall blond dude is captain of the tennis team, and the ripped dude who looks like Channing Tatum is the QB for the football team," said Rex.

"How about the third guy? He's no Adonis and doesn't seem to fit the mold," I said.

Rex and Amos giggled. "That's Addison D. Witt, the one everybody calls 'Dim Witt.' He's dumb as dirt and filthy rich, though his money isn't what she finds attractive about him, according to his wrestling teammates," Amos said, winking at Rex.

What he suggested didn't register immediately. "Then what is…oh, I get it. Enough said."

"You remember I told you about him, don't you, Uncle Danny? He's one of the three dudes who were giving me the evil eye till recently. I can't believe Mrs. Clarkson would want to spend time with that druggie idiot."

One thing I knew about Becky Clarkson: She was always calculating. What I didn't know was what was she doing with students besides filling out transcripts and seducing the occasional upperclassman?

Chapter Sixty-four

The day had been a success other than running into Becky Clarkson. Both Rex and Amos seemed to be even more determined to attend UVA, and the small-town atmosphere of Charlottesville was as appealing to them as it had been to me sixteen years ago.

Forward-thinking city planners had come up with a good plan when they closed the old downtown to traffic and created a thriving area of restaurants, businesses, and entertainment venues as an alternative to impersonal shopping malls. Walking along the bricked center street now devoid of cars, I noticed there had been a turnover of businesses from when I lived in Charlottesville, and I wandered through new antique shops and art exhibits while Rex and Amos sampled foods from various vendors. By the time we returned to the Clanton campus, we were all sufficiently fed with good food, a welcome break from cafeteria fare, and ready to enjoy the remains of the day.

The boys headed to the gym to shoot hoops and maybe find a pick-up game, and I went to my guest quarters. I needed to call Barney and run by him what I had noticed about the suicide note that Mr. Reasoner had left.

"Hello, Gladstone, are you at home? I hope I am not bothering you," I said when he answered his cell phone.

"Sure am, Danno…er, Danny. Naw, you ain't bothering me. Just about to watch some TV and have a brew. What's on your mind?"

I paused to choose my words carefully, not wanting to sound like I was prone to looking for coincidences that led to outrageous conspiracy theories. I felt pretty sure that JFK, Elvis, and Tupac were all dead.

"I have something to run past you, but I don't want you to mention it to anyone else, OK?"

"You can count on me to keep my mouth shut, Danny. Go ahead, spit it out."

Barney's choice of metaphor seemed unfortunately linked to his self-proclaimed oral discretion, but he probably didn't want to suggest that he knew how to shut up while asking me to tell all. Barney didn't seem prone to one-upmanship or dispensing insults.

"OK, Gladstone, but please don't laugh if you think I'm making a mountain out of a molehill. You remember Reasoner's suicide note, right?"

"Yeah, what about it? I thought it was clear as a bell even though he got a little wordy." Barney was dealing in paradoxical expressions this evening. Unintentionally, I was certain.

"If you'll recall, he used the phrase 'bloated misanthrope' to describe Mr. Wood."

"So? It's a school, Danny, and all them teachers went to college and know lots of big words. I know a few myself, Danny. I just don't see the point in using them."

"Slow down, Gladstone. What I was getting at was that I had heard that very expression to describe Mr. Wood long before reading that suicide note. Someone else either I or we interviewed may have said that."

"Ah, now I see where you're going with this. Too much of a coincidence that two people would use the exact same identical words." Barney was redundant, and language was not his strong suit, but that didn't stop him from grasping the significance of what I had told him. "Yeah, I think you're onto something, Danny. Problem is, I can't remember hearing anyone saying that."

"Damn, I had hoped you would, Gladstone. I have racked my brain trying to come up with a name to no avail. Oh, well, at least you agree with me, and that puts my mind at ease. I wasn't sure I was seeing something where there was nothing to be seen or trying to make things up because I couldn't find facts."

Ouch! My verbal skills had apparently taken leave.

"I'll sleep on it, Danny, and will get back to you if something pops into my memory. Good talking to you."

"Same here, Gladstone."

For the first time I felt I might be onto something. Maybe Mr. Mann could shed some more light on that tomorrow evening.

Chapter Sixty-five

Hank Mann's apartment was, surprisingly, furnished tastefully with antiques he told me he had refinished and repurposed and comfortable, upholstered blue-and-red striped sofa and chairs. My inaccurate preconceived notion was that his décor would match his way with words. Maybe there were other surprises forthcoming. That was my hope, after all, and my purpose for sharing his cheap wine.

"What's your poison, Danny? Red or white?" he asked me, intending to be gracious, I supposed, but maybe somewhat obtuse, given two of the recent deaths at Clanton.

I cringed only slightly as I weighed the options. Pinot grigio that tasted too much like water or the runny and bland pinot noir? I opted for the lesser of two evils, the pinot grigio.

Judging by his unsteady gait as he went to his kitchen, I guessed that Happy Hour had begun quite early for Mr. Mann today.

He returned with two huge goblets filled to the brim with pinot swill. "Cheers!" he said before downing a third of his glass in one long swallow. His Adam's apple bobbled as he drank.

Unless his tolerance for alcohol was enormous – and that was quite possible – I figured it should be easy to loosen his tongue.

Pointing to a cornucopia stuffed with artificial vegetables on his coffee table, I said, "I see you're ready for the upcoming Thanksgiving break. Do you stay on campus or visit family somewhere?"

He drained the rest of his wine as I sipped mine as slowly as possible. "Oh, I will stick around here, Danny. I have no family except my identical twin brother, and he is on a cruise in the Caribbean. He's a bachelor like me, and with no family responsibilities, he indulges himself. He adores cruising!"

No doubt, I thought, graciously refraining from making any comment that would serve to make him uncomfortable and thus less voluble.

He asked if I needed a refill, and when I told him I was not ready for another, he disappeared into the kitchen. In less than a minute he returned, this time with not only his filled-to-the-brim goblet but also a whole bottle that he placed on the coffee table.

"Grapes for your cornucopia?" I lamely joked.

He looked puzzled. "Huh? Grapes?"

"Wine is made of grapes, Hank. Weak joke."

"Oh, I get it! Maybe I've had a wee bit too much of the grape." He giggled. "Don't you think Thanksgiving is such a fesity occasion, Danny? I mean, all that good food and wine and turkey decorations. It's my favorite holy day."

Not the most stimulating of small talk, but I needed to put him at ease.

"It is, indeed, Hank. Next to Christmas, it's my favorite. Everyone is in a kind mood and thankful for his blessings."

He suddenly scowled, as if something had just dawned on him. "Not everybody, my friend. Not everybody," he said.

"Thinking of anyone in particular?" I asked, hoping that this might be a good vein to mine. I calculated that there was a fine line between letting his guard down and lapsing into a sodden state. At the rate he was guzzling, the line was fast approaching, and I wasn't about to let this assault on my palate by his wretched wine be in vain.

"Damn straight I am, Danny. You and everybody else probably think that Rollie Jenkins is a pillory of décor, but he isn't. No siree, he isn't." He took another long draft.

I feigned surprise. "No, you must be joking me, Hank. Mr. Jenkins would never be ungrateful. He's a class act."

"Class act, my ass. He's a spiteful man, Danny."

"Really?" I asked, eager for some sort of explanation that could confirm Jenkins's motive in the murder of Mr. Wood – and maybe the others. "Why do you say that?"

Hank Mann struggled to keep his balance as he awkwardly got up from his chair and almost shouted at me, "Danny, as I live and breathe, that man is evil personification. I can't say more than that, but you can write that down as truth."

He weaved for a few seconds and seemed deep in thought, though in his present state, thinking wasn't much of a possibility.

"You think he liked Mr. Wood? Ha! He hated his guts. Reasoner's, too. And probably mine."

With that, he plopped back into his chair, closed his eyes, and began to snore.

Happy Hour was over.

Chapter Sixty-six

As Danny Wright closed the door behind him and turned to go back to his quarters, he was startled by bumping into Rollie Jenkins.

"Damn, Mr. Jenkins, I didn't hear you coming up the steps. You scared the hell out of me," Danny Wright said.

Rollie Jenkins laughed, but not especially mirthfully. "I apologize – I guess. It wasn't my intent to sneak up on you. I am here to see if Mr. Mann would like to go out for a burger or something."

It was Danny's turn to laugh. "Trust me on this one: He is not likely to go out for anything. He's already out – cold, that is."

"Another of his three-hour-long Happy Hours, no doubt. Of late he's being doing them even on school nights. Did you get a chance to visit with him before he passed out?"

They started walking together in the direction of the Alumni House and Jenkins's nearby apartment.

Danny couldn't decide whether that question was innocuous small talk or prying. 'Better safe than sorry,' he concluded.

"Not too much, no. He was pretty far gone by the time I got here. He had asked me over for a glass of wine, and in the time it took me to sip mine, he went through a whole bottle. I have no idea how much he had consumed prior to my arrival. I gather it was quite a lot."

"Did he happen to mention me by any chance? He's been ignoring me lately, and I am wondering if I inadvertently offended him."

Danny knew it was not in character for Rollie Jenkins to be concerned about anyone's feelings. He was definitely prying.

Danny answered accordingly. "Not a word about you, Mr. Jenkins. Mostly he rambled on about his twin brother's retirement lifestyle and how much he envied that." He wanted Jenkins not to be in the least bit aware that he suspected Jenkins of dire deeds.

Rollie Jenkins snorted. "What a load of shit. Mann has more money tucked away than you and I combined. He doesn't drive a car. He rarely goes out to eat or to a movie. He never goes anywhere that I know of. He is content to stay here and drink himself into oblivion every night. In short, he has no expenses other than wine, and though that is probably a sizable monthly expense, the rest he has been saving and investing during his whole undistinguished tenure here. He could retire tomorrow if he chose to do so and live very comfortably."

The campus was essentially dark. The lights in each occupied room illuminated the dorm, and street lights about every hundred yards provided the only other break from blackness. For the next three blocks, the two walked in silence.

They reached Jenkins's apartment first, and he broke the silence. "Here's my place, Mr. Wright. I hope you enjoy the rest of the evening." He left the lighted street and walked toward the steps of his unlit porch.

'There's one person who won't be enjoying it,' he thought, peering through the darkness to see if he could spot Danny, who had continued walking toward his quarters. Unable to see him, he retraced his steps to the street. Far ahead he could catch a glimpse of Danny heading to his quarters.

"Time for a visit to Merrick," Jenkins said softly as he slipped into his car.

Chapter Sixty-seven

Merrick Bobson finished the last stroke of shaving every hair from his body and admired what he saw in the mirror. His thick thigh muscles and bulging pecs were still as firm as they had been in his football days, and the only concession to inevitable aging was the incipient tire replacing his once solid abs.

After striking a few narcissistic flex poses, he left the bathroom and entered his spacious walk-in closet. Concealed behind the row of expensive suits and sport coats was another rack on which hung a dozen floor length sequined gowns of various colors and one Jean-Louis lookalike blue dress with a white collar. Above them on a shelf were six women's wigs.

Fingering approvingly the wig identical to Judy Garland's hairdo in *A Star Is Born* when she sang "The Man That Got Away," he said to himself, "Esther Blodgett it is tonight." Reverently, he placed the wig of short dark hair on his bald skull and removed the ersatz Jean-Louis dress, size 18, from its padded hanger. Merrick Bobson knew how important the right hangers were.

Though the size seventeen blue flats were stretching at the seams, they completed the look he desired, and now fully transformed into a black and muscular Judy Garland, he headed to the living room. Opening the door to the cabinet containing vinyl recordings of his favorite divas, arranged in alphabetical order beginning with Aretha and ending with Whitney, he removed his coveted copy of Garland singing what the American Film Institute named the eleventh greatest song in American cinematic history, "The Man That Got Away." After placing it on his $30,000 VPI Classic Direct turntable, he opened his tablet to his favorite YouTube video of Garland singing the Harold Arlen classic and hit "pause" so that he could mute its sound while listening to his vinyl version. Merrick was a stickler for quality, and nothing compared to the purity of vinyl.

He situated himself in front of the large screen television and carefully placed the player's arm onto the record. The muted trombones that preceded singing washed over him, and turning on the muted YouTube video, he swayed as he mimicked Garland's every move and mannerism.

"The night is bitter,
The stars have lost their glitter,
The winds grow colder
And suddenly you're older,
And all because of the man that got away"

At this point, Merrick turned slightly as if looking into the camera.

"No more his eager call,
The writing's on the wall,
The dreams you dreamed have all
Gone astray"

By now he had perfectly synchronized his hand movements with Garland's and recreated her facial movements as her huge voice increased in volume.

Thoroughly engrossed in his performance, he didn't hear Jenkins slip into the room.

Jenkins had to slap his hand over his mouth to stifle his laughter as he stared at the burly ex-football player imitating the diminutive Garland. 'What an unforeseen and lovely prelude to his death,' Jenkins thought. 'I need to let this play out.'

"The man that won you
Has gone off and undone you.
That great beginning
Has seen its final inning."

'Not bad feminine rhyme,' Jenkins thought, now grinning.

"Don't know what happened
It's all a crazy game!"

As her voice soared above the instrumental accompaniment, Merrick became Esther Blodgett, coaxing every note out of his and her body.

"No more that all-time thrill
For you've been through the mill…"

Suddenly as Merrick turned as Garland had, he spotted Jenkins.

Jenkins clapped loudly and slowly three times.

"Quite a show, Merrick. Some chanteuse you are." He laughed derisively. "Who's that singing?"

Stunned that someone had invaded his private place, he stumbled for words. Finally he said almost inaudibly, "Judy. Judy Garland."

"As in Dorothy from 'The Wizard of Oz'?" asked the amused Jenkins. He was savoring the image of Bobson standing there with his massive frame squeezed into a very feminine blue dress almost as much as Bobson's palpable distress.

"Don't look at me that way, Rollie."

"What way, Merrick? I couldn't give a flying fuck if you're gay. I am more concerned about something much more important to me."

Merrick yelled, "I am not gay! I am straight, a musical interpreter of America's greatest divas."

"Yeah, whatever."

"Someday after I have perfected my act, I will perform in public, become the next Jim Bailey." He paused briefly to see if Jenkins would react obnoxiously, and when Jenkins remained stone-faced, he added softly, "Except I can't do my own singing like him."

"So in other words, you aspire to a career as a lip syncer?" With that Jenkins howled with laughter. "You're pathetic!"

Insulted, embarrassed, ashamed, and angry, Merrick turned on his blue flat heels and started retreating toward the bedroom.

"Not so fast, Merrick. We're not done here yet." Jenkins smiled at his timely understatement.

.

Chapter Sixty-eight

"I decide when we're done," he told Jenkins in a masculine, deep voice that seemed strange, given his appearance. Something in the tone of Jenkins's voice made Bobson stop and turn around He glowered at Jenkins in defiance, unaware of the almost comical figure he cut.

Jenkins retained his odd smile. "I think THIS decides when the conversation is done," he said as he pulled out his Springfield XDm 9mm pistol equipped with a silencer and pointed it at Bobson.

"What the fuck are you doing, Rollie? Put that thing away. You could hurt someone with that," Bobson said as he instinctively crossed his hands over his crotch as if they could stop a bullet.

Maintaining his calm demeanor and still smiling, Jenkins said softly, "But my dear Merrick, don't you see? That's exactly what I plan to do if you don't give me the right answers." He waved the pistol toward the chair Bobson had been sitting in. "Sit over there – *if* you can sit in that ridiculous dress."

Bobson shuffled sideways toward the chair, afraid to take his eyes away from Jenkins. Spreading his legs apart as far as the tight dress would allow, he gingerly lowered his bulk into the seat.

"Rollie, I don't understand what's going on here. Why are you acting crazy?" he said, his voice shaking.

"Just shut up, and I'll tell you exactly what's going on." Keeping his pistol aimed directly at Bobson's chest, he said, "You remember when we met and you convinced me to roll over much of my retirement portfolio, guaranteeing you'd double my money in five years? Foolishly I trusted you, believed you. I guess I was vulnerable, knowing I needed to increase my holdings if I ever hoped to retire from this goddamn shithole. And you zeroed in on that vulnerability like a heat-seeking missile."

Bobson interrupted him. "You're pointing that gun at me because I am making money for you?"

Jenkins laughed sardonically. "Oh, cram it, Bobson. I know exactly how much money you're making for me. I can see it in this lavishly furnished house and your Taj Mahal office."

"You're pissed off that I am spending the money I make for myself? That's crazy shit, Rollie."

"Bobson, let's stop the charade. A month ago I got wind that you and whoever else you're in league with in your Ponzi scheme have spent all our money. Every hard-earned cent. Our retirement funds have provided you with pricey box seats, a new BMW, a wardrobe that cost more than my annual salary, the opulent trappings of a sheikh, and God knows what else. Did you really think you would get away with this?"

"Whoever told you that was wrong, Rollie. Your money is safe and earning twenty percent even as we speak."

"Is that a fact? Don't take me for a fool. If it hasn't been spent, why didn't you refund it to me when I asked you for it a month ago?"

Bobson hesitated, feverishly improvising to avoid what he knew was coming if he couldn't convince Jenkins that his money was safe. "Rollie, you know we had to sign you on for five years. The money is invested in long-term instruments. If we withdraw the money prematurely, it won't generate profit."

"I know that's what you said, but I also know that those lucrative instruments you said you had invested in were just words on a page. You didn't invest a dime in anything but your lavish lifestyle. And for that you will pay dearly. Consider your death the reward for your efforts on my behalf."

Bobson started whimpering. "Please, Rollie, put the gun away. I swear I will repay you every cent."

"And how about the money you bilked from the others? You going to repay that, too?" Though Jenkins couldn't care less what happened to the funds of his colleagues, he felt the need to prolong Bobson's fear. He was enjoying this almost as much as he regretted losing his money.

"You're a greedy, scheming bastard, and there's not a day goes by that I don't regret recommending you for the CFO position here. Have you been skimming here, too?"

"You know I haven't, Rollie. An audit would show any misappropriation of funds." He slumped in his chair. "Rollie, I know I fucked you over. And the others, too. I don't know what got into me. I didn't start the venture with that in mind. But once I started tasting the good life, I couldn't stop myself." By now he was sobbing.

"Seems we have something in common, Merrick," Jenkins said, the smile never leaving his face. "Once I started killing, like you, I enjoyed it too much to stop myself. The others were just a prelude to the main event, Merrick, and that's you. Do you have any idea how much I am savoring the moment, watching you sitting there in that get-up waiting to die? Have you thought about what people will think when they find you dead wearing that ridiculous wig and dress? It's not enough just to kill you, Merrick. I need to kill your reputation, too."

Bobson, his face wet with tears and his chest heaving with sobs, struggled to lift himself out of his chair and rush Jenkins. Better to die trying than sit here and die a cowardly pussy, he thought. The dress was too restricting of his movements, however, and Jenkins laughed heartily watching Bobson flounder in his last attempt at foiling the plan Jenkins had so carefully laid out to exact revenge.

Exhilarated and finally fully satisfied, Jenkins slowly walked closer to Bobson, pointed the pistol between Bobson's plucked eyebrows, and asked, "Any last words, you pathetic son of a bitch?"

Bobson implored Jenkins with his eyes.

"No? Well then, meet your maker." The joy he felt pulling the trigger was ineffable.

Bobson slumped only slightly in the chair, the tight dress restricting his movements even in death.

As he had done after disposing of Reasoner, he made sure he left behind no fingerprints or traces of his ever having been there. One last touch he considered appropriate: He set up the YouTube video of Judy Garland singing her heart out to loop continuously. Whoever discovered the body should be able to figure out why Bobson was dressed as he was.

Turning at the door to survey the scene of his greatest achievement, Jenkins smiled and started singing softly, off key, along with Judy Garland.

"Good riddance, good-bye!
Every trick of his you're on to.
But fools will be fools
And where's he gone to?"

Chapter Sixty-nine

Groggy after nine hours of sleep, I assessed my options for dress: The laundry basket was overflowing, the closet empty. 'Either I stay here all day in my PJs, or it's time to go to the field house to wash my clothes and sheets,' I thought.

The only person I saw when I lugged the basket of clothes and sheets downstairs at the field house was unknown to me. A slightly overweight, short black man wearing thick glasses looked up from sorting what appeared to be basketball jerseys when he heard me enter his domain. I could tell by his questioning look that I owed him an explanation.

"Hi, I'm Danny Wright. I'm not trespassing or anything." I hoped he'd laugh, but he didn't. "You're probably wondering what I'm doing here. Well, it's simple, really. Mr. Madison gave me permission to use the facility while I am staying as a guest in the Alumni House. You can call him to verify if you like."

Looking at me, then my small mountain of dirty clothes and sheets, then back at me, he must have decided that I was not an interloper. Who'd make up a story like that?

"Go ahead, buddy. Do you know how to operate the industrial machines? Need any soap? Dryer sheets?"

"Yes, yes, and yes. I appreciate your offer. Thanks."

He shrugged and headed off to the bowels of the enormous field house to count jocks or something. I opened the large door of the cavernous washer and threw everything in, darks and whites together, knowing that they'd been laundered so many times that the darks wouldn't bleed. The wash cycle would take almost an hour, so I wandered upstairs to see if I could find anyone I knew to pass the time with.

I struck out at that quest, not unlike my batting prowess the one year I tried my hand at baseball. Next stop was the cafeteria for coffee.

Cafeteria Katie greeted me. Good to see you again, Mr. – er, um Mr. —"

I saved her the futile effort of trying to remember my name. "It's Wright, Katie. Danny Wright."

She didn't seem embarrassed in the least that she still couldn't remember my name, and I doubted she ever would.

"I'm bad with names, Mr. Wright. Always have been. Here for coffee? The food's all been served."

"Sure, if you wouldn't mind," I said as I walked toward the coffee machine, naively optimistic that this time the coffee would be better than sludge. It was probably my un-caffeinated brain, but the coffee seemed to pour out in glops. The first sip confirmed that it was thicker than gravy. Bogie liked his java strong, I seemed to recall, and I resigned myself to endangering the lining of my stomach.

"So, Katie, how have things been since the place quieted down?"

"Pretty much back to normal, though Mr. Bobson, he didn't show up for his usual huge breakfast this morning. Other than that, it's same old same old. The same folks comes in every day at the same time and eats the same things. I can't remember names, but I can remember what everyone eats."

Interesting, if not of much use to me. To kill time, I decided to pick Katie's brain. No telling what lingered there, but I figured there would be no harm in taking a peek.

"OK, Katie, I'll quiz you."

Her smile revealed the absence of a few teeth. "That sounds fun. Go ahead, quiz me. We're at a school after all." She guffawed at her best effort at humor.

I mentally listed the teachers I knew and began the game. "OK...Mr. Browning, the old English teacher."

"Breakfast is always scrambled eggs and two pieces of toast. Lunch is whatever cold cuts there is for sandwich. Dinner is fish if we have it. Mystery meat if we don't. Never eats a vegetable."

"Impressive, Katie. How about Mr. Rotherwood?"

"Oh, he's a big eater, that one is. He fills his tray with whatever we got and comes back for seconds. He even likes the spaghetti with corn in it."

Truly an undiscerning palate.

I rattled off a dozen more names, and she came up with instant answers. Even though I couldn't verify her accuracy, I tended to trust her memory.

"Great memory you have, Katie. One more before I have to go back to the field house. I remember you saying that Mr. Wood ate five hamburgers at a sitting, but what do his buddies Mr. Mann and Mr. Jenkins eat?"

I didn't expect any sudden flashes of insight. I simply wanted to know anything I could about Jenkins.

She harrumphed. "Mr. Mann turns up his nose at everything we serve. Tell you the truth, I think his brain is more pickled than our relish. I can smell alcohol on his breath at lunch. Mr. Jenkins? He don't really eat that much. He used to have a good appetite and would say hi to me. Now, he never says nothing to me, and most meals he just sits at his usual table drinking coffee and glaring at everybody. He must be allergic to smiling. He's probably the only person who eats here that I have no use for."

Nothing got past Katie.

"You have a great memory, Katie. A+ for you!"

Judging by her wide smile, I surmised that, that pleased her as much as if she had aced a Trig test.

"You made my day, Mr. Wright. See, I can remember names when I feel the need."

I gave that about as much a chance as my winning the lottery I never played. Walking back to the field house to toss my clothes into the dryer, it occurred to me that Katie had provided one valuable fact: Jenkins's behavior had changed lately. I needed to find out the reason for that.

Chapter Seventy

The industrial-sized dryer I used must have been as hot as Hades. My clothes dried in ten minutes and almost required asbestos gloves to handle them. No complaints, though. It was free, and idling in a cavernous room surrounded by stacks of stinky uniforms and discolored towels wasn't my idea of a good time. I folded everything and tried as best as I could to fit everything in the basket without wrinkling the clothes so badly I would have to resort to the dreaded ironing.

My mission accomplished, I headed to my quarters to drop off the laundry and check the fridge to see if I needed to make a run to Charlottesville. I was not pleased to see, walking directly toward me from his apartment, Mr. Jenkins, and there was no way I could avoid greeting him.

Uncharacteristically, he was smiling. "Laundry day, I see," he said pleasantly, unnecessarily nodding toward the basket.

"Yep. I figured I'd better wash everything before the mold count was cause for concern."

A weak joke, I knew, but Jenkins actually chuckled.

"You're in a good mood today, Mr. Jenkins. Did you win the lottery or come across the elusive well-written paper?"

"I *am* in a good mood, Mr. Wright. 'There is nothing either good or bad but thinking makes it so.' Do you recall that, Mr. Wright?"

I had to dust the cobwebs off my brain. I was in his class twenty years ago, after all, yet even now I wanted to appear less doltish than he probably considered me.

"Shakespeare, right?" I said with less authority than I desired.

"Correct, Mr. Wright. An 'A' for you if you can identify the play."

I narrowed it down to either *Hamlet* or *Macbeth* and went with my gut feeling. Projecting a false sense of confidence, I said, "Why, *Hamlet* of course."

"Right on target, Mr. Wright. There's hope for you yet. If only I could say the same for your nephew, whose appreciation for The Bard is less than enthusiastic."

"Give him time, Mr. Jenkins. He's more concerned about college admissions than anything else at the moment. He really is more appreciative than you may think. When he was a toddler, I read Shakespeare's sonnets to him at bedtime when I visited his house." That had not been the most astute discharge of my avuncular duties, but in my defense, I knew less about raising children than I knew about…well, anything.

I took Jenkins's silence as his tacit disapproval of my efforts. Methought he revered The Bard too much. To the point of obsession, maybe?

Changing the subject, I added, "So why *are* you feeling so chipper today?"

His eyes actually seemed to twinkle. "Mr. Wright, my world is right again."

I wondered what could have righted his dismal world.

"But now I must hurry off to class to fight the good fight against ignorance. Have a good day."

His moods were mercurial, that was for certain.

A bit puzzled, as I always seemed when dealing with Jenkins, I tried to brush aside my thoughts about Jenkins. True, I was frustrated that I didn't have the acumen or resources to uncover whatever evil Jenkins had done, but no one would hear me whining about it.

I didn't look to Shakespeare for words of wisdom. No, it was football coach Lou Holtz who summed up my attitude best: "The man who complains about the way the ball bounces is likely the one that dropped it."

Ball – and laundry – securely in hand, I would move forward and give it my best shot.

Chapter Seventy-one

Two bottles of wine and half a brick of cheese were the contents of my fridge. 'Enough provisions for another few days,' I thought and headed to the administration building to see H. Michael. Though I had nothing of interest to report, I wanted him to know that I was not idle. I liked those weekly payments of cash too much to trifle.

Miss Foss was so intent at pounding her keyboard that she didn't know I was standing in her office. I cleared my throat loudly to alert her of my presence and ruin her day.

I marveled that her permanent scowl could intensify into something other-worldly, which is what it did when she looked up to find me standing there, smiling broadly.

"What do you want?" she snarled.

"Good morning to you, too, Miss Foss."

She bristled. "Get to the point, Mr. Wright. You're interrupting me."

"Has anyone told you, you look like Cate Blanchett, Miss Foss?"

She glared at me. "No."

"Of course they haven't."

I thoroughly enjoyed her indignity. Since I last saw her, she had changed her hair color to an unfortunate shade of burgundy. I wondered if her stylist knew that his efforts were like gilding a turd.

Ignoring her huffing, I said, "I need to see Mr. Madison. Would you please buzz him."

"Too bad, Mr. Wright. He won't have time for you today. He's in conference." She cocked her head to give me a "so-there!" look.

So much for my plan to endorse myself.

"Damn," I blurted. "Say, when you flew to work this morning, where'd you park your broom? There's not an open parking space anywhere outside this building."

"That's so funny I forgot to laugh," she said.

Her puerile comebacks were good for my ego.

"As always, you're in the dark. Obviously you have no idea why the FBI is in his office." By the gloating smirk on her hatchet-like face, I surmised that she cared more about knowing something that I didn't than about what was probably another crisis.

"The FBI? Why are they back here? I thought they considered the cases closed after finding Mr. Reasoner's suicide note."

She aimed her death rays at me and smugly said, "For the life of me, I can't figure out why Mr. Madison, who is the smartest man I have ever known, would employ you to do any detecting. You'd get lost in a two-car funeral." She maintained her death rays, waiting, I supposed, for some sort of reaction. She could wait till her next bad dye job for that to happen. My expression remained blank.

"The FBI is here, you moron, because of yesterday's murder."

That news stunned me.

"Another murder? Who?"

For the first time this morning, she dropped her defensive stance. "Mr. Bobson. He was shot in the head at his house. That's all I know. Everyone in the administration building is devastated. He was one of our own. An important asset to Clanton Academy. A true Christian."

It figured that the current administration valued their work and minimized that of the faculty.

"That's terrible news, Miss Foss." I meant that. "In my dealings with him, he seemed like such an outgoing, competent person. What possible motive could there be to murder him?"

It was appallingly clear to me that unless the FBI or I could uncover motives, the killer or killers would have a free hand.

"Or Mr. Reasoner," I added. He had spent most of his adult life working at this school, and his death, which I couldn't accept as a suicide, was every bit as tragic as Mr. Bobson's.

At that moment a disturbing thought occurred to me: Had Mr. Jenkins's rare good mood been caused by his having committed…

I was so deep in thought that I hadn't heard Sloane approach me. "Well, well, Mr. Wright. Seems that murder follows you like night follows day," said Sloane, whose interruption of the unthinkable was welcome even if he wasn't.

"Always a pleasure, Mr. Sloane," I responded, trying my hardest not to show how much he annoyed me. "As always, you're a day late and a dollar short."

I did a quick run-through of my memory bank to see if I could come up with the name of someone I disliked more than this self-important toad. I couldn't. Even Miss Foss excited less disgust, and that was saying something.

I turned my attention to Agent Parker, who stood behind Mr. Sloane with two other Feds I hadn't seen before.

"Agent Parker, if you have a minute to spare, could I talk with you?"

I looked directly at Sloane and added, "Privately."

Chapter Seventy-two

Parker didn't even bother looking at Sloane for his permission – or his reaction. It was against the odds that Sloane's abrasive personality and peremptory manner would engender any loyalty from his peers; that is, if he considered anyone worthy of the status of peer.

"Sure thing, Danny. Lead the way."

Did he refer to me by my first name to annoy Sloane? I sneaked a brief glance at Sloane to see his reaction and was rewarded by his frown and squinted eyes. Parker was definitely growing on me.

"Let's go to the reception lounge where we'll have some privacy," I said loud enough for Sloane to hear as we walked away.

It took less than a couple minutes to reach the lounge, and, as usual except when prospective parents were visiting campus, it was empty. Parker sat in a Martha Washington chair with striped upholstery, and I positioned a nearby ladder back chair to sit across from him.

"I have a good idea why we're here, Danny. You want information about the latest murder, correct?"

"Of course. This one has really thrown me for a loop. It doesn't fit any pattern. Is there a psychopath on the loose here?"

"You realize, don't you, that I shouldn't share any information with you? If Sloane should find out, my ass would be fired." He paused and then broke out in laughter. "But it's because of that arrogant SOB that I will tell you anything you want to know. Just don't broadcast it, though, OK?"

"Mum's the word," I assured him. Parker was the only source of information I had, and I wouldn't jeopardize it by crossing him. "Can you give me any details about the scene of the murder?"

"Danny, it was totally weird. And unexpected."

"How so?" Was there more to it than a simple shooting?

"The bullet hole between his eyes was nothing out of the ordinary. But the circumstances were more than a little unusual. You know how huge and fit Bobson was. He looked as if he could still play NFL football. Well, when we found him, that 250 pounds of muscle was crammed into a tight blue dress, and above his body was playing a YouTube video of Judy Garland singing a song from one of her movies. In it she was wearing a much smaller version of the same dress Bobson was wearing. Perched on his bald head was a slightly skewed wig identical to her haircut, too."

I had a hard time processing this. I just couldn't see Bobson dressed like that. And why the YouTube video?

"Are you adding all of this up, Danny? Do you understand what Bobson was almost certainly doing when he was shot?" He waited for me to answer, and when I didn't, he continued. "Danny, he was lip syncing that performance. Merrick Bobson liked dressing up as female singers and imitating their performances."

"Performances? Singers? As in plural?" I asked incredulously.

"You got it, Danny. When we checked out the huge closet in his bedroom, we found a whole lot more than dozens of Armani and Hugo Boss suits and Bruno Magli shoes. Hidden behind his suits was a rack of sequined dresses and women's wigs. Now, I don't keep up with what's going on in the popular culture too much, but Eddie, one of my colleagues, does, and he identified them as hairstyles that Cher, Whitney Houston, Bette Midler, Christina Aguilera, Diana Ross, and a few others whose names I can't remember wore at one time or another in their careers."

I concentrated on not allowing my jaw to drop.

"Eddie's IDs were confirmed when we found vinyl albums and CDs of all of their biggest hits and videos of them singing them stored on his open laptop in a file he called 'My Babes.' Mr. Merrick Bobson, it seems, was a female impersonator of sorts."

I remained speechless.

"And, Danny, he wasn't a pretty sight. Whoever killed him made sure that when we found him, he'd look pathetic. And that he was."

"Damn!" I finally managed to speak. "I can't wrap my head around this. He seemed…well, so masculine. And, according to Mr. Madison, he was a devout Christian. That's why he hired him."

"Danny, we have come across every imaginable situation over the years. A little old grandma who had whips and chains in her bedroom. A famous serial killer with a DVD collection of Walt Disney animated movies.

Devout Christians? How about a priest with a satanic bible by his bedside? Or a televangelist with obscene naked Teletubbies plastered all over his bathroom walls? There's no formula for how people live. Yes, we were nonplussed initially because it seemed so out of character for him, but as professionals, we knew that there are no real surprises when it comes to human behavior."

I couldn't claim to approach this news like the professional he was. I kept shaking my head as if to delete the image of Merrick Bobson crammed into a dress with a bullet through his head.

Parker's patience was commendable. He didn't speak for the long seconds it was taking for me to work through this and start thinking logically.

I finally spoke. "Did you make any determination regarding the murder? Any insights about whoever did it?"

He hesitated.

"Well, yes and no, Danny. Sloane's theory is that it was a hate crime. That whoever killed him came across him doing his thing, assumed he was gay, and was overwhelmed by his homophobia."

"Overwhelmed to the point of killing him? Isn't that a stretch? And how was he in Bobson's house to observe him?"

"We think alike, Danny. I brought up those same points to Sloane."

"And?"

"And nothing. He spouted all the statistics we already knew about the difference between premeditated and impulsive murders. Any rookie investigator knows that it's not too bright to hang around with a guy with a low IQ who abuses drugs or alcohol. That guy is more likely to snap than someone with a higher IQ. But it's the guy with the higher IQ who plans violent acts. It's a cognitive skill at work."

"So, what is *your* conclusion, premediated or impulsive murder?" I was confident I knew what his answer was.

"Premeditated. Merrick Bobson was not the type of person to hang around with dimwits. No, whoever did this was someone he knew. Probably another professional. Likely someone we have met, too."

And I had a good idea of just who that was.

What I didn't know, I suddenly realized, was Parker's first name.

"I agree with you. And not just because I would like to think that Sloane is wrong because he's an asshole. Even assholes can be right once in a while. You know, Parker, we didn't get off to a good start, and maybe that was my fault. I don't even know your first name."

"Joshua. It's Joshua. But everybody calls me Parker, and I prefer that."

"OK, Joshua," I said and laughed.

"Wiseass," Parker said, laughing.

It felt great to have an ally. But what good was having an ally without knowing a killer's motive? In this cloistered place, everybody had means and opportunity. Though Jenkins was still my choice of suspects, what possible evidence was there to confirm that?

Not a damn thing.

Chapter Seventy-three

Recapping the murders – and I was convinced that Reasoner was also a victim – I couldn't find any pattern. Two by poison, one by a belly bomb, another by gunshot. Where was the MO? If Jenkins was indeed guilty of all four murders, I couldn't find a thread that connected them.

Doubts began to cloud my thinking, and, as much as I hated to admit it, my brain was telling me that I should entertain the possibility that Jenkins hadn't killed all four of them, that another person had killed at least one, maybe two, of the victims. The odds of multiple murderers living and working at this tiny school nestled in a rural setting were surely off the chart.

The Feds, or Sloane, at least, seemed disinclined to recognize those odds and were approaching each murder by acknowledging only facts, even though the meager facts they had gleaned led to no definitive conclusion that I could discern. To them, there could be one murderer or two. Reasoner's convenient suicide note ostensibly proved them right about the first three deaths, and Bobson's murder was an unfortunate, unrelated hate crime. Their logic seemed convincing. It was known that murders do occasionally occur in clusters.

With nothing concrete to disprove or support those odds, I, on the other hand, figured that following my instincts seemed better than relying on logic. Jenkins would remain at the top of my list of one.

I dreaded a meeting with H. Michael, whose stress levels I assumed would also undoubtedly be off the chart. He was paying the piper, however, and I made my way to his office to share what I knew, which was nothing. My hunch was getting expensive for him, and I was certain he wanted more than my instinct for the cash he was laying out.

With no time to annoy Miss Foss, I broke her protocol by bypassing her and entering H. Michael's office after only a perfunctory knock. She started to object, then must have thought better of it, concluding that for reasons unfathomable to her, he would welcome me.

H. Michael looked briefly up from his computer, nodded to my usual chair, and resumed typing for a long thirty seconds, long enough for my attention to linger on the British fox hunting prints that hung in the center of each of the three walls beside and in front of his large desk. Each showed a dozen or more traditionally dressed huntsmen in scarlet coats astride horses glistening from attentive grooming. Missing were the terrified foxes, the object of the impossibly civilized yet savage ritual. That H. Michael surrounded himself with representations of order that concealed ugly reality and that he had built a protective moat of willingly sycophantic yes men to shield him from potential discord spoke to his creation of a life driven by manipulation of the elements that composed it, not unlike the prints he had chosen to establish the deliberately orderly milieu in which he comfortably and efficiently reigned. Life might be festering on the inside, but to the outside observer, everything was controlled and well managed.

It also explained his religious zealotry. If he sometimes weaponized religion or fended off potential criticism or an angry parent with prayer, he did so knowingly. Essential to his very existence was an overwhelming need to be in control. And, to me, that was less a character defect than it was a contrived leadership style that worked well for him and, by extension, Clanton Academy. His professional life was a fox hunt to H. Michael. So powerful was his self-creation that I couldn't even imagine what his personal life was like. I could imagine, however, that he considered having a personal life irrelevant.

Finished with his messaging, he made eye contact with me, his tacit green light for me to speak.

"I am sorry to bother you, Mr. Madison. I know how busy you are – and will be – after this latest disaster. I won't keep you but a minute."

"Get on with it, Mr. Wright. What brings you here? I'm sure it's too much to hope that you bear good news."

H. Michael's posture was erect and his voice strong and unwavering. If he was experiencing a case of shot nerves, I couldn't see it.

"I have little news about the latest murder, unless you consider my hunch newsworthy, but I do have a nuts and bolts question."

"Nuts and bolts first, Mr. Wright."

How could I phrase this so as not to appear crass? Deciding on the direct approach, I said, "Mr. Madison, now is not an auspicious time, I realize, to discuss remuneration, but the weekly checks Mr. Bobson cashed for me were – er, make that are – the only source of income I have at the moment. Will his death affect my payments?"

Before talking with Parker, out of respect for Mr. Bobson, I wouldn't have been able to bring up such an indelicate matter, but the circumstances of his death, and his life, for that matter, made me see him in a much less sympathetic light.

My concern over my financial needs in these turbulent times didn't seem to agitate him in the slightest. "Mr. Wright, rest assured that you will continue to receive your compensation as long as it's necessary. When I hired Mr. Bobson, I didn't want him to be inconvenienced by mundane bookkeeping matters, and to make sure he wasn't, I hired six assistants to take care of payroll, retirement accounts, and so forth. I have promoted Mr. Powell to replace Mr. Bobson. He is already ensconced in what was Mr. Bobson's office."

Efficiency or callousness? Too close to call.

"That is a relief, Mr. Madison. I'm sure Mr. Powell will acclimate himself to the opulence of his new office."

"Make no mistake, Mr. Wright. I didn't approve of Mr. Bobson's extravagances. But since he paid for them himself, I allowed him to indulge himself."

His choice of words fortuitously opened the door for my next question.

Unnecessarily lowering my voice, I asked, "Seems that expensive décor was not Mr. Bobson's only indulgence. May I assume that the Feds shared with you the details of Mr. Bobson's death?" I hesitated briefly and added, "And his little secret?"

I scrutinized H. Michael's face for any sign of surprise or humility. Nothing. His blank affect was chilling.

"Of course I was apprised of all details. Mr. Bobson's unusual proclivity was indeed surprising, considering his strong Christian beliefs, but Satan has managed to corrupt even the strongest among us. I have no doubt that when I hired him, he was pure of spirit and only subsequently succumbed to perversion. Naturally, the circumstances need to remain in-house. And by 'in-house,' I mean only the Feds, Bobson's next-door neighbor who discovered the body, you, and me. Understood?"

Begrudgingly I had to admire his ability to keep calm in a crisis and distance himself from any blame for anything that happened. The thought surely never occurred to him that he had misread Bobson.

"Mr. Wright, there is something you should realize about me: I always swim upstream." Judging by his ability to insulate himself from doubt or guilt, I had no doubt about that. Besides, I could relate to that, having swum upstream for much of my life myself. Nothing like having a drunk for a father and poverty for my companion to provide adversity in abundance.

"I guarantee you that we will get past this, and Clanton Academy will persevere. It is the Lord's will."

For the sake of my alma mater and my nephew, I hoped he was as prescient as he was confident.

"Now, if we are finished here…oh, I forgot. You said you had a hunch about the murders?"

At the risk of looking like a fool, which wouldn't be the first time for me, I said, "No doubt the Feds will dismiss my hunch as unfounded amateurism, but I do have a suspect in mind."

That got H. Michael's attention. "Really, Mr. Wright? And who might that be?"

"Mr. Rollie Jenkins," I said firmly.

For the first time in a long time, maybe ever, Mr. H. Michael Madison was speechless.

Chapter Seventy-four

H. Michael was not one to be flummoxed for long, and in only a few seconds, his self-assurance resurfaced.

"Are you in jest, Mr. Wright, or have you taken leave of your senses? Mr. Jenkins has had an impeccable career at Clanton Academy and has never once given me cause for concern. Moreover, he has personally shared with me his deep spirituality, and I have seen him attending chapel services regularly even when they are not required."

And what were the chances that Jenkins knew exactly when H. Michael would be in attendance? I would never underestimate Jenkins's calculating cunning.

"No, I am not in jest, Mr. Madison, nor have I lost my mind. I have good reason to think he's guilty of four murders. I haven't shared this with anyone else because I haven't discovered possible motive, but as soon as I find out what has triggered this insane killing spree, you will be the first to know."

His head shook back and forth several times. I knew that his tut-tut body language was a prelude to his disapproval. What I had no way of knowing was just how low I had sunk in his estimation. I hoped it wasn't so low that he'd pull the plug on my monetary compensation for services rendered.

"Mr. Wright, I hope this hare-brained theory isn't the extent of your investigation. I expect more than this for the money I am paying you."

Maybe I had erred in sharing my hunch. It was time to recoup any potential losses. "Of course that's not all, Mr. Madison. I have established a pipeline to the Feds, and I have access to whatever they discover."

Well, at least one Fed. Why quibble over the letter "s"?

"But I can't reveal more about Jenkins at this time. Suspend your disbelief for a while, please, and do not share this with anyone. There's a very good chance your discretion will be amply rewarded – by bringing a foul murderer to justice."

"Oh, of that you can rest assured, Mr. Wright. Do you think I would make such a groundless speculation and risk a slander law suit? Not in a million years."

He gave me a steely look.

"I need to terminate this meeting now. The future of Clanton Academy depends on my ability to contain this damage and thwart Satan's plan. By tomorrow the local newspapers and television stations will renew their assault. It appears that destroying Clanton Academy is their highest priority. Any information you can feed me as I keep them at bay would be much appreciated, Mr. Wright."

He either couldn't or wouldn't accept that four murders at a small private school was news. Big news. The media didn't have a vendetta against Clanton Academy.

"You can count on it, Mr. Madison," I said and left his office, relieved that my income was intact.

Miss Foss didn't bother looking up at me as I passed her office on my way to find Rex. The sound of the battering her keyboard was enduring followed me. I had observed before how her keyboard almost bounced as she slammed her bony fingers against it. Her hatred of me and probably dozens of others had found a harmless outlet. Why is it, I asked myself, that most people learn to deal with even the most intense malice in harmless ways, while others resort to violence? If I could figure out the source of Jenkins's hatred, maybe I would be able to force his hand through face-to-face confrontation.

Chapter Seventy-five

Knowing that the place would become a maelstrom once the media started reporting on Bobson's death, I thought a few quiet moments in the teachers' lounge would be a good idea. The calm before the storm and all that. I might even filch a cup of their decent coffee if they didn't object to sharing with a layman.

An assortment of mismatched but comfortable looking overstuffed chairs and two sofas could provide seating for at least a dozen teachers, but today only four were occupying the lounge. Deep in serious conversation, they took no notice of me, so I made my way to the coffee station and availed myself of a cup of coffee that didn't have the consistency of sludge. Though I tried to be as unobtrusive as possible in taking a seat across the room from them, one of them, my former Civics teacher, noticed me. Still short, squat, and given to wearing ugly ties, his appearance hadn't changed much over the years.

"Sorry to bother you. Do you remember me, Mr. Gore? Danny Wright. I was in your class as a freshman over twenty years ago. I'm here visiting my nephew and needed to get off my feet and grab a cup of your coffee. I hope you're OK with that."

I didn't expect him to remember me. Unlike his appearance, mine had changed enough that unless his ability to extrapolate how the effects of aging would alter my appearance was extraordinary, I would need to offer more than a name to revive his memory.

Adjusting his glasses as if that would help his memory, he looked me up and down, his brow furrowed from concentrated effort, then shook his head to indicate that he didn't recognize me. "Sorry to say, Danny, but I'm drawing a blank. But you're welcome to relax here as long as you want – if you don't mind listening to a bunch of irate teachers having a bitch session." He laughed. The other three, whom I did not know, remained silent.

"Thanks for the hospitality, Mr. Gore. Just ignore me and carry on. I won't stay long."

Almost immediately they resumed their intense conversation, though now in more hushed tones. We students had always wondered what teachers talked about in here. Did they share stories of our foibles? Carp about their salaries? Argue about their favorite sports teams? Share their summer plans? After all the intervening years, the mystery was about to be solved, long after I gave a rat's ass.

I tuned out their talking and let myself fall into a state of relaxation.

That is, until the words "that fucking Bobson" jarred me. Eavesdropping as subtly as I could, I strained to follow the conversation.

"How much did he get from you, Alec?"

"My entire retirement fund!"

"Ditto." That voice I recognized; it was Mr. Gore's.

"Whoa, that bites. I lost only $40 thousand."

"*Only* forty thousand? What are you, another Bill Gates?"

"Anyone know who else besides us got taken by that sonofabitch?"

A few seconds of silence.

"I heard rumors. Jackson, Watson, maybe Mann."

"I heard that Jenkins lost everything."

Jenkins had lost everything? Now, that was more than a little interesting.

I couldn't leave the lounge without hearing more. Tossing manners aside, I intruded. "Please excuse me, but I couldn't help overhearing snatches of your conversation. Am I right in thinking that some teachers at Clanton were victimized?"

All four just looked at me, uncertain, I gathered, about whether they should bother answering a question about something that was clearly none of my business. Mr. Gore finally broke the ice.

"What the hell, no harm in sharing what that asshole did to us."

When I asked if "asshole" was a synonym for Merrick Bobson, they simultaneously confirmed my question with rancor.

"Asshole is too good a word to describe a man who did what he did, Mr. Wright. That bastard screwed a bunch of us out of our retirement funds with his damn Ponzi scheme," said a lanky, bespectacled teacher with enough volume to qualify as yelling.

"I'm ashamed to admit to a total stranger that I was one of those gullible enough to be suckered in by Mr. Bobson," said the black middle-aged teacher sitting across from Mr. Gore. "When I received a letter from the SEC, I shivered before opening it, as if I knew it would be bad news."

"You can have no idea how disastrous this is for us, Danny," said Mr. Gore, his eyes downturned. "I have only ten years till when I had hoped to retire. Now I'll have to work till they bury me." He looked up at me with sad eyes. "But it's no concern of yours. Please excuse our anger."

I objected sincerely. "But you're wrong, Mr. Gore. When something bad happens to a Clanton teacher or student, it hurts all alumni. We're a family connected by this school. All the murders and now this…I am deeply concerned about the future of Clanton and its students and teachers."

"That makes five of us, Mr. Wright," said the bespectacled teacher, sighing.

I hoped they accepted me enough to keep sharing information.

"Those other teachers' names you mentioned…how reliable are the rumors? For instance, do you really think Mr. Jenkins lost everything? He was one of my teachers twenty years ago," I asked.

"I haven't talked to him yet, but I'd bet what was once my retirement fund that he lost everything. He was with me at the seminar where Bobson made his pitch, and he stayed behind to talk with him after I signed the papers that have consigned me to poverty." He smiled weakly. Gallows humor, I supposed. "I'm sure he signed on that day, too."

"And Mr. Mann, the librarian? Any reason to believe he didn't get taken in?" I asked.

"Don't know for sure, but I heard he had invested forty or fifty thousand. Not that it would make a dent in his retirement. He's rich as Croesus," said Mr. Gore. "Come to think of it, I'm pretty sure of that. After Bobson was hired here, he started enlarging what we now know was a Ponzi scheme and told anyone who was interested in investing with him to check with Mr. Mann and Mr. Jenkins, who could attest to the lucrative gains his investments were making."

The middle-aged black teacher spoke up. "I do believe you're right about that, David. I remember hearing that, but, fool that I am, I signed on without checking any references. I mean, if I couldn't trust Mr. Madison's hand-selected CFO to take care of Clanton, who could I trust? Besides, I don't much care for Mr. Jenkins. He's a cold fish. And Mr. Mann? I wouldn't ask that idiot for the time of day."

"Thank you for taking me into your confidence, gentlemen. I hope there is a possibility that you'll be able to rescue some of the funds," I said, knowing that a small recovery of lost funds would offer little solace. Even selling off all of the expensive toys and furniture that Bobson had bought with his ill-gotten funds would do little good. Used furniture and clothes wouldn't fetch much at auction.

"The SEC lawyer I called after I received the letter told me that there was little chance of that. I have resigned myself to an uncertain retirement. I wish I hadn't been so desperate for a better retirement that I rolled over everything, but that's blood over the dam," Mr. Gore said.

The glum looks from his peers silently announced that they shared his sentiments.

I felt a profound sadness that Bobson had destroyed the futures of these good men and probably others here.

I also felt that I finally had found a motive that could undo Jenkins.

Chapter-Seventy-six

It took less than a few minutes to jog to Rex's room, which was unoccupied and in its usual disarray. He needed to hear my latest discovery for his own safety. If I confronted Jenkins or convinced the Feds to interrogate him, I felt certain that Jenkins would target not only me but also Rex for murder Number 5. I left a note on the top of the piles of graded essays and tests on his desk asking him to call me as soon as he read the note, then headed to the administration building to find Parker.

There was very little activity on the first floor and on the second, almost none. The administrative staff H. Michael had put in place seemed paralyzed whenever a crisis arose. Perhaps that suited him just fine – it ensured that no one would dare challenge his decisions – but to me they seemed a waste of money when Clanton Academy could ill afford any excess expenditures.

Gathered outside Mrs. Clarkson's office were Sloane, Parker, and several men I didn't recognize, though their dark suits and buzzed heads screamed Feds. Mrs. Clarkson had their undivided attention, but I wasn't close enough to hear what she was saying to them.

Just then Parker caught a glimpse of me and must have excused himself from the pow wow because he broke off from the group and headed my way.

"I see that Mrs. Clarkson has captivated yet another group of..." I started to say.

"It's not like that, Danny. She was filling us in on today's schedule. We have a lot to do before the media swarm here. I do admit, though, that she is easy on the eyes."

"Oh, she's easy all right." I regretted saying it as soon as the words left my mouth. "Forget I said that, Parker. I have something I want to share with you."

"Here? Or should we go somewhere private?"

"Definitely private. Let's go to my guest quarters."

On the way to the Alumni House, Parker filled me in on what they knew, which wasn't much. Forensics confirmed that the cause of death was a gunshot wound to the head and that Bobson had ingested no drugs or alcohol.

"Excuse the mess," I told Parker as we entered my quarters. "I could lie and say I didn't have time to tidy up, but the truth is that I tend to be a slob. Just toss me the dirty clothes on that chair and have a seat. Can I get you a soda or water?"

I caught the two shirts and one pair of pants that Parker threw to me and got right down to voicing my finding after he declined the offer of beverage. I doubted I had a soda left, anyway.

"Parker, I am one hundred percent sure that I know who killed all four victims." Hoping for a sign that he was eager for me to continue but getting none from the dispassionate Parker, I continued anyway. "I have suspected that one man, a teacher, had killed them but couldn't find a motive for the life of me. Till half an hour ago, that is."

Parker remained expressionless.

"Are you interested in hearing it?" I asked. "You seem bored or unimpressed."

"I am neither, Danny. I am a little skeptical, however. Convince me I am wrong."

As succinctly as I could, I laid it all in front of him – the changes in Jenkins's behavior coinciding with the murders, the opportunity for him to have inserted the belly bomb into the sausage he gave to Wood, his callousness at Thomason's funeral, Hank Mann's alcohol-induced revealing of Jenkins's spitefulness, Jenkins's unlikely friendship with Bobson, the abrupt change from dour to elated state after Bobson's murder, and the *piece de resistance*, his having been a victim of Bobson's Ponzi scheme that wiped out his retirement fund.

"All circumstantial, I realize. But it all adds up to one conclusion."

I studied Parker's face to see if it revealed even a hint of expression. Nada. A blank. Unpolished granite. He made the Sphinx look animated. Though a bit miffed at his lack of enthusiasm, I had to admire his well-honed ability to show no reaction.

"Well? Am I onto something, Parker? Say something, for crissakes."

More long seconds of silence. Either he was processing what I had said, or he was trying to find an inoffensive way to tell me I was full of shit.

Finally he spoke. "Danny, I think your theory is better than anything we have come up with. It does make sense. But…"

I knew there would be a "but."

"Without any evidence, we can't do a damn thing. Unless he confesses to the murders, which is highly improbable, we have nothing but speculation and weak-at-best circumstantial evidence."

I would have preferred a high five, but his agreement that Jenkins was a suspect was enough to keep me moving forward.

"I know you and your fellow Feds can't commit yourselves based only on my observations, but can I count on you at least to help me if I pursue this myself, Parker?"

"Sure thing, Danny. As I said, we have nothing better to go on anyway. Sloane plans on tearing the place upside down if he has to, to find some hard evidence, but I doubt he'll find any. Jenkins or whoever did the murders made sure of that."

"One more thing, Parker. Please don't share with Sloane or anyone else what I said. I will figure out some way to get him to slip up, but I don't want him to be even more on his guard, which is what will happen if you call him in and confront him."

"OK, Danny, but don't put yourself in harm's way. You don't carry a weapon, do you? What if he attacked you? Unlike you, I *do* carry a weapon and know how to use it. When dealing with potentially dangerous persons, it is always advisable to be prepared for the worst. Jenkins, as you said, may be a cold-blooded killer, and if he is, he won't hesitate to add one more victim to his tally. Promise you'll call me before doing anything. Going after him alone and unarmed is unwise."

I assured him I would – and I might even do so. If it was the last thing I ever did, I was going to take that bastard down with or without the Feds' help.

Chapter Seventy-seven

Walking back toward the dorm, I saw Rex heading to class and flagged him down.

"Sorry I didn't call you, Uncle Danny. Didn't have time and can't be late for Mr. Jenkins's class. He will have my ass in a sling," Rex said as we walked briskly toward the academic building.

"That's OK. We can walk and talk at the same time," I said, almost out of breath as he picked up the pace. I hadn't done a lick of exercise since the first day I returned here, and it was showing.

"Actually, it's Mr. Jenkins I wanted to talk with you about."

He abruptly stopped walking and turned to me. "Why do I have the feeling that this is not good news?" he said.

I tried to ease his tension by half jokingly saying, "Because it isn't."

He frowned, and I knew him well enough to realize it wasn't because of my lame attempt at casual humor.

"Rex, we don't have time to discuss this in detail. I just wanted to warn you that he could be dangerous. And that danger extends to you if things progress as I think they will. Try never to be alone the next couple days. Hang out with your buddies until it's time to go to bed, and lock the door to your room then."

He was visibly shaken. "Me? Why would I have anything to fear from him? I haven't ever done anything to get on his bad side."

"You haven't, Rex, but I will definitely be on his bad side soon, and I am sure he'll direct his anger to you if he gets the chance. If you feel that you can't handle this, I will call your mom immediately and have her take you home for a while. With the continued exodus of students after Mr. Bobson's murder, it won't be as if you're alone in being afraid."

That would probably be a prudent thing to do, especially if he allowed teenage bravado to warp his thinking to the point he felt invincible.

"I admit that you're scaring me, Uncle Danny. I mean, after four faculty deaths, who feels safe here? But I am not going to let Jenkins or anyone else here decide how I live. I am not going home now. Period. I will hang out with friends all day, every day, when I am not in classes till this freaking nightmare is over."

Was this typical teenager's posturing? Or did he fully understand the implications of being a target of a crazed killer? I couldn't afford to get it wrong. Sending him home now would definitely be the wisest choice, and that was what I decided I would do immediately after classes.

"Rex, I am rethinking this whole situation. I think it's best that you spend some time away from here. If anything bad happened to you that was my fault, I don't know how I could live with myself."

He suddenly dropped his books to the ground and hugged me. Hard.

Releasing me from a long hug, he said, "Uncle Danny, I know you love me, and I know you are thinking of what's best for me, but I am not running away. I am going to stay in my classes and keep my grades up. If I run away from this and jeopardize my chance to get into UVA, I would never be able to forgive myself. I promise I will not put myself in danger. I'll spend every waking moment with friends, and instead of locking my door at night, I'll sleep on the floor of Amos's room. No one – not Jenkins or anyone else – will know where I am."

Damn it, the boy was becoming a man, and I had ambivalent feelings about that.

"But right now, Uncle Danny, I really have to haul ass to get to class."

"Go ahead, Rex. I need time to think about this. I'll see you right after your class is over, OK?"

He hugged me again, picked up his books, and sprinted to class.

Feeling more nervous that I had ever felt before, I trailed after him.

Chapter Seventy-eight

I waited till the hallways were empty of students and made my way to Jenkins's room to wait till his class was over to collect Rex. As usual, his door was open, and I positioned myself to be out of his view in order to eavesdrop. If nothing else, I was curious how a man who I was convinced was guilty of four murders would conduct himself.

The class was discussing *Macbeth,* a play I had enjoyed when I was in his class.

"All right, you not so budding scholars, who volunteers to give me a quick synopsis of the plot? Don't get bogged down in details. I simply want to know if you understood the sometimes difficult language of that era."

From my vantage point, I could see only the first five seats of each row, and if the other students were like the ones I observed fidgeting with purposely dropped pens, thumbing aimlessly through the book, digging in pockets to find handkerchiefs for nonexistent sinus drips – anything to avoid eye contact with Jenkins – I didn't foresee any volunteers any time soon.

"Just as I figured. Worthless waste of air, you are. Did *anyone* bother to read it?"

Every hand immediately shot up.

"Sir, we all read it. It's just that the language is difficult," one of the braver students said.

A chorus of other voices concurred, including what I recognized as Amos's and Rex's.

A short redheaded boy in the first seat of the row directly in front of Jenkins raised his hand cautiously.

"Do *SparkNotes* count?"

What I could see of the class intently watched Jenkins to see his reaction. They seemed reluctant to venture forth a guess or laugh or even answer a question. It wasn't like that when I was in his class. He was impatient, sometimes sarcastic, back then, but he did seem to care if we learned something or not. Now I sensed a large gulf between him and his students. Whether that was caused by his being burned out or by a change in personality I didn't know, but I suspected it was the latter. Coldblooded murders changed even Macbeth and his wicked wife.

He shrugged his shoulders and flashed briefly a half smile, at which point, giggling ensued.

"Let's hear what you remember from old Sparky. Does anyone bother to give a nod to the omniscient Cliff anymore?" He scanned the classroom. "No? Well that figures. *Cliff's Notes* look too much like a book to you. Go ahead, your recitation, please, Mr. Griffin."

He didn't look or sound like a cafeteria Griffin, and his succinct summary of the plot seemed on point as far as I could remember.

"Quite accurate, Mr. Griffin. You will make a fine plagiarizer someday."

A few students in the rows not in my line of vision chuckled, but only briefly, as Jenkins proceeded.

"Well, then, class, now that Mr. Griffin has reminded you of what you accessed on your damn computers, let us move along to more important issues than simple plot, not that Shakespeare's plot is anything short of perfect."

Jenkins fired question after question to the class, which, in my opinion, answered with reasonable accuracy and depth of thought. Jenkins must have agreed with me because he gave the class his version of a compliment.

"Class, I must say that you have outdone yourselves and attained close to mediocrity today. We have only a few minutes left of class till the bell rings like the porter's knocking at the gate, so I don't expect an answer right now. Your homework for tonight is to answer in 750 words whether you think Macbeth was innately evil. Consider whether it is possible that he was a good man corrupted by the influence of the witches and Lady Macbeth. Was his self-proclaimed tragic flaw of vaulting ambition the cause of his descent? Or did he perhaps not recognize the evil within himself? Speculate on whether a man can be born evil or be made evil by circumstances. And, as always, go to the text to support your answers."

After a hasty assembling of books and notebooks, the students sat stiffly, eager for the bell to end their misery. Mercifully it came within seconds, and they filed rapidly out into the hallway. I stopped Rex and whispered to him to meet me in the lounge in the dorm in a few minutes.

Exhaling a deep breath, I entered Jenkins's room.

"I have an answer to that question, Mr. Jenkins," I said, getting his attention. "Care to hear it?"

Jenkins seemed self-assured as usual and answered, "Twenty years is a long wait to be answered, Mr. Wright, but I'm all agog. Enlighten me, please."

He sat back in his chair, looking at me with what appeared to be amusement.

"A man *can* become evil through circumstances, and a man can also be innately evil. And you're living proof of both, Mr. Jenkins. Just when did that evil get the better of you? When you somehow found out that Bobson had deprived you of your retirement? Or have you always known you are capable of evil and quashed the impulse till then?"

I couldn't foretell what reaction I had to deal with and didn't much care. I had let him know that I was onto him, and, if nothing else, that knowledge would require him to act. Sooner or later he'd slip up.

He burst into a maniacal laugh that was disturbing in its vigor. Not quite what I expected.

"Wrong answer, Mr. Wright. Your creativity is surprising. I had you pegged as a paint-by-the-numbers thinker."

The smile left his face abruptly, and he glared menacingly at me as he spoke with deliberate, calm articulation of each syllable. "Besides, Mr. Wright, if I am as evil as you say, don't you think you are making an error in sharing that with me? A man as evil as you think I am could easily kill you, too." He leaned forward slightly. "And enjoy it."

For a few seconds he had shown a slight crack in the façade he had cultivated over the years, and that was my cue to leave the room.

If his evil required a trigger to activate it, I hoped I had just pulled it.

Chapter Seventy-nine

Odd how random thoughts pop up at the strangest times. One of the few things I remembered from my Latin classes at Clanton Academy was Caesar's declaration when about to cross the Rubicon River: "*Alea iacta est*" –"the die has been cast." Granted, I was no Caesar, and confronting Jenkins was not tantamount to starting a civil war. Nevertheless, setting in motion a chain of events that would either result in a murderer being brought to justice or...I didn't want to consider the alternative. I hurried to meet Rex in the lounge of his dorm. I knew I would be targeted but wanted to make sure Rex wasn't.

He was waiting for me in the empty lounge. Sitting in a ratty chair, his legs were pumping up and down like a jackhammer, as they often did when he was nervous or impatient. Today it was probably both.

Standing up when he saw me, he said, "Uncle Danny, — "

I stopped him before he could say another word.

"Rex, sit back down and listen carefully to what I say. After you left Jenkins's classroom, I went in to let him know that I was aware that he was a murderer. I now know why he killed Mr. Bobson, and although I don't have any proof that he killed the others, I'd bet my life – and I probably have already done so – that he is guilty of four murders."

"Uncle Danny, I have never doubted or questioned anything you said, but this is some deep shit. If what you think is true, aren't you afraid you've set yourself up to be another victim? Can you get the Feds to protect you?" By the tone of his voice, I knew he was obviously agitated and alarmed.

"Settle down, Rex. I know what I'm doing."

Did I really? I couldn't afford to let doubt infect me at this point. The Rubicon was behind me, and I needed to let this play out.

"You see, Rex, because there is no evidence to charge him with any crime, I need him to confess or catch him in the act of another attempted murder, and the only way I could think of for him to do that was to paint him into a corner and force him to come after me. I am going to enlist the aid of Agent Parker, so you needn't worry about my safety."

He shook his head rapidly back and forth. "Not worry? You gotta be kidding!"

"Rex, trust me, I will be fine. That bastard is going to pay for everything he has done. If anyone should be worrying, it's him." Maybe a little too Clint Eastwood of me, but it was how I felt. My only concern for safety right now was for Rex.

"And that brings me to you, Rex. He might try to get at me by harming you, and that isn't going to happen. I understand your insisting that you remain at Clanton Academy, and I am going to allow that. But on my terms."

He didn't object, so I pressed on.

"As soon as we're done talking here, I am going to see Coach Rotherwood and ask him if you can stay at his house till Jenkins is no longer a threat. With him and his three sons to protect you there, you'll be safe from Jenkins. You will not eat in the cafeteria – I'm sure his wife won't object to having one more mouth to feed – and I will get permission from Mr. Madison for you to cut Jenkins's class. Are we clear on the conditions of your remaining here?"

With no other option, Rex acquiesced. He scurried off to his next class, and I left to find Coach Rotherwood and meet with H. Michael before calling Parker.

If my hunch was right, Jenkins would not waste time in trying to eliminate me.

Chapter Eighty

After Coach Rotherwood readily agreed to the unexpected house guest with no explanation from me other than that I'd fill him in later, my next stop was H. Michael's office.

Miss Foss intentionally ignored me, not even looking up from her desk as I hovered over her, repeatedly clearing my throat. I was more than OK with that, as I had no time to waste on her. For the time being, at any rate. If I survived my plan intact, I would continue to be a source of vexation for her, pleasure for me.

"Nice to see you, too, Miss Foss. I'm going in to see the boss unless he's in conference."

She grunted. Her guttural approval, I assumed.

H. Michael barked a loud "Enter!" when I knocked on his door.

"Oh, it's you," he said quietly when he saw me. "Excuse my rudeness. I had instructed Miss Foss to keep everyone out for the next few hours."

"She must have forgotten. She sent me right in," I replied, hoping to erode her favor with the man she admired to the point of hero worship.

"Well, now that you're here, I'll take a short break from putting out brush fires." He became lost in thought momentarily. "Forest fires, actually. What's on your mind? Progress of some sort?"

"You might say that," I answered. "If all goes well, Mr. Jenkins will be behind bars, probably sooner than later."

His cocked head indicated skepticism. And why not? He was only joining a growing crowd that doubted my wisdom. Or was it sanity? No matter. There was no turning back.

"And what makes you think that, Mr. Wright?"

I felt no need to fill him in with details of a still murky plan.

"Because I think he is going to try to kill me."

I wanted that to sink in for a few seconds before getting his permission for Rex to skip Jenkins's class and informing him that I took the liberty of arranging for Rex to stay at Coach Rotherwood's. "Act first, apologize later," a wise man once told me.

"Oh, my, Mr. Wright, I don't like where this is going."

"You don't have to like it. Just trust me. What have you got to lose? The Feds have come up dry, and the school has lost half its enrollment. If what I said is true, then what's another murder? Better yet, if I'm right and Jenkins ends up behind bars, then Clanton Academy can start healing."

I was acting casual, if not brave, on the outside while my guts churned on the inside.

"Remember this conversation and share it with Agent Sloane if Jenkins succeeds in his fifth murder. Maybe then they'll focus their attention on him."

Showing me his well-practiced stern face, he said with gravitas, "I'm afraid I have to order you to refrain from any foolhardy acts, Mr. Wright, even though I don't think for a minute that Mr. Jenkins is a murderer. Clanton Academy simply cannot endure any more death. The grim reaper —"

I risked censure by interrupting him.

"With all due respect, Mr. Madison, I have to ignore your order. You see, I have already confronted Jenkins with what I know, and I am a hundred percent certain he'll come after me."

H. Michael groaned. "What a fool I have been to allow you to intrude on the FBI's investigation." He slumped in his chair. "I hate sports metaphors, but since I can come up with nothing better than 'the ball is your court,' can you *please* keep me in your godforsaken loop?"

"Of course. By the way, my loop, as you called it, includes only you, my nephew, and Agent Parker at this time. I will also include Sheriff Dixon later. I would appreciate your keeping this under your hat till I inform you otherwise."

"Of that you can rest assured, Mr. Wright. Do you think I would risk my reputation telling anyone that I approved of this madness? I hope you realize that if I weren't in such dire straits right now, you'd already be out of here on your butt."

"Your vote of confidence underwhelms me, Mr. Madison, but in all fairness, I understand your skepticism. I have two more things to run by you. One, I have already convinced Coach Rotherwood to keep Rex at his house till whatever happens, happens. I know I should have gained your approval first, but I just don't have time to follow protocol. Two, I need your permission for Rex to cut Jenkins's class. I wouldn't be at all surprised if Jenkins attempted to get at me though him, and I don't want Rex to be near him."

"Anything else you want, Mr. Wright? Access to petty cash? Your own office, perhaps?"

"No need for you to resort to sarcasm, Mr. Madison. All I ask for is a little trust in me and permission for Rex to stay away from that one class."

H. Michael sighed dramatically. "The latter is granted. The former? I'm afraid not. Your life is in God's hands. I wash my hands of this."

"Isn't that what Pontius Pilate did?" I asked.

That struck a nerve, as I knew it would.

As I hurriedly exited his office, I heard only "Blasphe —" before the door closed behind me.

As angry as I had made him, I half expected him to say, "Don't let the door hit your ass on the way out," but his piety prevailed. I briefly wondered what it would take for it to crack.

Chapter Eighty-one

Parker was proving to be elusive. A thorough search of the
campus produced only tired feet and the need for a long,
hot shower. When I arrived at my guest quarters, the first
thing I noticed was an envelope that someone had slipped
under the door. Curiosity got the better of caution, and I
tore it open. Inside was a note made of letters cut from
magazines. I had always thought that method of
communication occurred only in television shows, but here
it was, short and not so sweet.

Your a dead man if you keep metaling.

What was I to make of the egregious spelling errors?
Was the writer truly only semi-literate? Or was this an
attempt to conceal the writer's literacy? Jenkins sending me
a warning, perhaps? Maybe the bully that Rex had jacked
up in defense of his friend being hazed was trying to
retaliate by threatening me? Highly unlikely that a Clanton
Academy student could be that dim. Who else had a bone
to pick with me? No one but Rex, Amos, and H. Michael
knew I was snooping around about the drug trafficking, and
that seemed to have stopped, anyway. I was drawing a
blank, but I just couldn't imagine that Jenkins's hubris
would tolerate illiteracy even as a disguise. The only

conclusion, if it could be called that, was that either someone felt threatened by me or a student was exercising his right to be stupid. Regardless, whoever sent it would be disappointed to learn that I was not going to stop "metaling."

Tucking the note into the back pocket of my only pair of relatively clean pants, I decided to postpone the shower and check the campus again to find Parker. Hygiene and laundry had to take a back seat to my meddling.

My first stop was the administration building, and on the second floor I saw Sloane and two other Feds conferring. Not among them was Parker, and that bothered me. If he had been reassigned because he had incurred the disfavor of Sloane, I was worried about how I could fend off an attack from Jenkins without a firearm.

Somewhat desperate now, I checked every building except the field house, which I figured would be the last place I'd find him. For once I was happy to be wrong: Parker was working out in the weight room. I didn't announce myself immediately and observed his intense sets with free weights, impressed with his strength and privately embarrassed that I had been remiss in working out myself the past couple years.

As he was putting back hand weights, he caught sight of me and walked over to see me.

"Hey, Danny. Here to work out? I'm done and can spot for you if you want," he said, wiping the sweat off his face with a towel draped around his neck.

"Thanks, but that's not why I am here. You said to call you before doing something to take down Jenkins. Well, that's not exactly the way it worked out."

He stiffened, clearly not pleased, but allowed me to finish what I had to say.

"I went to his classroom and confronted him. I told him that I knew he had murdered four people. It was the only way I could think of to scare him into action."

Parker threw the towel to the floor and said between clenched teeth, "Have you lost your fucking mind, Danny? Do you realize how foolhardy you have been? How do you think you can defend yourself if he decides to come after you when you're alone somewhere? And what about your nephew? What will happen to him if Jenkins goes after him? This stupid plan is incredibly ill-conceived, Danny."

He hadn't said anything I hadn't already thought of myself.

"My nephew is safe. I arranged for him to stay at Coach Rotherwood's, and I got permission from Mr. Madison for him to cut Jenkins's class. I'm the only one that is vulnerable. If you'll help me, we can get him, Parker."

"And how could I possibly help you? I can't follow you around like your shadow."

"I know that, Parker. Listen to the rest of my plan, OK?"

My fingers were crossed.

"I want you to wire me and be in hiding nearby when I set myself up as a target in the Alumni House. If he takes the bait, you will be able to hear what he says, maybe even a confession, and keep him in your sights. I hope he chooses to overwhelm me physically rather than shoot me like he shot Bobson, but even if he does pull out a gun, you could shoot him before he pulled the trigger, right?"

"Danny, you have been watching too many reruns of 'Murder, She Wrote.' Your plan can go wrong in too many ways to count. I am an excellent shot, but what if I don't have an angle to shoot from? What if he doesn't bother talking first and just shoots you? It's just too risky. And how could I possibly justify involving you to Sloane? He'd have my head on a platter even if this insane scheme should work. The FBI never recruits outsiders. Never."

Everything he said made sense. But that wasn't about to stop me. If he wouldn't help me with this plan, I'd come up with something else. What choice did I have? Jenkins was going to try to eliminate me, I was sure.

Accepting that I had no choice but to continue on my own, I said, "You're probably right, Parker. I shouldn't have asked you. Forget I brought it up."

He picked up his towel and wiped off the remaining sweat from his brow. I turned and started to leave the field house when he yelled at me, "Get back here, damn it! You can't do this alone. I'll help you even it means my job. No one ever said I was the sharpest knife in the drawer."

I had no doubt that he was the smartest of the Feds working this case, but it wasn't his IQ that concerned me.

Could he wire me skillfully enough so that Jenkins wouldn't suspect it? And, more important, could he shoot accurately enough to take down Jenkins if necessary?

My life depended on it.

Chapter Eighty-two

Lined up in three chairs opposite the empty desk of The Boss, Witt, Jensen, and Van Verdenburg nervously looked at each other, afraid to break the tense silence.

Finally, Jensen spoke. "Anyone have a clue why we got called in today? Did we fuck up again somehow?"

The other two mumbled denials of any knowledge, clearly agitated and fearful.

The Boss entered silently behind them, walked behind Witt, and slapped him hard across the back of his head.

As Witt winced, The Boss said, "Witt, did you do everything I asked you to do last week? I haven't heard back from you."

Witt turned to answer, but by then The Boss had filled the empty seat behind the desk.

"Quit sitting there with your mouths hanging open. Have any of you learned how to speak yet?"

Witt spoke with the ill-advised confidence that dim-witted people unaware of their intellectual shortcomings often feel. "Boss, I always get the job done. You know that. I didn't come by cuz of the FBI creeps hanging around, and Hardy's uncle is like a stain that won't go away."

"What does he have to do with anything, Witt? He hasn't said a word about drugs."

Witt replied, "Well, he don't belong here, and I hate his nephew."

Somehow that seemed like a logical answer to him.

It soon became clear to him that The Boss thought otherwise.

"Is your stupidity bottomless, Witt?" Jensen and Van Verdenburg giggled. "Shut the fuck up, you clowns. What makes you think you're any smarter? I haven't seen hide nor hair of you, either. Are you afraid of Hardy's uncle, too?"

Thinking that rebuke provided an opportunity to redeem himself, Witt said, "Yeah, you tools. At least I did something about it."

The Boss sat in stony silence for fifteen seconds trying to figure out what moronic maneuver Witt had made.

"What exactly did you do, Witt?" The Boss asked calmly.

"You're gonna love this, Boss. I wrote a threat to kill him and slid it under that punk's uncle's door. I bet he's so scared that he'll hightail it right outta here." He swelled his athletic chest and gave his cohorts a smug look to indicate his minor victory.

The Boss sat stunned, mouth hanging open, thinking, 'If that fool has jeopardized my operation, I will kill him.'

"You say you wrote a threat. Just what was this threat and how did you write it? Even you can't be so stupid that you wrote it by hand. And please tell me you used spell check."

Witt, still unaware of what storm lay behind The Boss's calm, said, "You gotta have more confidence in me, Boss. I cut letters from magazines I stole from the library and glued them on a page. Told him he'd be a dead man if he didn't stop metaling." His face broke out in a broad smile as he waited for the praise he knew was forthcoming.

"Metaling? What the fuck is metaling, you idiot?" said Jensen, laughing until The Boss stared him down.

"You think you're so smart, Jensen! Ha! Metaling, like, you know, like 'stop metaling in my affairs.'" Witt gloated.

The Boss erupted. "Good God, you total moron, you complete idiot, you cretin! Do you know what you've done? You've now added one more person that I will have to deal with."

"Huh? How do you figure?" Witt managed to eke out.

"Think, if that's possible, Witt. He will want to find out what prompted someone to tell him to stop snooping around when he wasn't doing any such thing. I have been super-careful to make sure that we kept such a low profile that no one would suspect any drug activity here. He is no dummy like you, Witt. As soon as he saw 'metaling,' I guarantee he assumed that only a student, and a bad one at that, would misspell 'meddling.' With your reputation as the anti-scholar at Clanton, how many people will he have to ask before your name comes up? He may not know anything about drugs at this point, but once he starts asking around who might have written that note, that might change. And then we're in deep trouble. Do you get it now, Witt?"

Witt's handsome head dropped to his chest. "I'm sorry, Boss. I was just trying to help."

Even in anger, The Boss knew better than to push him further. It was possible that Witt could complicate matters even more by trying to make things right.

"No sense in crying over spilt milk, Witt. Forget about it. With Feds crawling all over the place, we need to suspend our sales again anyway. You three lay low till you hear from me again. And do *not* even think about doing anything – I repeat, A.N.Y.T.H.I.N.G. – without seeing me first. Now, get your asses out of here. I need to think about how to deal with Mr. Wright."

Chapter Eighty-three

I left Parker shaking his head and probably wondering what he was letting himself in for. When he had offered to lend me a Kevlar vest, the reality of what I was about to do sank in. My confidence was shaken if not my resolve.

A long, hot shower that I had already postponed promised to revive me physically, but I wasn't sure if it could work its magic on my flagging confidence. Heading to my guest quarters, I decided to postpone it for a few more minutes and dropped in to see Hank Mann.

Mann was hustling around his domain like a fussy Merry Maid, straightening the stacks that saw little action in these days of technology, placing magazines back in their proper place, and clucking when he found chewing gum wrappers beneath the computer stations. When he finally saw me standing by the check-out desk, he immediately abandoned his cleaning duties and hurried over to see me.

"Danny, so good of you to visit me here. I haven't seen you since our last Happy Hour. I hope I didn't offend you by dozing off. Hadn't slept a wink in days and just conked out."

He got the "conked out" part right, but both of us knew the cause of his sudden somnolence had nothing to do with sleep deprivation.

"Not a problem, Hank. We all need to get our sleep when we can." I smiled to defuse any potential for embarrassment he might have felt.

"True, but I apologize anyway. It was rude." I waved off the necessity to apologize, and he changed gears. "Hey, I suppose you heard about Bobson. Who knew he was a Judy Garlic fan in *that* way?"

My heart skipped a beat. No one other than the FBI, Mr. Madison, and I knew about Bobson's activity prior to his death, and I couldn't imagine either the Feds or H. Michael sharing that information with Mann. No, there was only one way he could know that.

"Hank, listen to me very carefully. No one but the killer and four others knew about his being dressed like Judy Garland."

He cupped his hand over his mouth, and his eyes widened. It was a portrait of panic.

"Tell me how you know this, Hank. And don't even think about lying. If you don't come clean right now, I am going directly to see Agent Sloane, and you'll be arrested as an accomplice to murder or, at the very least, an accessory after the fact."

Mann swooned, and I caught him under his armpit just as he was about to succumb to what my great-grandmother called "the vapors."

"Hank, catch your breath and fess up. It was Jenkins who told you that, wasn't it?"

Breaking into sobs that caught the attention of the three students at computer stations, he started to babble indistinguishable words.

"Not here, Hank. Let's go to your office." I turned to the three curious students and told them to mind their own business, that Mr. Mann had just received word of a death in the family.

Inside his office, Mann regained his composure and told me in a strange, slow monotone the whole story.

"Jenkins came to my apartment right after he had murdered Bobson, bragging about how *we* had avenged Bobson's treachery. 'We?' I told him. 'We?' I had nothing to do with any of your horrible murders!"

When he paused to wipe the tears from his face, I nodded for him to continue.

"He laughed at me, Danny. Laughed at me like I was some sort of joke. When I asked him what was so funny, he poked me in the chest and said I was. And then his face turned hard like I'd never seen him before, and he said if I even thought about telling anyone anything about…" He shivered. "He said he'd kill me, too, Danny. I was – I am – so scared. What should I do? He's a crazy man, Danny. He would kill me without batting an eyelid."

"Were you aware of the other murders before they occurred, Hank?"

"Just Wood's, I swear. When he told us —"

"Us?" I interrupted.

"Yes, us. Reasoner and me. I didn't really believe he would do any of it. He was always just a, you know, just a quiet guy, a teacher, for God's sake. Who knew he would turn into a madman?"

"Why did he kill Reasoner if he was in on it?"

The pieces were falling in place, and Mann's testimony would be the damning evidence.

"Because Reasoner told him he wouldn't go along with it. Jenkins knew if he didn't get rid of him, he'd be caught.

It was when he killed Reasoner that I knew Jenkins was crazed. And I knew if I said anything, I'd be the next to die."

He broke down again, and this time I let him cry while I figured out the best way to use Mann's knowledge.

"Hank, you'll be safe as long as he doesn't think you'll share what you know about him. Don't worry about me – I won't tell anyone. Yet. But if I need you to fess up to put him away, you'll have to testify. Understand?"

It must have dawned on him what testifying would mean to him. "But wouldn't that mean...wouldn't that make me an exercise after the fact?"

"What's worse, Hank? Some possible jail time or certain death at the hands of Jenkins?" I hated to go all existential on him, but if Jenkins wouldn't confess while I was wired, Mann's testimony would be vital. Besides, it was impossible for me to summon up much sympathy for a man who could have prevented at least three murders by coming forth with information.

His body shook as if it had tremors. "All right, Danny. Whatever you say. If it comes to that, I have enough money to hire a good lawyer." He closed his eyes and croaked, "And Jenkins doesn't." He laughed and sobbed simultaneously. A minor Pyrrhic victory, all things considered.

"Just keep your composure if Jenkins comes around to check on you. If you don't, you won't have to worry about a lawyer. You'll be a dead man."

As he resumed his waterworks, it felt gratifying to twist the knife a little deeper. Helping to bring Jenkins down wasn't enough to absolve him entirely of his part in the brutal killings.

It was time to set my plan in action. Bogie would approve, I felt certain.

Though it was becoming obvious that maybe a film hero was insufficient defense against a real-life villain.

Chapter Eighty-four

A quick call to Barney, who, unlike Parker, was on board without need of convincing, was the last detail I needed to complete before meeting Parker.

Parker sat in the rear of the cafeteria and seemed deep in thought as I approached him.

"Can I spring for a cup of coffee? I hear this place rivals Starbucks," I joked, intentionally interrupting his reverie that, unless I missed my guess, was full of doubts and anxiety.

He looked up at me without smiling. His hair was mussed and bags were starting to form under his eyes.

"Parker, I want you to know how much I appreciate your putting your career on the line to help me. I wouldn't put you in this position if there were any other alternative, believe me."

He looked at me coldly, his non-expressive face in place.

"Danny, let's get one thing clear. I know what I'm doing. You aren't holding a gun to my head. I know Sloane well enough to know how stubborn he is. He will cling to his theory that Reasoner was responsible for the first three deaths and that Bobson was the victim of a hate crime till...

well, till forever. He'd rather let a killer go unpunished than accept that you might be right."

Even I hadn't considered Sloane that flawed, but Parker knew him better than I did, and I had no reason to doubt him. If his opinion was right, in my eyes, Sloane was almost as malevolent as Jenkins. He'd eventually get his comeuppance, if not during this investigation, then down the road. An out of control ego had no place in enforcing the law.

"So here's how it'll go down. In my car is a Kevlar vest for you. I'll meet you at your quarters in fifteen minutes and help you put it on so that it won't show under a sweater – you have a sweater here, I hope?"

I assured him I had one.

"And then I'll wire you. You'll have to show me the best place for me to conceal myself but still have a clear path to shoot him if necessary. Do you have a place in mind?"

"Yes, I do. I will arrange the few pieces of furniture so that I will stand in front of two chairs to deter him from sitting if he should want to do that. You can crouch behind the divider between that room and the kitchenette. In the unlikely event that he goes to the kitchenette and finds you… well, as you said, you know how to use your weapon. If I do my part, that won't happen, though."

His eyes looked upward at nothing in particular, as he seemed to be processing that part of my plan.

"That seems doable, Danny. I'll check for myself, of course. I do have actual experience, you know. If I think it can't be done in your quarters, we'll come up with Plan B."

"Works for me," I said, relieved that we were within an hour or two of hopefully lancing the boil that was Jenkins.

"Oh, and one more thing, Danny. If he gives up without a fight, I will not involve myself with the arrest process unless it's absolutely necessary. I can't officially be involved as an FBI agent without Sloane's approval, and we both know that would never happen. If I arrest him, it'll be my last collar as an FBI agent."

I had seen this one coming.

"Got you covered on that one, Parker. I already arranged for Sheriff Dixon to be concealed in the bedroom while all of this goes down. My little insurance policy. Figured an extra gun couldn't hurt. He can cuff him and deliver him to the Charlottesville police, and you won't have to be involved. You OK with that?"

He didn't hesitate.

"I don't think the sheriff is all that astute, Danny, but if he can keep my career in the FBI intact, he'll go up a few notches in my esteem. At the moment, he's my only option, so count him in."

Before I exited the cafeteria, I reminded Parker to leave a few minutes later and stop by his car to pick up the vest I hoped I would not need, then proceed to the Alumni House five minutes behind me. What was going through his mind, God only knew, but during my short walk, I rehearsed in my mind what I was going to say to Jenkins to entice him to my quarters.

How I baited the trap was the key to my survival and Jenkins's demise.

Chapter Eighty-five

In the five minutes I had before Parker would arrive, I hurriedly picked up scattered clothes and stowed dirty glasses and my one used dish in the sink before it occurred to me that Parker probably couldn't care less about my housekeeping. "Relax," I ordered myself.

As soon as he entered the tiny living room, Parker began assessing it for placement of both me and Jenkins, then moved into the kitchenette. Ducking below the room divider, he called out, "Am I totally out of sight, Danny? Can you hear me if I move?"

I answered "No" to both questions and waited for him to help me with the Kevlar vest and wire. His expert hands accomplished both in under ten minutes.

"Check yourself out in a mirror, Danny, and let me know if you think the vest and wire are totally undetectable. They look perfect to me."

I went into the bathroom and scrutinized my image in the mirror over the sink for any tell-tale bulges or bumps. Not a one. I looked possibly a few pounds heavier, though I doubted even my sister could notice that.

Returning to the living room, where Parker was arranging the two chairs on the windowless side of the room, I said, "Looks perfect to me. I do have to ask, though: Are you sure something so thin can stop a bullet at close range?"

"From experience I can vouch for its effectiveness. I have been shot several times, yet here I am." He smiled broadly. "Depending on the power of the weapon, it can knock you down, however, and you'll have the wind knocked out of you and sore ribs. Small price to pay for saving your life, don't you think?"

No need for me to answer that question, obviously. Still, I preferred not to test its effectiveness. My fervent hope was for Jenkins to give up without a struggle once he knew the game was up.

Parker set up the recorder that he laid on the floor beneath the sink and asked me to speak in a normal tone of voice to see if the wire was working. It was.

"OK, Parker, I'm off to confront Jenkins. I'll get back here as soon as possible after that. If all goes well, he should be here within an hour, maybe sooner if he decides to cancel class."

Parker scanned the place for what must have been the tenth time and looked me up and down once again to see if he had succeeded in doing his part of this operation. Then he pulled out his Glock 22 to check that for the tenth time, as well, and returned it to the black holster on his belt.

"Look, Danny, it's not too late for you to back out. I may be able to convince Sloane to consider bringing in Jenkins for interrogation."

"And then what? If he denies everything and there's no proof of his killings, he'll be free as a bird and cagier than ever." Ordinarily my irony meter would have registered and prompted me to add "no pun intended," but at the moment, irony seemed insignificant. "No, the only hope we have is for him to make a move against me with a recording and you and Gladstone to witness it."

I had no way of telling if he was more concerned for my safety or his career, or even if he was as adamant as I that justice be served, but I gave him the benefit of the doubt when he told me I was probably right.

"Wish me luck, Parker," I said as I headed to the door.

"The FBI doesn't believe in luck, Danny. We believe in preparation and perfect execution. God speed. I'll be waiting for you here."

As soon as I closed the door behind me, Barney advanced toward me.

"Everything ready?" he asked.

"Ready as we'll ever be, Gladstone. Go on in. Parker's already there and will show you where to hide yourself."

Oddly enough, I felt a sense of determined calm despite the surge of adrenaline, and I knew at that moment I was cut out for this kind of work.

If I survived.

Chapter Eighty-six

Hank Mann was placing books back into the stacks when I tapped him on the shoulder and whispered, "Hank, you have to find somewhere else to be for the rest of the day – for your safety. Unless I miss my guess, Jenkins will soon be looking for both of us with evil intent. Is there a place you can take refuge for a while?"

Mann's face lost its color. "You don't really think he'd try something in the libary, do you? I thought I'd be safe with people around."

I led him back to his checkout desk and told him as emphatically as I could without being overheard, "Make some sort of excuse to get rid of the students and leave immediately." He started to say something, but I cut him off. "Unless you want to end your days here, possibly in front of others, who you will also put in harm's way. Haven't you already done enough damage by not turning in Jenkins before he went on his killing spree?"

He visibly wilted. "You're right, of course. I know a place where he'd never think to look." Giving me his cell phone number, he pleaded, "Please call me when I can come out of hiding. Please."

I assured him that I would call him, though I knew there was a chance I might never be able to call anyone again.

Less than five minutes later, I was standing at the end of the hall where Jenkins's class was in session. Taking several deep breaths to calm myself, I approached his room. As usual his door was open, but this time I had no intention of listening to his discussion with his class.

I cleared my throat loudly to get his attention. When he saw me, he frowned.

"Is there something I can do for you, Mr. Wright? As you can see, I am busy teaching."

"I can come inside your classroom if you prefer, or you can step into the hall, Mr. Jenkins. What I have to say won't take long." I tried to keep my voice as expressionless as I could, and that was no small task with my heart beating so fast I thought it would burst.

It didn't take long for Jenkins to understand that it would be to his benefit to talk privately. He turned to the class and directed them to turn to a page of the textbook and continue reading silently for a minute, then walked briskly to where I stood waiting. Softly closing the door behind him, he said to me, "You're really pressing your luck, Mr. Wright. If you have more harassment in mind, I suggest you desist, or I will have to report you to Mr. Madison."

I paused several seconds before calmly saying, "Oh, I can save you the bother of that, Mr. Jenkins. I'll be reporting to Mr. Madison myself very soon. And to the FBI and the local law authority." I stopped speaking to let that sink in.

"More of your delusions, Mr. Wright? We both know you don't have a shred of evidence to connect me to any crime. If you try to impugn my good name, they'll laugh and I'll sue."

I smiled to annoy him.

"I doubt they'll laugh, and it will be hard for you to sue anyone from behind bars. You, see, Mr. Jenkins, I now have proof that you murdered four men."

He didn't flinch or bat an eyelash. I had to give it to him – he was unflappable.

"Proof, my ass, Mr. Wright. You have nothing. Now, if you'll excuse me, I have a class to teach."

He turned on his heels to leave.

"Does Mr. Mann's testimony qualify as proof, Mr. Jenkins?"

He stopped abruptly and swung around to say something but couldn't seem to find words. Finally, he regained his composure and said, "Who'd listen to that sot? They'd chalk it up to his alcoholic hallucinations."

"Yes, everyone knows Mr. Mann drinks too much, but his testimony, which I have on tape, is lucid and provides details that only the murderer and the FBI could have known. No, Mr. Jenkins, your killing spree stops now. As soon as I am finished here, I am going to send Mr. Mann into hiding where he's safe from you and get my recorded testimony to deliver to Mr. Madison and the Feds. In a couple hours, you'll be arrested and put where you belong – behind bars. And if you think that running will save your ass, forget about it. You can't outrun the resources of the FBI."

He stood rigidly, but I could feel his rage emanating from every pore of his body. If we weren't standing in the hallway with students coming and going from other classrooms, he'd undoubtedly have already attacked me.

"Oh, by the way, if you're thinking that if I had real proof, I would not be telling you this now instead of turning it in, you can quash that thought. The reason I am telling you this, Mr. Jenkins, is that I have a small hope – a very small hope, I admit – that you have a molecule of decency left in you and will turn yourself in before I turn in my evidence to spare Clanton Academy further embarrassment of a public arrest in front of students."

In a muted but intense voice, he said, "Fuck you and fuck Clanton Academy." Returning to his class, he slammed the door in my face, the only tell he'd shown.

But it was a big one. I expected a visit soon.

Chapter Eighty-seven

Walking briskly back to my guest quarters where this would end one way or another, my senses seemed to have intensified. In my previous excursions in and out of my quarters, I hadn't taken notice of the piles of crimson and gold leaves raked carefully by someone in maintenance and waiting to be bagged and disposed of. In the dying moments of autumn, the campus appeared ready for winter yet unaware of the uncertainty of its survival for the next autumn. I could relate to that.

Parker was busily adjusting his recording equipment while Barney paced nervously around the perimeter of the living room. He barely acknowledged my presence, concentrating on whatever was going through his mind. When he passed by the divider between the living room and the kitchenette where Parker was working, Parker bolted upright.

"Gladstone, go to the bathroom right now and wash off your cologne. If I can smell it from here, Jenkins would be able to smell it, too!" he said firmly.

Parker's voice broke Barney's intense concentration, and for a second, he looked confused. I couldn't help thinking that this assignment might be beyond Barney's pay grade. Parker, on the other hand, seemed in total control, and that was minimal reassurance that maybe I hadn't done the most boneheaded act of my life. I was counting on Parker to keep me alive.

Parker must have noticed that I was mulling things over more than I should be doing at this juncture.

"Danny, this is no time for thinking what-ifs. There's no room for even a hint of weakness if Jenkins decides to take the bait." Parker's voice was steady and encouraging, not reproachful.

"You're right, as usual," I said, and I was as sincere as I have even been before. "I think some deep breathing will calm me down."

Barney returned from the bathroom and, rubbing the back of his neck, said to Parker, "I scrubbed my neck till it was red, Parker." Realizing his unfortunate choice of words, he quickly added, "And no redneck jokes, please."

We all laughed, breaking the tension, in all probability most of it mine, that had filled my quarters. As I began some deep breathing exercises, Barney started fondling his Glock 22.

"Gladstone, would you mind stopping playing with that thing. I'm nervous as it is," I said.

Once again, a voice seemed to jar him from his thoughts. "Sorry about that, Danny," he apologized. "It's a nervous habit. It's got nothing to do with doubting my shooting skills, Danny. I been shooting since before I went to kindygarten. It's just that…well, I ain't never shot a person before."

Parker broke into our conversation.

"There's a good chance you won't today, either, Gladstone. If Jenkins has good sense, he will give up peacefully, and no one will have to fire a shot. And even if he goes stupid on us, I will get off a shot. Consider yourself an insurance policy."

I couldn't tell how being relegated to backup status settled with Barney, whose facial expression didn't change, but at the moment, I didn't care about anyone's ego being bruised.

Looking at my watch, I realized that Jenkins's class period was about to end.

"Classes are over in less than a minute, guys. Gladstone, it's time for you to take your position in the bedroom. Crack the door slightly. Parker, time for you to remain hidden. I'll take my position in front of the chairs. Jenkins could be here any minute."

Maintaining a calm demeanor, I assumed my position and waited.

Not for long, though.

Chapter Eighty-eight

Jenkins silently let himself into my quarters, his pistol pointed directly at me. Or should I say "slithered into my quarters"? His face was contorted into an ugly mask of loathing, and I was sure that I was the object of it.

"My dear Mr. Wright, please forgive my lapse of manners for not announcing myself by knocking." His measured voice seemed at odds with his venomous countenance.

I pretended to be startled.

"Oh, my God!" I blurted. "Put that gun away."

"I see your humor is intact. Too bad your brain isn't. Did you really think I would let an amateur like you take me down? The tape, Mr. Wright, give me the tape."

I threw up my hands shoulder high, palms facing him. Did I look convincingly panicked?

"What makes you think it's here, Mr. Jenkins? I already turned it in to the FBI and told Mr. Madison everything. If you know what's good for you, you'd better cut bait and get out of here as fast as you can."

That must have amused him greatly. After his laughter subsided, he said soberly, "I gave you more credit than you deserve, Mr. Wright. You're dumb as a fence post. I passed Mr. Madison and Agent Sloane on my way here, and they both greeted me like rain in a desert. No, Mr. Wright, you gave that tape to no one. I want it *now*."

I blinked several times as if I were considering my options. Rush him? I knew before he came here that, that would be foolish. Give him a fake tape? He was too smart to accept it without listening to it. These options I had eliminated hours earlier.

"If I give it to you, what will I get in return, a bullet?"

"Think, Mr. Wright, think. If you *don't* give me the tape, I'll shoot you right now and find it myself. If you do give it to me, who knows, maybe I'll just tie you up and depart for parts unknown? The odds of the latter must seem better than immediate death, don't you agree?"

I paused as I had rehearsed. This was going exactly as I had imagined it would.

Sighing, I said, "I guess I overestimated my crime-solving skills and underestimated your cunning, Mr. Jenkins."

He smiled smugly. "I hope that doesn't surprise you, Mr. Wright. You haven't exactly acquitted yourself like…damn, I can't recall even a single competent sleuth. The point is that you are a bumbling fool, and if you don't give me that tape immediately, you will pay dearly for your meddlesome ineptitude." His face hardened, and I noticed his trigger finger was twitching.

I tried to produce a few tears or at least a welling up of my eyes, but crying was not in my nature, and I never was good at acting.

Instead I slumped as if in defeat. My body language had better be convincing.

"OK, Mr. Jenkins, you win. I'll get the tape. I know now I was in way over my head. Do you think you would…"

I purposely stopped myself from finishing my sentence, hoping he'd want to hear it finished.

He did. "Think I would what, Mr. Wright?"

"I understand I'm in no position to ask anything of you except to please spare my life, Mr. Jenkins, but I just have to know why you killed Wood, Reasoner, and Thomason? I get it that Bobson did you wrong, but what did those other people do to deserve to die?"

"You mean Mann didn't fill you in on that? Not surprising. He can barely remember his own name these days." He looked hard at me for several seconds. "Guess there's no harm in filling in the gaps, Mr. Wright. I am a teacher after all." He laughed lustily at his idea of humor.

"About a month ago I overheard Bobson talking with his corrupt business partner. The bastard was actually whining about having to find new suckers because they had had spent every cent of the money that other Clanton teachers and I had entrusted to them. I knew at that precise moment that I would kill him for destroying my life. I didn't know how at the time, but I knew if it was the last thing I ever did, he'd pay with his life."

I listened intently, hoping that the wire was picking up every word.

"I shared my discovery with Reasoner and Mann because I knew that they had also invested with Bobson. It became apparent within minutes, however, that neither of them would be of much help to destroy Bobson. I did manage to convince Reasoner to devise a belly bomb to kill Wood, but after that, he balked and became a threat to me because he knew too much. Mann is a wimp, and I made my only miscue in not eliminating him, thinking he was too much of a coward to betray me."

"But why did you kill Wood and Thomason? They weren't any danger to you."

"I needed to deflect any link that might lead to me after Bobson, Mr. Wright. Because I wanted the authorities to think there was a serial killer at work, I needed a couple sacrifices. Why Wood? Why not, Mr. Wright? As you certainly realize, he was a despicable human being. Did you see even one person who was upset in the least by his death?"

Once he decided to talk, there was no stopping him. All I needed was to keep the flow coming.

"Choosing Wood I can understand on some level, Mr. Jenkins, but Mr. Thomason? He was a decent, good man. Why him?"

Without so much as a glimmer of remorse, Jenkins continued. "Thomason never did anything to harm me or anyone else that I know of. It was for that reason I chose him. A psychopathic serial killer doesn't select his victims logically, and I knew that he was so unlike Wood that the authorities would see no link between them. As for Reasoner, I thought staging his suicide was a stroke of genius, giving me time and a clear path to get Bobson."

He hesitated, and I wanted him to add more details. "How did you manage the Bobson killing? He's twice your size."

"He may have been bigger than me, Mr. Wright, but squeezed into a tight dress, he was ironically trapped in a device of his choosing. When I came upon him dressed as a woman lip syncing her song…well, it was downright providential. I could kill him and ensure he'd be remembered only as a pitiful loser. Delicious."

He frowned.

"Do you know how pissed off I was when the FBI chose not to reveal what he was doing when he died? I had even hoped for photos in the media. I didn't fret too much, though, Mr. Wright, because as my plan unfolded, I learned something about myself: I enjoy watching people die at my hands. Yes, I suppose that makes me a psychopath, and I have no problem with that. So, you see, Mr. Wright, killing you would be not only easy for me but also enjoyable. Time for our pleasant conversation to end. Get me the tape!"

Before I could answer, Parker must have lost his balance and, in trying to steady himself, made enough noise that Jenkins wheeled around facing the kitchenette. "Whoever is there, you'd better —"

Barney's first shot went through Jenkins's heart, and before Jenkins's body dropped to the floor, a second pierced his neck.

And just like that, the nightmare was over.

Chapter Eighty-nine

Jenkins lay at my feet, blood seeping out of his chest and neck. I stared at his lifeless body, unable to speak or breathe, or so it seemed. Voices that seemed vague and distant were calling my name.

"Danny, are you all right? Speak to me, buddy," said Barney.

"Snap out of it, Danny," said Parker. "We have work to do before I slip away from here."

"What do you think, Parker – is he in shock? What should we do?" Barney said to Parker.

"Let's wait a minute to see if he responds. In the meantime let me show you how the taping machine works, and I need to fill you in on how to wire someone and stuff. You never know if someone will ask you for details. We don't have much time before this has to be called in."

The voices gradually became focused, and I moved my attention from Jenkins to Barney and Parker in the kitchenette. "Hey, guys, let me in on what you're doing over there," I said weakly, trying to blot out of my mind what had just happened long enough for me to collect my wits and proceed with my plan.

"C'mon over here, Danny. I was just showing Gladstone how the wire and tape machine work," Parker said to me.

I involuntarily pawed at the wire and Kevlar vest and started to remove them. "Where should I put these?" I asked Parker.

"Whoa, hold on! Don't remove them. Remember, you need to be wearing them when Sloane and company, including me, arrive here after you make the necessary calls. Give me five minutes after we're done here for me to join Sloane and the others. Do *not* touch or move the body." He turned to Barney. "Gladstone, do you have any more questions about how *you* set this up?"

Barney was steady and calm, seemingly unaffected by his having just drilled Jenkins with two deadly shots. If he hadn't, maybe both Parker and I wouldn't be alive.

"Piece of cake, buddy. Bring on the Feds!" he said to Parker. "No offense, buddy. You're one of the good guys. Gotta admit, though, that I am really looking forward to seeing that prick Sloane's face when he realizes that he was bested by Danny and me."

Parker smiled. "No offense taken, Gladstone. I owe you big time. I had no idea you are such a marksman, but I sure do now."

"Make that two of us, Gladstone," I added.

Barney's smile could light up a room. Puffing out his bony chest, he said, "I know I ain't the biggest guy to come down the pike – maybe not the smartest, neither – and I ain't never investigated nothing like this before, but one thing I know I can do, and that's shoot. I can pick off a mosquito coming at me." He laughed at his hyperbole.

"When I saw that Jenkins was gonna shoot Danny, and then he turned to fire at you…well, no way in hell I was gonna let him shoot my two buddies." That was as close to sentimentality as I had heard at this school in over a month.

An awkward silence ensued for long seconds. "Well, Gladstone, I hope you realize that both of us are in your debt," Parker said. "But time for gratitude later. I have to get out of here. Give me at least five minutes and call this number."

He handed me what I assumed was Sloane's cell phone number and exited my quarters, leaving Barney and me to congratulate ourselves on a job well done.

Waiting an extra couple minutes for good measure, I made the most gratifying phone call I had ever made.

Chapter Ninety

The first to arrive was Sloane, with three Feds, including Parker, in tow, and his scowl was enough to tell me he wasn't pleased by the results of my plan.

"Come on in, Mr. Sloane. Mr. Dixon and I haven't touched anything," I said in my most serious tone of voice.

Sloane surveyed the small quarters in seconds, then turned his attention to the corpse in the middle of the living room.

"I see two entry wounds. Who did the shooting? Just two shots fired?"

Barney answered that he shot him before Jenkins had a chance to shoot at me, and two shots were all that were necessary.

"Let's start at the beginning, shall we?" Sloane said testily as Parker and two other Feds examined the living room and kitchenette. "Why was Jenkins here, armed? And why are you wired and wearing a vest, Wright?"

I resisted the urge to tell him that *he* was the reason that Jenkins was here and why I was wired and wearing a vest. Instead, I relayed the details of my plan and how I had come to suspect Jenkins even if Sloane didn't.

Snorting, he then turned to Barney and said, "And just how did you come to be here, Dixon? I thought I made myself clear when I told you that this was FBI business, not yours."

Sloane's irritation at being sidestepped didn't deter Barney. "Well, you see. Mr. Sloane, I didn't intend to get involved, but when Mr. Wright here told me what he had said to Mr. Jenkins, I knew sure as I'm standing here that Jenkins would come after him. No offense, Mr. Sloane, but your track record here in preventing murders ain't been all that good, and I decided that with no time to find you before Jenkins found him, I needed to protect him. So I wired him up and recorded the conversation so as to have some evidence. But I slipped a bit hiding in the kitchen, and Jenkins heard me and turned to shoot me first. Well, I don't mind saying, Mr. Sloane, if anyone's gonna shoot at me, he'd better be quick cuz I ain't waiting to get plugged. I dropped him like a bad habit in two seconds."

"And am I supposed to take your word for that?" said Sloane.

"No, sir. I suggest you listen to the conversation I recorded. That oughta make things good and clear."

From the kitchenette, Parker announced, "Hey, Sloane, the tape's here, all right." He turned it on, and I relished watching Sloane's scowl dissolve into a slow burn.

Within fifteen minutes, Jenkins's body and Sloane and his fellow Feds were leaving the quarters, headed to their typical black SUVs to retreat to DC. Sloane said nothing to either Barney or me on his way out, but Parker did. "Of course you'll have statements to sign and so on. I'll stick around and get them, OK, Sloane?" Sloane didn't bothered answering.

As soon as the SUVs were out of sight, the three of us in unison breathed sighs of relief. Barney and I gave Parker our rehearsed version of the attempt on my life with the occasional editing by Parker.

"This one is cut and dry, men," Parker said as he closed his briefcase. "You'll get all the credit for solving four murders, and my career will be intact. When I leave here, I am going to the administration building to call the Charlottesville police to alert them because I am pretty sure Sloane hasn't. I'll meet them there, and of course you two need to hang around campus to answer any questions they might have after reading my report."

I erroneously thought he was done speaking and asked Barney if he wanted to grab a cup of coffee with me. Before he could answer, Parker continued.

"You realize, I'm sure, that Sloane will never forgive you for upstaging him, but somehow I don't think that'll bother you. The guy's an arrogant asshole who could be a decent investigatory agent but never will be because his ego always gets in the way. Someday I'd like to team up with agents without the bullshit baggage – like you."

He shook our hands and departed. Barney said he'd meet me at the cafeteria after he called in to his office, and he, too, left. I took a long, hard look around at my now empty quarters and felt better about myself than I had ever felt before.

It was now time to see H. Michael and Rex with good news for a change.

Chapter Ninety-one

Amos was busy cleaning Rex's dorm room when I arrived, and as much as I hated to interrupt what was probably an annual event, if mess and dirt accumulated at the same rate as they did at my place, I wanted to share the good news.

"What's the occasion, Amos? Isn't Rex still at Coach Rotherwood's house?" I said, looking around for the usual piles of clothes and debris.

He must not have detected the surprise in my voice and continued frantically cleaning. "I am cleaning his room before his mom arrives next week to take us to his house. I'm spending the Thanksgiving break with them," Amos said while throwing dirty socks and underwear under Rex's bed.

"Hmmm, aren't you a bit premature?" I said. "You think this place will stay clean for a week?"

"It will because he'll be at Coach's house," Amos replied.

I tapped him on the shoulder to stop his frenetic housecleaning mission. "That's why I came here, Amos. I hoped to find him getting books or a change of clothes to tell Rex he can return to his room now."

That finally stopped his cleaning. "Huh?" For a smart kid, his verbal skills occasionally lapsed into monosyllables.

"Long story, Amos. Do me a favor and find Rex and tell him he no longer has anything to fear. I will be busy for the next hour or so, but if he can give me a call on the cell phone he doesn't have, I'll fill him in." He shot me a puzzled look. "I'll fill you in later, too, of course. Good job you're doing, by the way. If you hire out, my place could use a good cleaning, too."

When he started to reply, I quickly cut him off. "Just kidding, Amos. Later."

'I hope H. Michael is in. This news is too good to wait,' I thought as I left Rex's almost unrecognizable room and headed to the administration building.

In the best mood I had been in for months, I stopped briefly to bother Miss Foss. She must know when I am nearby by the smell of my cologne or something because she didn't look up as I hovered over her.

"Typing away as usual, Miss Foss. You are a real workhorse," I said, feigning sincerity. Unlike Jenkins, she didn't take the bait.

"I'll spare you the futile effort of trying to think of a new insult, Mr. Wright. You need to see Mr. Madison, right? Go on in. Ruin his day instead of mine," she said drily, her eyes never leaving the keyboard enduring its daily pounding.

Her not providing me an opportunity to rattle her cage was a minor defeat on an otherwise glorious day.

H. Michael took a page out of Miss Foss's book and didn't look up from his computer when I entered his office. "Ever heard of knocking, Mr. Wright? It's been a social convention for some time now," he said.

Given all the stress he had been dealing with, I couldn't blame him for being testy.

"I have good news you might want to hear, Mr. Madison," I said.

His attention changed from his computer screen to me. "That's something I haven't heard in weeks. What is it?"

I held a smile for a few seconds before answering. "Clanton Academy no longer houses a murderer, Mr. Madison. Jenkins is dead. His body is being transported as I speak to DC."

He looked stunned. "Say that again, Mr. Wright. Jenkins?"

I couldn't let pass the opportunity to rub it in that I had been right all along and relayed the events without leaving out a single detail. He absorbed my report quietly, his face remaining expressionless.

"A thank-you would seem to be in order, Mr. Madison," I said. Getting no response, I said, "And maybe even an apology for doubting me."

Neither was forthcoming. H. Michael ignored my presence and called Miss Foss. "Miss Foss, call all local newspapers and television stations and tell them we are holding a press conference here tomorrow morning at ten to announce the apprehension of the murderer that terrorized Clanton Academy."

He turned his attention back to his computer and rapidly began typing and talking at the same time. "Well, Mr. Wright, why are still here? I have work to do. Be here at 9:55 sharp. And try to wear a decent coat and tie for a change. You and I and your cohort Mr. Dixon will answer their questions, though I think you'll agree that it would be best if Mr. Dixon said as little as possible."

What a prince he was.

His ingratitude was boundless.

Chapter Ninety-two

Flanked by H. Michael to my left and Barney to my right, I fidgeted nervously, adjusting and readjusting my tie repeatedly while waiting for the first press conference I had ever participated in to begin. Or even attended, if truth be told.

At ten o'clock sharp, H. Michael read a brief statement saying that the "Clanton Assassin," as the media had dubbed him for several weeks, had been killed by Sheriff Dixon yesterday while he, Mr. Rollie Jenkins, was attempting to murder Mr. Wright, an alumnus of Clanton Academy who had been leading the investigation of recent murders on campus. He then announced that we were open to questions. I wasn't prepared for the onslaught of questions bombarding us.

Panicking, I looked at Barney, who shrugged his shoulders and said nothing, then at H. Michael, who not surprisingly maintained his composure.

"Ladies and gentlemen," he addressed the noisy throng. "Please, one question at a time. And please designate whom you want to address. We will gladly answer any of your questions for the next fifteen minutes."

The news anchor from the NBC television station fired the first one. "Mr. Wright, how did you come to suspect Mr. Jenkins? Was he a former teacher of yours? Was he a long-time employee here?"

I answered him succinctly and began to relax as I fielded several more questions from other media representatives. I was getting the hang of it and started to enjoy my fifteen minutes of fame. Barney, on the other hand, seemed unwilling to say anything more than "I defer to Mr. Wright."

Finally, a reporter from a county journal read by at most three or four hundred local citizens, directed a question to H. Michael.

"Mr. Madison, I am sure you're relieved now that your school and the rest of us in the county are safe from that evil man. Tell us how you figured in apprehending him."

'This should be interesting,' I thought.

"It goes without saying that Clanton Academy has much to be thankful for this Thanksgiving. The Lord has been with us throughout this trial." He shared his most pious smile with them.

"I'm sure He was, Mr. Madison," she said, "but what part did *you* play in his capture?"

H. Michael patted me on my shoulder. "The only part I played was giving this fine young man my complete confidence to pursue the evil infecting my beloved school. My faith in him never wavered. When the FBI doubted him, I stood firmly behind him. In these three terrible weeks, I have to come to look upon him as a son who came to my rescue when I most needed him." Without turning to see him, I knew he had applied his pious humble-face that he could summon at will.

Cameras directed at me, I knew better than to cringe. I smiled blandly.

After answering more questions and directing my praise to Barney's marksmanship and astuteness while minimizing the FBI's role in bringing the murderer to his deserved fate, I took advantage of a brief lull in the questioning to make my unsolicited announcement.

"Most likely none of you know that I am a detective by profession." Several reporters began to address me. I cut them off and proceeded. "But this was the first experience I had in dealing with crimes of this magnitude. Working with the FBI and Sheriff Dixon, I surprised myself by calling on my instincts that ended with this successful resolution. It was an epiphany of sorts, and I realize I had found my true calling. With Sheriff Dixon's urging, I have closed my office in Virginia Beach and am opening shop in Charlottesville. Let your readers and viewers know that I am available as of a week from now to take on cases of any type."

Shameless self-hype, I knew, but I readily forgave myself.

Chapter Ninety-three

Rex was receptive to both the good news about Jenkins's demise and my forthcoming move to Charlottesville. "That's great, Uncle Danny. I'll be there the next four years, and we can chill together."

While I admired his unswerving and possibly unfounded confidence that UVA would accept him, I was only guardedly optimistic about his chances. Still, I didn't want to say anything to dampen his good spirits. He looked a few pounds thinner than he had three weeks ago, but maybe that had less to do with dealing with stress and more to do with the cafeteria fare, which did seem worse than usual, if that was possible.

"When should you hear from UVA, Rex? You applied for early action, right?"

"Yes, I did. I should hear by the end of January. When are you moving to Charlottesville? Have you found an apartment or house? Office?"

"I need to close my office in Virginia Beach first, probably this coming week. Your mom has suggested I stay with her and you over Thanksgiving Break while I look around for an apartment and an office. I have an area of town in mind. You and Amos are welcome to join me in the search if you like. Could give you a chance to familiarize yourself with more of the area."

The thought occurred to me that it would more than a little awkward if only one of them was accepted by UVA, but I wasn't about to give voice to that thought, either.

"I would like that, and I'm pretty sure Amos would, too. Oh, by the way, I haven't had a chance to tell you before now, but I think that drugs are back on campus again. And I am positive that Witt, Jensen, and Van Verdenburg are moving them."

In my elation over taking down Jenkins, I had almost forgotten about the drugs. In truth, I was wondering if I even should get involved. If a case came my way in Charlottesville within the next two weeks, I would accept that and cut my financial arrangement with H. Michael.

I couldn't let on to Rex that I was less interested in dismantling a drug operation, however. After all, I had recruited him and Amos to help me.

"Why do you think those three are guilty, Rex? Have you seen something I should know about?"

He looked me squarely in the eye and said, "You know how you went with your instincts about Mr. Jenkins? Well, I am doing the same with those three. It all adds up. The past couple days I have seen them going in and out of five rooms of guys who often seem stoned, and they're always together, even when they should be in different classes. If they're not dealing, I will eat my shirt, Uncle Danny."

I knew immediately how important it was for me to be supportive of him, having been doubted by the FBI and H. Michael myself the past couple weeks.

"I think your instincts are valid," I said. "Have you seen them hanging around any adults here? They can't be doing this on their own."

"Nope, haven't tailed them or anything like that."

"And make sure you don't," I said. "Let me see what I can dig up. I have to go now, but make sure you call me if you see anything suspicious. You have been indispensable eyes and ears for me, Rex."

He thanked me, put on a clean sweatshirt, and headed to his English class, which I assumed was being taught by a substitute teacher or someone recruited from the ranks of idle administrators. I once more admired his orderly room and headed to the academic office to check on the progress of Rex's college admissions.

Before I reached the office of the academic dean, I was greeted overly enthusiastically by Becky Clarkson. Even though her cleavage was not on display as usual, her shirt was so clinging and tight that it was instantly noticeable that she wore no bra. Every step she took produced provocative motion, and hard as I tried, I couldn't not take notice.

She raised her eyebrows and said flirtatiously, "Well, my, my, if it isn't the hero of Clanton Academy in the flesh. And such attractive flesh."

I hoped I wasn't blushing. How could I take on a deranged murderer and be unsettled by Becky Clarkson?

"You're too kind, Mrs. Clarkson," I said, avoiding eye contact. "The reason I'm here is that I need to see the dean about my nephew's college admission process. Is he in?"

Whether it was for effect or she was trying to decide what to say, I couldn't tell. All I knew was that I was embarrassed as she eyed me up and down before finally saying, "I'm afraid he's in conference and won't be back for at least an hour or two, Danny. But I can help you. Let's go to my office, and I'll bring up his file."

I reluctantly followed her to her office, forcing myself not to watch her undulate down the hallway.

"Sit down, Danny," she said, pointing at the one chair across from hers behind the keyhole desk. "This may take a few minutes. Make yourself comfortable and take off that sports coat."

I was feeling a bit overheated, though not because the room was too hot, and handed over my wrinkled, navy blue all-purpose coat that she carefully hung on a hook on the inside of the door.

In four or five minutes, she accessed his files and relayed that everything was in order, all letters of recommendation had been submitted, his transcript sent, and his essays written and included in the packet sent from the guidance office.

"Thanks, Mrs. Clarkson," I said getting up from my seat.

"Call me Becky, remember?" she purred and started to approach me.

I had to leave before it got even more heated up. "Sorry, gotta run," I blurted.

Bolting out of her office, I almost ran into Addison D. Witt who was standing outside the open door.

"Excuse me," I mumbled and beat a hasty retreat toward the exit.

Once outside, I breathed the crisp air deeply and started toward my quarters when I realized I had left my sport coat in her office. No way I was going back there now, though. It could wait.

I already knew that Addison D. Witt was one of Becky Clarkson's boy toys. Since Rex was convinced that Witt was dealing drugs, could it be possible that she had other business with him as well?

Chapter Ninety-four

After calling Katherine to update her on the status of Rex's application and Julia to alert her of my relocation to Charlottesville, I wandered around the campus for a few hours. Gray, almost desolate with leafless trees and soggy ground from recent showers, it was uninviting, and I couldn't prevent myself from pondering its future. Potential patrons would probably consider Jenkins's murder spree as a one-and-done, an aberration in an otherwise unblemished existence, but what effect would more sensational headlines about drug trafficking have on their thinking? Adverse, at best, I concluded. If there was a way to eliminate drugs on campus without the media swooping in like jackals, I hadn't thought of it.

By seven o'clock, the campus was dark and free of activity, a good time to sneak up to Becky Clarkson's office to retrieve my sport coat. The hallway on which her office was located was deserted, and with not even ambient light to aid my vision, I had to run my hand against the right hand wall to help me find the door I hoped would be unlocked. Counting four doors down, I arrived at her office and turned the door knob. It was unlocked.

I let myself in, and without turning on the light, I found my coat hanging on the hook. I snatched it and started to leave the office when I heard muffled voices and laughing. I quickly ducked back inside her office, my heart beating faster by the second, when I realized the voices belonged to Becky Clarkson and H. Michael.

'Damn,' I thought, frantically thinking of a possible excuse for my being in her dark office. There was none. Only one option came to mind: Hide under her desk and pray that she wouldn't stick around or need to use her computer.

Scrunched up in the small space, I tried not to gasp when I heard them enter the office.

"You may release me now, Samson. I have never been carried down the hall before. You are so powerful," she said breathlessly.

The thud above me verified that he had plopped her on her desk. The next sounds I heard were zippers and rustling of clothing.

"Oh, Master Mikey. What are you doing?" she cooed. "Have I been a naughty nurse?"

H. Michael replied hoarsely, "You have been very naughty, bitch, and now you must pay."

"Please be gentle, Master. I promise I'll be good." There was a brief pause. "Oh, my, Master, you are too big! You will hurt me," she said.

"That's what you deserve, Naughty Nurse! Now shut up and be prepared to be punished as you never have been before."

Possibly the most pitiful sex talk I had ever heard. I willed myself not to gag.

After less than two minutes of thumps and exaggerated moaning by Becky Clarkson, it was over. Two minutes of my life I'd rather forget.

More rustling of clothes and zippers accompanied by H. Michael's catching his breath broke the silence.

"As always, Mikey, you were the champ," Becky spoke softly. I could envision her looking up coquettishly at H. Michael.

"You bring out the best in me, Becky. Same time for Happy Hour tomorrow evening, OK?" he said in his normal voice. "Wear your leather skirt."

"Whatever you say, Mikey," she said. "Now hurry along. I need to make a quick phone call and get home."

A second after I heard the door close, Becky's voice replaced the silence. The number she called must have been on speed dial, as I heard no sound prior to her saying, "Confirming tomorrow's shipment. I won't be there to meet you. Will send my three carriers to pick up the order. 6:00 sharp behind the usual spot in the parking area by the cafeteria. The tall carrier will have the cash." A pause. "Yes, all twenties. If you spot anyone, leave immediately, and we'll do it the following night. Any questions?" Another pause. "Good. Be prompt and be smart."

The room became dark again and the door closed softly.

If I had been standing and heard that conversation, I could have been knocked over by a puff of smoke.

Becky Clarkson was the leader of the drug operation on campus.

Chapter Ninety-five

It wasn't entirely clear to me if my strategy was ethically pure, but, determined to spare Clanton Academy any more injurious headlines, I put my latest plan in motion. My first call to Barney was quick – he was instantly on board and had no qualms about coercing the three students to aid us in exchange for not being arrested. If the simple plan succeeded, Witt, Jensen, and Van Verdenburg would withdraw from Clanton Academy, leaving behind written confessions as guarantees that they'd keep their mouths shut about their part in drug trafficking.

My next call was to Parker, repayment for the debt I owed him.

"Parker, I don't have a lot of time to fill you in on details, but I can give you drug dealers for your own collar – no sharing of credit with Sloane or anyone else. Interested?"

He was very interested. Who wouldn't be? This could be the break he needed to get free of Sloane and advance in the ranks of the FBI.

"I'll be at your quarters in three hours, Danny. Thanks for looking out for me."

Now all that remained was to wait impatiently for six hours or keep busy. I opted for the latter, and walked to the dorm to fill in Rex and Amos of my plan. They wanted to be there for the arrest, but I nixed that immediately. Their safety was more important than what they called their desire to help but which really was more like thrill seeking.

I strolled around campus, avoiding any contact with Becky Clarkson or H. Michael. As much as I dreaded seeing him, I did need to see Hank Mann one more time, and stopped by the library.

He was busy helping students who needed help finding sources about the Electoral College for their U.S. Government class, I assumed.

"Ooh," he said in his effeminate voice. "You must be in Mr. Harland's class. His students are always asking for information on the electrical college at this time of year."

Oblivious to the rolling of eyes that followed his latest malapropism, he directed them to computer stations and told them which database to search. He then noticed that I was standing by the checkout desk and frowned.

I motioned for him to join me, and when he was near enough to me that he could hear me whisper, I told him, "Hank, this isn't open to discussion. Tomorrow you are going to see Mr. Madison and resign immediately. Make up any excuse you want – death in the family, need to look after your brother, whatever." When he pursed his lips and started to object, I cut him off. "As I said, Hank, this is a done deal. I can easily inform the FBI of your connection with Jenkins. Is that what you want?"

Clearly it wasn't, and he agreed reluctantly. I had zero sympathy for him. He had plenty of money – more than enough to drink himself to death – and he had no business being a part of the school he had helped put in its current precarious condition.

With those two loose ends tied up, I returned to my quarters to pace the floors for another few hours.

Chapter Ninety-six

Parker somehow managed to be prompt despite dealing with the usual traffic glut in Northern Virginia. Eschewing his usual dark suit, he was dressed for action in black corduroy pants and a gray hoodie. Unfortunately I had few choices from my scant wardrobe and wore what was available, polyester navy blue slacks and my ratty UVA sweatshirt. I doubted Parker cared a whit about my ensemble.

"OK, Danny, time to fill me in on what's going down," he said, his jaw firm, a look of calm determination on his face that bolstered my confidence.

I was explaining the logistics just as Barney arrived in uniform, and I repeated myself for his benefit. An hour later, Barney headed to the dorm to round up the three soon-to-be accomplices in the dismantling of the drug ring, and Parker and I headed to the cafeteria parking lot to position ourselves behind a row of large boxwoods that served as a wall between the parking lot and the access road leading to it. From our position, we would have an unobstructed view and were close enough to hear any dialog.

Forty minutes later, Barney arrived with the nervous accomplices. He again instructed them what to say and do and pointed out ominously that we would be only ten feet away. He stroked his gun for emphasis. They shuffled in place and mumbled; Barney joined us and was short enough that he didn't have to stoop as we did. We remained silent for another ten minutes before a Lexus SUV glided almost silently into the parking lot and stopped ten feet from the three boys.

Three bulky men dressed in dark hoodies climbed out of the SUV and approached the three boys. "No time for small talk, guys." Pointing at Witt who was holding a large red duffel bag, he asked, "Is that the money?"

Witt nodded that it was and tossed the bag at the feet of the thug who had addressed him.

"Where's the stuff?" Witt said tremulously.

The other two drug dealers went back to the SUV. Each grabbed a large bundle that they carried back to the thug who stood silently staring at the three nervous boys.

"I ain't going to count this money right now. If it's short, I know where to find you, and you don't want that."

"It's all there," squeaked Witt. "The Boss don't ever make mistakes."

As Barney had instructed, the boys picked up the bundles of drugs and walked toward where we were hidden. As soon as they were behind the boxwoods, both Parker and Barney exploded from behind their cover, guns out.

"Freeze!" Parker barked. "Make a move and you're dead."

The thugs hesitated for less than a couple seconds before raising their hands.

Parker cuffed them while Barney grabbed the duffle with the drug money. He called out to the three boys, "OK, fellas, you can come out now."

As they walked uncertainly toward Barney, the thug who appeared to be the leader shouted, "You just made the biggest mistake of your life. I'll hunt you down no matter what hole you crawl in."

The boys couldn't summon words, but Parker easily could.

"Highly doubtful, scumbags. You'll be locked up till they're on social security."

Amidst their curses, I joined them and asked Parker if he needed me to stick around and told Barney to take the three shaking boys away.

When Barney herded them toward the sidewalk to take them back to his police car, Parker said, "No problem, Danny. I got everything covered. I'm taking them to DC right away." Turning toward the thug who was the driver, he demanded the keys to the Lexus and instructed me to move it somewhere till he came back the next day. As I turned to leave, he asked, "Where are you headed?"

"I have a date with Mary Astor," I said and didn't bother to look back to see if he any idea what I was talking about. It didn't matter. Bogie and I knew what I meant.

Chapter Ninety-seven

The administration building had only two offices with lights on – H. Michael's and Becky Clarkson's. I needed to catch my breath after sprinting to get there before their scheduled liaison. Then I quietly padded down the hall to Becky Clarkson's office. She was sitting at her desk, filing her perfect nails.

Closing the door quietly behind me, I took three steps to her desk and said nothing when she looked up at me with questioning eyes. Tugging her leather bustier to sit on her hips as she stood, she said, "Danny, what a pleasant surprise. But I'm afraid I have a previous —"

"It's over," I said soberly. "The game's done. Kaput. You're finished."

Her face flushed, but only briefly. Walking up to me from around her desk, she said, "Whatever do you mean? Don't talk in riddles, Danny."

I stared her down till she began fidgeting.

"The sheriff has your three stooges in custody, and the Feds are on their way to DC with your drug dealing pals in handcuffs."

For almost a minute she said nothing and stood motionless, staring into space. Suddenly she burst into tears and grabbed my hoodie, pulling me toward her.

Shaking me desperately, she sobbed, "Danny, what are you saying? I don't know anything about drugs. You have to believe me. You know you're special to me, I love you. Stop scaring me."

Despite the tears streaming down her face, she looked as gorgeous as ever. The thought crossed my mind that those tears were as calculated as her batted eyelashes, her coy upturned looks, her provocative walk whenever she was aware a man was watching her. Her body was a weapon, and I was having none of it this time. I pushed her back to the edge of her desk.

"Save the sob story for someone who cares, Becky. You're going down."

She grabbed my hoodie again. "Danny, Danny, oh Danny,' she cried. "Don't do this! I have money. Lots of money. We can go away together. You'll never have to —"

I shoved her back harder than before, and she grabbed the front of the desk to steady herself.

"I won't play the sap for you. You're going over for it," I said, channeling Bogie.

Her tears stopped as suddenly as they began.

"Now what? The police?"

"Becky, I'm going to give you a break you don't deserve. If you cooperate."

"Anything, Danny, I'll do anything!" she said almost in hysterics.

"Pull yourself together, Becky. Here's what you're going to do. In your own handwriting you will now write a detailed account of the drug operation, naming names. Not just the students but also the suppliers."

"I don't know the suppliers' names, Danny. I swear. They don't know mine either. All I know is a phone number."

"That's good enough. Include that in your report. And make it fast before you know who comes looking for you."

She wrote fast, and as soon as she signed it, I snatched it from her trembling hands, folded it in half, and stuffed it into my back pocket.

"That's a good girl, Becky. This will never see the light of day under one condition: You leave here as soon as you can pack your clothes and go as far away from here as possible. One word of this, and the Feds will have this confession, and they *will* find you. Make no mistake about that. Understood?"

She shook her head up and down so vigorously that I thought she'd get whiplash.

She tried ineffectually to wipe her wet face with her bare arm. "But what about him?" she said, nodding her head toward H. Michael's office.

"Leave him to me, Becky. Now get out of here," I said coldly.

For the first time since I met her, I didn't admire the view as she walked away. By the time she was out of the office, I was on my way to see H. Michael to finish the last part of my plan.

Chapter Ninety-eight

I had long believed that those who assuage ennui – a self-imposed affliction, in my opinion – with excesses of alcohol, drugs, or promiscuity are little different from those who look to religious zeal as a cure. Till very recently I had assumed that H. Michael embraced his ersatz religious fervor to serve his quest for power, but after learning – in a most distasteful way – of his ongoing tryst with Becky Clarkson, I wondered if maybe he was filling some sort of void as well. Whatever the reasons for his false piety, he was going to abandon it or observe it elsewhere. The future of Clanton Academy rested on the ability of whoever held the office of school head.

I didn't bother knocking and let myself into H. Michael's office. Expecting Becky Clarkson, when he looked up from his computer, his leer was replaced by a guttural noise. "What are *you* doing here, Mr. Wright? I have important business to attend to. Leave now and come back tomorrow morning. I'll let Miss Foss know I'm expecting you," he growled, making little effort to disguise his displeasure in seeing me instead of Becky Clarkson.

Maybe he sensed that something was about to happen that he wouldn't like, or maybe he had elevated his opinion of my abilities after exposing Jenkins. In either case, he seemed to reconsider his tone and added, "If you promise to make it quick, tell me what's on your mind that would warrant this rude intrusion."

Collecting my thoughts, I hesitated briefly before launching into my ultimatum.

"I thought you might like to know that I just broke up the drug operation on campus. Three students are currently in custody of Sheriff Dixon, and three drug suppliers are on their way to FBI headquarters."

H. Michael's mood instantly brightened. "Unbelievable! You mean to say that you have solved this problem so quickly on the heels of solving the Jenkins affair? I must say, your detective skills have far exceeded my original estimation." He ran his hands up and down his expensive lapels, which to me seemed an odd reaction. "Hard to believe that students could run such an operation. What are their names?"

"They didn't run it," I said, purposely not identifying who did. I wanted him to have to ask.

"If not them, then who? Surely not someone on staff," he asked.

I focused on his eyes to make sure I didn't miss his reaction. "Oh, the ring leader was definitely someone on staff, Mr. Madison." I stood in silence for several seconds, enjoying watching his curiosity overcome his customary composure.

"Spit it out, for God's sake! Who was he?" he said.

"Not *he*, Mr. Madison. *She*. As in Mrs. Clarkson."

The color drained from his face, and he sputtered sounds, not words, till he pulled himself together sufficiently to speak.

"That can't be true, Mr. Wright. There is some terrible mistake here. She is one of my most competent and trusted employees."

I suppressed a laugh. Time to lay my cards on the table.

"Mr. Madison, we both know she was more than your trusted employee. Now, here's how this will play out. Listen carefully!" I said harshly.

"How dare you use that tone with me, Mr. Wright!"

"Oh, there's not much dare involved," I said calmly. "Is there now, Master Mikey?"

His gasp told me that there would be no more protestations. "As I just said, this is how this will play out. I am not about to stand by and do nothing while Clanton Academy goes up in flames. This drug operation will never be reported by media unless I choose to do so, and that will depend on you."

H. Michael seemed confused. "Me? What possible —"

"Shut up and listen. Your job and the future of Clanton Academy depend on your doing what I say. One, your leather-clad paramour is on her way to parts unknown. I have in my possession her hand-written confession of her drug smuggling operation. If she ever makes it public, I will share her confession with the FBI. Mrs. Clarkson may be many things, but she is not stupid. She'll keep her mouth shut. At least to talk."

I gave him what I thought a reasonable amount of time to process that.

"Two," I continued, "because of Clanton Academy's plunge in enrollment, you will downsize personnel, beginning with axing all those administrative sycophants you've surrounded yourself with. Three, you will replace Mrs. Clarkson, Mr. Thomason, Mr. Wood, Mr. Reasoner, and Mr. Jenkins with people whose qualifications have nothing to do with their alleged religious convictions. Oh, and add to that list Mr. Mann, who will tender his resignation shortly – don't ask why. To aid you in this undertaking, you will create a personnel committee consisting of Mr. Rotherwood, Mr. Harland, and Mr. Gore, all of whom I trust to recognize competence and potential value to Clanton Academy. All future hires will also be assessed by those criteria. The den of iniquity, as you referred to it when we first met, was a much better place than Clanton Academy became under your watch, and as for iniquity…well, you know more about that than I."

He started to object but must have thought better of it and stopped in mid-sentence. "Any other stipulations, Mr. Wright?" he asked, his voice dripping with rancor.

"As a matter of fact, yes," I said, handing him a folded piece of paper with Julia's name and phone number written on it. "You will call Julia Hawthorne, an extremely competent administrative assistant, and give her the right of first refusal for the position of your personal assistant after you inform Miss Foss that she has been reassigned as Julia's assistant."

Had H. Michael agreed without trying to save face, I would have been shocked. He hadn't gotten this far in his career without overcoming adversity along the way. Which is precisely why I wanted him to remain at the helm if he could agree to my changes.

Looking at me with his jaw slightly jutting, he said, "I underestimated more than your detection expertise, Mr. Wright. I didn't figure you for an extortionist. And what if I don't agree with this blackmail, Mr. Wright?"

"The choice is yours, of course. The Board will certainly take a dim view of Clanton's president playing 'Naughty Nurse' with the academic secretary and drug kingpin – or is that queenpin? – but I'm sure someone of your resilience should be able to find a new position, though probably not at a school. Sex scandals tend to look bad on resumes of school heads."

He seemed to be sizing me up, saying nothing while repeatedly pulling at his incipient double chin. It was probably my imagination, but I sensed a new measure of respect from H. Michael. Not enough to qualify as a worthy adversary but more than he gave to the grovelers he surrounded himself with.

"Seems as if I have little choice in this, do I? Very well then, Mr. Wright. I agree to your terms, but understand it is not out of fear. No, it is because I know you are motivated by the best interest of Clanton Academy, not personal gain. Believe it or not, Mr. Wright, so am I."

I didn't believe a syllable of that, but I figured that leaving him with a shred of dignity couldn't hurt.

"That goes without saying," I said. "Tomorrow Sheriff Dixon will escort Mrs. Clarkson's three student dealers to your office and will turn over to you their written confessions. In whatever manner you like, you will allow them to withdraw from Clanton Academy with the stipulation that if they ever tell anyone that they dealt drugs here, you will prosecute them. They aren't smart enough to know that isn't possible, but if one of them is stupid enough to challenge you, tell Sheriff Dixon to press charges against them. I think we both prefer to keep the drug situation out of the media, but no punk is going to call the shots. The drug dealers may point a finger at Becky Clarkson, but all their transactions were done without names, and if you provide a cover for her sudden departure, the Feds won't have much to go on."

We shook hands, not to say goodbye or to seal a deal. It just seemed the thing to do. An ending, as it were.

Bringing an end to a murder spree, eradicating a drug ring, and helping my alma mater overcome almost impossible odds…my resume was shaping up.

This ending was my beginning.

Chapter Ninety-nine

Five months later, I was settled in my new office in Charlottesville and actually had a few successful cases under my belt. Nothing as important as the "Clanton Assassin" or thwarting a drug ring but a whole lot better than being a peeping Tom for insurance companies and hotheaded spouses. On a rare day off, I decided to visit Rex and see how Clanton Academy was doing.

With apologies to T. S. Eliot, April is not the cruelest month, at least not in Central Virginia. Springs in Central Virginia are often spectacular, and this one was exceptional. The campus was in full bloom, and the manicured lawns were emerald green. Strolling leisurely around the grounds before looking for Rex, I took stock of this place's influence on my life. It had saved me as a teenager by preparing me for UVA, and five months ago it had afforded me the opportunity to explore my potential for a better career. I owed so much to Clanton Academy, and I hoped H. Michael could help it survive the enrollment crisis.

My wandering led me to the track. Coach Rotherwood was working with hurdlers, and it was readily noticeable that he had fewer athletes to work with this year. Yet I felt certain that somehow he would manage another league championship despite being shorthanded. Having inherited an anemic track program, he had begun his Clanton career with smoke and mirrors, and as he had done then, he'd find a way to win. I waved at him and yelled across an expanse of green, "Just checking things out, Coach. Thanks again for everything." When I couldn't hear his reply, I realized he hadn't heard mine, either. I made a mental note to see him before I left campus later today.

Next stop on my trip around campus was the administration building. Though H. Michael wasn't brimming over with delight to see me, he did report that he and the Personnel Committee had successfully filled all positions, and found no fault with his new Administrative Assistant, Julia. His idea of praise was not to criticize her. Like adding a footnote, he said, "And, incidentally, half of the students who withdrew during the dark days have re-enrolled. We probably won't open next September at full capacity, but we'll make budget. We've stopped the bleeding."

I knew he withheld that information till the end of our conversation to annoy me, and he gave me no credit for the turnaround, but it was music to my ears nevertheless. The guy just couldn't help being a prick.

On the way out, I poked my head into Miss Foss's new office, a tiny windowless room that used to house the copy machine.

"Didn't know you had a new office, Miss Foss," I lied. "How do you like your new arrangement? Did you know that Julia once worked for me?"

"She reminds me of that all too often, Mr. Wright. And I keep reminding her how she's gone from rags to riches."

I laughed. "Touché, Miss Foss."

"This new job doesn't take full advantage of my skills, but I still get to work for the marvelous Mr. Madison, so I have no complaints. The man is a saint."

"Saint Bacchus, maybe," I said.

"I'm not Catholic, Mr. Wright, but I assume Mr. Bacchus was a great man," she said. "Say, I do have a question for you. I know you took an interest in Becky Clarkson. She just up and disappeared without a word to anyone. Poor Mr. Madison, he had to find a replacement for her on top of everything else going on."

"Trust me on this, Miss Foss, she is in a better situation. Mr. Madison will soldier bravely on without her. Last I heard, she was living at The Tarantula Arms in Mississippi."

"What an odd name for a hotel. Oh, well, as long as she's happy. She was such a sweet young thing. Mr. Madison admired her greatly."

"That he did, Miss Foss, that he did."

I felt much more optimistic about Clanton's future after hearing that student defections had been reversed and left to find Rex.

As so often was the case, Amos was hanging out in Rex's room.

"Fric and Frac taking it easy today?" I said, entering the room that had resumed its former state of decay. "Your room looks like a compost pile. And smells like one, too," I said only half in jest.

"Nice to see you, too, Uncle Danny," Rex said as he hugged me.

"So, men, how's everything going now that you're future alumni of UVA?" Both had been accepted at the end of January, but I had been too busy working a case to offer congratulations in person.

"Couldn't be better," Amos said grinning. "No more stress. No more SATs. Life is sweet. Say, guess what we did over Spring Break."

Such a loaded question. I wasn't about to venture a guess.

"Don't have a clue," I said. "But I hope it was legal."

"Ha, ha, Uncle Danny. Very funny. What we did was take your advice and watched some old movies. They weren't totally bad."

"Damning with faint praise doesn't become you, Rex," I said smiling. "They'll grow on you. I just wanted to stop by campus to see how things are here and congratulate you both in person for being accepted by UVA. Who knows? Maybe next year when you're First Years, you can assist me in cases now and then. We made a pretty good team."

"Pretty good? We were awesome!" Amos crowed.

"Oh, and speaking of growing on you, I got a new dog over Spring Leave. You'll love him. He's a Wire Fox Terrier," Rex announced.

"I'm surprised my sister approved of that. What's his name, Rosebud?"

"Good guess, but nope."

"Well, what is it?" I said mildly exasperated.

"Asta."

"Hmmm...Bogie and Myrna worked together in 1931, pre-Sam Spade and Nora Charles, but not bad, Rex, not bad at all. You might have the makings of a detective after all," I said.

"I could say the same of you, Uncle Danny," Rex quipped.

"Here's looking at you, kid," I said, smiling at my protégé.

I could barely wait for my next case.

As long as it wasn't at Clanton Academy.

The End

Made in the USA
Middletown, DE
08 November 2019